CHANGES IN ATTITUDE

OTHER BOOKS BY KATHLEEN SHAPUTIS

The Crowded Nest Syndrome

also

50 Fabulous Places to Raise Your Family, 3rd Edition
Grandma Online

Visit www.Shaputis.com to order books

Changes in Attitude

A novel by

Kathleen Shaputis

Second Printing

CLUTTER FAIRY PUBLISHING
P. O. Box 11056
Olympia, WA 98508-1056

Library of Congress Cataloging-in-Publication Data
Shaputis, Kathleen
 Changes in Attitude / by Kathleen Shaputis.--1st ed.
    p. cm.
 ISBN 0-9726727-1-0
 1. Title.
 PS3619.H35634C47 2005
 813`.6--dc22
                              2005023740

Cover design by Kathryn E. Campbell

Printed by Gorham Printing
Rochester, Washington

To my favorite Parrot Head,
Bob

Chapter 1

"I want one of those." Allie Thompson pointed her soda across a busy aisle of the department store, and a dozen thin metal bracelets clinked together. Surrounded by Saturday afternoon shoppers, Allie's words came out calm, a statement of fact, to her best friend. Calm unless you noticed the minor detail of white knuckles locked around her Diet Coke.

"One what? I can't see anything," said Soozi. A woman in her late twenties, leaning on the handle of a baby stroller, blocked Soozi's view of the jewelry department's display case. Soozi's three-year-old son firmly yanking on one arm for attention didn't help her angle of vision either. "How can you see from here?"

Once more Allie stretched a tanned arm in front of her, the bracelets clinking again like a small wind chime in a breeze. "Sooz, right in front. Check it out." Allie felt her face muscles tighten, anticipating what? Some kind of loud, hysterical response to her heart-revealing remark? A five-minute patronizing soliloquy from Sooz? No taking the words back from the cosmos now, too late, no regrets. Where's a dramatic soundtrack when you need one; where are the violins and cellos?

"What? Gold? Ruby slippers? What am I supposed to see?" Soozi asked.

"Not even close, girlfriend." Allie stared over at Soozi, her accomplice to most of life's doings. Soozi seemed ditzier than usual this afternoon. Was early menopause or midlife dullness striking her once again overdressed friend?

Why the hell am I nervous? I'm only stripping my soul naked and exposing it to possible humiliation in front of God and strangers. In a shopping mall, for heaven's sake. What was I thinking, safety in numbers? Sooz wouldn't dump a barrage of insults on me in here, would she, and risk being thrown out? On the other hand, has a crowd ever stopped Sooz from doing a Mount Saint Helen in the thirty-some years we've known each other?

I'm forty-something and fairly attractive by magazine standards of the late fifties. And tall, if that counts for anything. Okay, significant patches of solid padding here and there accentuate my figure, but I'd be considered slender during the Baroque era, damn it. I can do this. I want this. Allie mentally stamped her foot.

Soozi turned and said sharply to her son, "Lenny, for the umpteenth time, stop pulling on my arm. I can't understand what Aunt Allie just told Mommy. Obviously, my arm is connected to my ear because I could have sworn Aunt Allie is saying she wants what's in front of the expensive baubles." Soozi sniffed as she straightened back to her full but diminutive five foot three height. "And that's certainly not possible."

Allie let go the breath she'd been holding, as a soft smile crossed her face. Her dark brown eyes twinkled in an unwavering gaze at the woman in front of them pushing a blue-patterned stroller slowly back and forth, rocking a tiny towheaded rider to sleep.

"Uh-huh." Allie could almost feel the padded handle in her own long-past-puberty hand as she watched, not caring they were blocking the traffic flow of harried mall shoppers. Get over it people, go around us.

"You've gone too long without eating again, Allie. Let's sit at the café and discuss these sudden maternal hallucinations of yours. Besides, Lenny needs to give my arm a rest. I think it stretched two inches in the last half hour." Soozi bent over, creatively shifting her shopping bags away from the child while balancing on high heels, and encouraged Lenny to rush toward the store's corner café with visions of peanut butter and jelly sandwiches.

Allie watched the slight, wiry boy with baggy shorts and well-worn sneakers run across the floor, arms and legs competing for forward motion. Her stomach tightened as a strange fluttering sensation painted her firm torso with invisible energy. She quietly inhaled and found her arms crossed over her stomach, her sacks and leather purse dangling in front. Someday my child could run like a gangly newborn colt ahead of me.

The two best friends leaned their shoulders together and followed the boy's lead.

Soozi and Allie, as partners in crime and pleasure, went back together to early grade school. Two Southern California girls, growing up with Disneyland in their backyard, and endless hours of television, had the magic of living down the street from one another. Mutt and Jeff, the tall and the short of it, Pete and Repeat were only some of the names the neighborhood adults tagged on them in those early years. Walking, roller-skating, or biking to each other's house at least once or twice a day, with countless trips on the weekends. No dark winter nights or drenching summer rains deterred the friends from spending every possible moment together.

Growing up they shared every juicy, horrendous, or confusing insight. From loud kindergarten disgust when they saw Joey Peterson with his pants down peeing in the girls' bathroom (and discovered boys were weirdly different), to Soozi's first embarrassing stains of menstruation on the back of her skirt in junior high.

"I just want to die, Allie," Soozi had whispered in the nurse's office. "It's okay," Allie reported. "We're women now."

Last year the duo even shared the miracle of birth. When Soozi delivered her second child, a petite baby girl named Zoe, both her husband and Allie were in the delivery room. Allie, freaked yet fascinated, stood at the head of the hospital bed while Soozi's husband, Randy, cut the umbilical cord, freeing the soggy, screaming infant from its mother. Allie's opinion of the meek male Soozi chose to wed long ago changed in that magical moment as he handled his new daughter with an amazing confidence.

Sooz didn't have a clue how much those maternity moments had affected Allie. How could Allie explain to her best friend the sight of a gooey newborn and exhausted mother united for the first time had set off a strange tug of war in her own heart. A queer emptiness snuck up on her late at night while watching television. An invisible force, a sudden pounding of her heart making her nauseous, could shatter the rare solitude in her hectic world. Who'd have thought I had an ol' cliché biological clock inside? Not me, not "I don't need anyone slowing me down, thank you very much," Allie.

Months rolled by and instead of the wanting evaporating, the desire increased, jumping out at her, sniping at her in random, painful waves when baby food commercials appeared on television or an ad for toddler toys pop-upped on her computer. The crazy wanna-be maternal secret screamed for verbalization to the one woman who meant the most to Allie and might understand this insanity the least. Being a mom was Soozi's job, always had been since childhood. Soozi played with dolls, Allie played with office supplies. If the subject had to be broached, right here in the safety of consumer-land seemed as good a place as any to detonate the explosion.

The trio settled at a small Formica table in the crowded café, and a young waitress in a black skirt appeared to take their order.

"Two tossed salads with ranch dressing on the side, and a cold washrag for my best friend here. She doesn't look too good," Allie said, fanning the simple plastic menu back and forth in front of her face, a teasing grin across her painted lips.

"I think you're the one needing the cold shower of reality." Soozi smoothed her short dark hair with her hand. "I can't believe your implications."

"What? That we're having salad for lunch?" Allie asked with mock innocence.

"You know what I'm talking about."

The waitress wrote up the food order between the feuding women and pulled a small box of crayons out of her apron pocket for Lenny.

Soozi waited a split second after the woman left before attacking. Leaning toward Allie, she spoke with clenched jaw, "You're never home, Ms. My-Career-Means-Everything-to-Me. You live in your office eighteen hours a day. What in the world would you do with a baby in your life?"

"Hel-lo. Next banal question, please." Allie rolled her eyes, smoothing an invisible wrinkle in the front of her blouse, trying hard to steady the nerves in her hands. "Is this the best you can do in the lecture department, Ms. Ph.D. of Motherhood? I am disappointed." Allie smiled and shook her head making her dangling gold earrings tinkle softly in her ear. "I expected more gunfire and Hail Marys out of you on this subject."

"Okay, not only didn't I think having a baby was on your top ten list of things to do before you reached fifty," Soozi's voice dropped, "but you're not dating anyone right now. In fact, I don't remember your last date. How many months has it been? Ten, eleven? Let alone any action in the bedroom. Zip. Zero. Nothing on your dance card since macho what's-his-name flew through town eons ago." Soozi reached across the table with perfectly manicured nails painted a Southwest blue and turned Lenny's hand-decorated placemat over to give him a fresh page to draw on. "Where is this baby supposed to come from, Ms. Almost-a-Virgin-Again?"

"The Internet."

"Pregnancy by cybersex?" Soozi screeched.

Lenny lifted his head up at the sharp tone of his mother's voice.

"Warning, warning!" Allie grinned back at her friend's shocked face.

Soozi smoothed a strand of hair out of the young boy's face. "You started this conversation. Lenny hasn't a clue about s-e-x. And I'd like to keep it that way for a while if you don't mind. Keep the conversation at a PG level, please."

"I meant an artificial insemination process I can sign up for on the Internet. And don't give me that blank look, young lady," Allie said. She started to choke, giggling at her own words. "Didn't that sound like a mom thing? See, you're not the only one around here that can wear pablum-stained apron strings." Allie shifted her weight in the straight-back chair, tucking sandaled feet underneath. The rungs of the wrought iron chair felt cold against her long, bare legs. The café's air conditioner hummed at full blast, but the adrenaline of the conversation kept Allie more than warm enough.

"AI is great. I've been studying it on quite a few different sites. You should see it all, tons of information. I've e-mailed with a dozen women who conceived their babies through AI. It's incredible the choices you have." Allie waved her hands for emphasis in the air between them. "And I know my own pathetic dating record, thank you very much. Don't rub my nose in the lack of physical male contact."

The women stared at each other across the short distance.

"Think about it, Sooz, what do I do best in my *other* spare time? Shop. I'm probably one of the best online shopaholics in Southern California when it comes to quality and affordability; you have to give me that much. I can research and thoroughly scope out my choice of male partnership genes, and let modern science and nature do the rest."

Soozi leaned in, resting bare elbows on the cool tabletop. She stared hard at Allie's familiar face, the usual slapped-on makeup and the lack of fine lines or crowsfeet around the eyes despite their similar ages. The dark brown eyes of her friend spoke volumes. "My gawd, I think you're serious. It's hard to believe." A sigh escaped her. Placing her hand flat against Lenny's back, she rubbed in small circles and for a moment her eyes clouded. Allie watched tiny wrinkles of concentration form between her brows.

"Okay, let's suppose your crazy scheme about computer fatherhood actually works, and you get pregnant. What are you going to give up in that hectic schedule you call a life to make room for this baby?"

"Give up what? I may have to cut back some hours and a few meetings, but get serious. I can do the hard work involved in raising a little squirt. I've watched you enough over the last three years with Mickey and Minnie Mouse to know most of the routines."

The waitress interrupted Allie and set two glasses of water, each with a slice of lemon, in front of them. She brought a Roy Rogers with two cherries for Lenny. Neither woman noticed her.

"A few hours—excuse me? You are wired twenty-four/seven on stress. You're locked in a glass and steel office, what, ten to twelve hours a day, every day, by choice? You created a successful company from nothing but sweat and sacrifice. And now you want to throw a baby into the mix?"

Allie blinked. Did she hear a note of bitterness? Couldn't have.

"Where's the baby going to be, Ms. CEO, at a sitter's? You know we are talking about a real baby, the kind with stuff running in one end and out the other. An infant needs real time with its mother. Like, on a daily basis is the nationally approved concept."

"Okay, okay, I'll hire a nanny." Allie flinched from her own rash comeback as soon as the words came out. She hated delegating, in any respect of her work or existence. How could she turn over something this important, like raising her child, to someone else? *Maybe I can remodel the office space next to mine, a pseudo-nursery with an efficient set-up and rocking chair for the* nanny. Something soothing yet fun, maybe in blues and mauves, do they make mauve teddy bears? At least the baby would be there in her office every day during those first critical years, and—

"Earth to Allie, you're zoning on me. Another thing to think about is the total lack of freedom once the baby's born. Do you know how jealous I get when you ramble on about sleeping in late on Saturday mornings? You can scratch that off your list of doable things for at least two to three years with a brand new baby." She snapped her fingers. "Lenny is an all-night alarm for anything from a runny nose and cough, to m-o-n-s-t-e-r shadows in his closet. And don't get me started on baby sister's nocturnal habits." Soozi cast her eyes toward the ceiling and let out a deep sigh. "Zoe doesn't have a clue about sleeping when it is nighttime. The child thinks the dark is more exciting for playing pat-a-cake."

Allie reached up, her bracelets jangling, and pulled a strand of strawberry blonde hair back into the shell clip on the side of her head. Let the games begin. She might as well get comfortable, Soozi was wound up like a giant rubber band. She knew this would be her best friend's reaction when she finally got up the nerve to break the 180 degree flip of baby decision to her. Turning in her seat, Allie crossed tanned legs beside the table.

"Children do not care about adult timetables. They wake up with the sun. There are cartoons to watch and noise to make. Infants are the worst, their tummies growl every two to four hours around the clock, nonstop. Very few cooperate with any concept of sleeping through the night for a long time." Soozi tapped her fingernail on the table for emphasis, and then checked the painted porcelain for damage, a slight frown creasing her forehead.

"I don't sleep in every weekend." Allie took a phony swipe toward her friend. "I guess it's a luxury of sorts, but so is picking up a baby and crawling back into bed on a cold Saturday morning. Inhaling scents of Johnson's Baby Shampoo and old milk first thing in the morning sounds more enticing than fresh-brewed coffee to me. Thoughts of snuggling with a tiny bundle in bed almost gives me goose bumps."

How long can kids draw on a blank sheet of paper, Allie wondered as she glanced across the table. Lenny's head was down, ignoring the women around him. His eyebrows furrowed in concentration on his colorful work of art.

Allie leaned in closer to peak at his masterpiece in progress.

"No, no. Don't!" Lenny stretched the last word into three long syllables, as he plopped his compact body on top of his drawing. Allie straightened up in her chair, surprised by his whining pitch.

"Lenny—mind your manners, be nice to Auntie Allie." Soozi turned back to Allie. "Okay, having a baby is full of Beatrix Potter kinds of stuff, agreed. But your single lifestyle hasn't been cruel and unusual punishment, you've enjoyed other ways of contentment. Once you make the Grand Canyon leap into parenthood, Al, there's no changing your mind. No returning them back to the store for a refund."

The waitress stepped up and began to set their salads and sandwiches on the table. She looked over the boy's shoulder and admired his colorful work. Lenny beamed at the woman's attention. Allie tilted her head at this casual exchange across from her. Why had Lenny refused her looking at the picture, yet allowed this stranger not only to see, but rewarded her with a crooked smile? Allie shook the negative thoughts from her mind; this is nothing personal about any lack of maternal genes on her part. I will make a good mother; I can be a good mother. Lack of experience does not constitute failure, and I refuse to be a failure at anything.

Soozi picked up her fork with one hand and rearranged Lenny's artwork and sandwich with the other, then tucked a paper napkin into the top of Lenny's shirt with well-practiced skill before Allie made a move toward her own lunch. Multi-tasking never looked so good. Mothers did it long before someone made a catch phrase out of it.

"You'd have to child-proof your forest hide-away. All those ceramic Lladros you've got out on tabletops would have to be put away or hung from the ceiling for safekeeping. You won't believe the enormous reach a kid has when grabbing across an end table, for God's sake, at the five-hundred-dollar art object Randy picked up in New York."

Allie ran her finger against the edge of the saucer of Ranch salad dressing to catch a drip. "Hmm, that sounded a tad acidic, girl. What did your miniature shadow break this time?" She licked the droplet of dressing off her fingertip.

"Only the most gorgeous gift Randy ever gave me. I had this incredible

Waterford angel out of the gift box for no more than a minute. I turned to pick up the wrapping papers off the couch, when a set of sticky fingers came over the back and I saw this flash of blue T-shirt flying behind me. I'm telling you, two seconds tops, and Lenny ran out of the room with the angel in his hands."

Lenny ducked his head down closer to the colored placemat during his mother's outbreak, a wad of sandwich burrowed in his cheek. Allie couldn't see a fraction of daylight between him and the drawing.

"Before I could jump off the couch, Lenny trips over God knows what, and he and my angel land hard on the entryway tile. He's lucky he didn't slice his face open. I didn't know whether to kiss him or kill him. So much for my romantic bauble from the never-home-anymore husband." Soozi stabbed her fork hard at the romaine lettuce on her plate.

"Hey, the mere male tried to be nice."

"Lenny doesn't know Waterford glass from Fisher-Price plastic. Pretty is pretty to a three-year-old." Soozi continued her tirade, taking further vengeance on her plate by cutting her lettuce with knife and fork. Her words matched the rhythm. "I'm telling you, your house is a minefield for children to destroy. Why do you think I rarely bring any of the herd along when I come to visit?"

"Because *mi casa es su* insanity sanctuary. You leave the kids with dependable ol' Randy when you come over, standard operating procedure. I don't have anything to run *back* to, like you do, when you've replenished yourself in my house. By the end of our gab and wine sessions, you're chomping at the bit to go home and make sure Randy hasn't put them outside with the dog or forgotten to feed them."

Soozi nodded with her mouth full. Randy had a good heart, but not a lot of common sense in the parenting department. How many Randy-bashing stories had Allie sat through, regarding his lack of paternal skills?

"I want that constant thinking of someone. I want to experience the process of loving someone and being anxious about their every move. You only get it through being a mother. I didn't think I had any of the maternal instinct we're supposed to have somewhere in our genes just because the doctor announced 'It's a girl' when we were born."

Allie laid her fork down and leaned toward her friend. "Aunt Kitty always said I'd never make it as a mom, and I believed her. Finding buried treasure in the South Pacific or successfully running for state governor, no problem. A mom? Never." Her eyes dropped as she took a sip of water. She felt vulnerable speaking Aunt Kitty's name, ripping the band-aid off the past, but Allie needed to get Soozi to understand.

"I find myself wandering into the infant department of Target and touching these soft, fuzzy sleepers. Or wondering what theme I'd put together for its first birthday party." Allie smiled. "I want to know what happens to your heart the next morning the first time they sleep through the two o'clock feeding."

Soozi stared at her friend with half-closed eyes and dabbed at her mouth with the napkin. "You actually put those considerations through that business blender you call a mind? Girl, I've seen you go in and out of some pretty bizarre fads, but, you know, this one stays with you if you actually go for it. There's no going 'oops' a few years later if you're not up to croupy coughs and droopy drawers." She laid her fork across the plate. "If this is what you really want to do…" she paused a split second of eternity, "I know a thing or two about changing diapers and wiping runny noses to help you over the rough spots, I guess. Just let me know what you decide to do. I'm president of your fan club."

Allie squealed. "Remember how you wanted to be president of a *That Girl* fan club?" She laid her hand on top of her best friend's. Before the howl of Soozi's children, before the separation of Allie going to the University of San Luis Obispo, they had their television idols.

"If I couldn't be Ann Marie at six years old, the least I could do was be her best fan. I thought you were going to be Ann Marie for the both of us when we grew up. Single, great career, a few minor scrapes here and there to keep you grounded, and a smile to paint away anything else. God, I loved that show." Soozi continued to reminisce about the favorite sitcom with her mouth full of breadstick. "Your hair was so straight, doing a flip on the end didn't create a problem for you. You seem pretty Ann-Marie-ish now. The only thing lacking is a Donald in your life."

"Maybe that's my problem. No guy lived up to the sweetness and flexibility of Donald. Maybe I've been trying to find his twin brother between the sheets all these years." Allie laughed at the possibility, and then challenged Soozi with, "Do you remember the theme song?"

"Like I'm going to remember. Ask me the words to Sesame Street's theme song and you're on." Soozi leaned back in her chair. "I won't bet, 'cause I'm sure you *do* know all the words in that categorized portion of your body that science would call a brain. How do you keep so much info in there without it all spilling out?" Soozi dabbed at her mouth with the napkin and then took a swipe at Lenny's without missing a beat before she put it back in her lap. "Don't impress me, I know you know it."

Allie faked a pout.

"Hard to imagine *That Girl* having a baby." Soozi sighed with heaviness, feeling an age she couldn't remember obtaining. "I feel like I'm in an episode of *The Twilight Zone* or something. How weird, thinking of you being a mom after all this time. I'm the mom, you're the working woman, forever and always, amen…"

Allie tweaked her head toward the ceiling and with a sharp inhale interrupted Soozi. "Do you hear that desecration?"

"Is this one of your questions where I won't have a clue?" Soozi strained to hear heaven knew what around the buzz of the crowded mall on a Saturday afternoon.

"Listen. They're playing *Margaritaville* over the speakers. How dare they destroy the integrity of Jimmy's song by recording it in elevator music!" She smacked the top of the table, and Lenny jumped in his chair across from her. "Sorry, Lenny." A die-hard Jimmy Buffett fan since the early seventies, Allie had dressed in Hawaiian shirts and anything with parrots in high school and early college years. Jimmy Buffett's Caribbean rock-and-roll songs blasted from her dorm room, much to the dismay of many roommates.

"Oh, sure. It's okay if they use 90 percent of Barry's songs to drown out the noise of mass shoppers, but let them use just one of Jimmy's and you have a fit and fall in it," Soozi sniffed. She picked up a piece of Lenny's sandwich and popped it into her mouth. Lenny made a fist and smashed the rest of the bread slices into flat objects, the jelly oozing out the sides. Soozi changed her mind about taking any more.

Allie smirked at Lenny's behavior. "Muzak and Mannilow are made for each other. Barry probably gets an enormous kickback from the company for providing the majority of their material over the last gazillion years. You can't compare the mighty Buffett man with balladeer Barry. Not even in the same league, my dear."

"Don't start. You don't want to go down the road of who has the most albums and the most hit records. Sold-out concerts might be a draw."

"Right, like hypnotized women between the ages of thirty-two and fifty-two, who buy his platters regardless of taste, are of a concern to me. Remember the New Year's Eve concert in Los Angeles you dragged me to? I couldn't tell one song from the other with those rowdy Oreo-eaters sobbing in my ears."

"Hey, at least I've supported my hero by attending multiple concerts."

"Ouch." Allie faked a sting to her heart. "I was surprised you didn't name your daughter Mandy. Remember how you wore out the grooves of the record you had?" The women squealed in unison and traded stories of cheap studio apartments and eating green beans out of a can for dinner during Allie's college days and Soozi's impoverished first year of marriage.

"Mommy, I'm done." Lenny picked up his empty plate.

Both women were startled. The boy had been quietly engrossed in his sandwich mash-then-eat routine and they had forgotten him. Allie caught Soozi's eyes across the table and a slight nod. "Good for you, Lenny. What a good eater." The boy blushed and tucked his chin into his shirt collar, stretching the cotton threads.

The waitress came over touting visions of sugar-rich desserts as she collected the empty plates.

"Why not? Let's celebrate."

"We'll *share* a piece of cheesecake," Soozi said. "You may not be worried about your waistline right now, but I'm still carrying around extra baggage from Zoe's birth."

The waitress brought back a single slice with three salad forks.

Allie raised her fork, heavy with white gooey calories and graham cracker crust. "Here's to the next Thompson generation, to Internet donations, and whatever precious surprises life holds in store for all of us."

Soozi raised her fork in salute. "I must agree, sperm shopping will be right up your alley, my friend. You always come away with the best bargains." Both of them laughed and enjoyed the deliciously rich concoction.

After a few bites Lenny laid his fork and head on the table. "I think it's time to get this miniature shopper home for a nap," Soozi said, lowering her voice.

Allie grabbed the bill while Soozi dipped her napkin into her glass of water to unceremoniously clean Lenny's horizontal face one last time. It's a mother thing, Allie thought, watching her friend struggle with an uncooperative and tired little boy. How she had hated it when her own mother or aunt spit on a handkerchief in public and scrubbed for blood against her cheeks. Not much change in this part of the post-maternity ward in the last forty-some years.

In the packed parking lot Allie gave kisses to Lenny's weary face, and the women soon parted. The hot afternoon sun had slipped into evening, sinking its bright yellow neon globe into the brown western haze. Colors and hues of an infamous Southern California pink sunset painted the sky on the last cheery notes of daylight. Toward the north Mount Baldy's peak stood majestic in a mountain range, mirroring the glow and standing guard over the valley area. The Inland Empire radiated the coming of summer.

The engine of Allie's Toyota turned over on the first try of the key, and the air conditioner filled her face with hot air as Allie sat and replayed the baby conversation in her mind. "I think it went well. Sooz didn't faint from a heart attack, no dialing 9-1-1. She didn't criticize me with as much venom as I thought she would on the baby subject," mused Allie out loud. She reached behind her shoulder and grabbed the seat belt. "I swear you never know what that woman is going to say in a situation. When you least expect it, she puts up a great support fence to our friendship." With the belt snapped in place, Allie put her car into reverse.

As Soozi punched the gas pedal of her mini-SUV at the intersection's green light leaving the mall, she reached down to dial her cell phone between the seats. She stayed over in the slow lane and adjusted her earphone. Before the car reached second gear, she heard the other phone pick up.

"Randy? We're on our way home, and Lenny's about to fall asleep on me. You will never, ever guess who wants to have a baby."

Chapter 2

As the elevator doors glided opened, Gillian Nation stepped into the well-decorated fourth floor hallway of the Dagot and Johnson Building. He took a last look in the reflective siding of the elevator. Everything practically perfect as usual; no Monday drudgery in this gorgeous temple. Before he could appreciate the feng shui energy of the decor as he did first thing every morning, the smell of fresh-brewed Kona coffee assailed his nose.

"Damn. What time does that woman get out of bed?" Gillian rushed down the carpeted corridor. "She might as well live here." His slender, muscular legs led him in lengthy strides toward the office where he worked as an assistant to Allie. Five years down the same hallway. His haste made his streaked blond ponytail bounce against the starched collar of his pale blue, expensive shirt. Roughly pushing the glass entrance door, he left a perfect, enormous handprint just below the printed logo, Novel Software, Inc.

Relentless, Gillian tried keeping up with Allie's diligence and dedication, and found himself always a step or two out of sync with his workaholic boss. It wasn't necessary to overachieve in his world, a grandiose lifestyle subsidized by a generous inheritance. He enjoyed the technical challenge and the schmoozing that went along with his work in this small firm. He admired Allie's forthrightness and stamina as a woman and a corporate business owner. Gillian wanted to be just like her when he grew up. If he ever grew up, which he highly doubted.

Allie assured him in their first interview that imagination and intelligence would work best in her company. A touch of childlike curiosity mixed with a heavy dose of technical skill was what she needed for the position. Gillian Nation was a master of both. Working for an older woman didn't dampen his enthusiasm, though he would never be catty enough to remind her of the fifteen-year difference in age between them.

"It's only Monday, dragon lady of the almighty paycheck—did you bother going home at all this weekend?" Gillian yelled toward her office. He set down his leather briefcase on the front desk. A fresh stack of programming, covered in penciled scribbles, had been placed near his computer, which was booted and ready for data input.

"It's seven-thirty in the blessed morning out here in your dreary suburb. I've only had one cup of coffee yet. That's vicious. Do you just go into screensaver mode in your office after I leave on Friday?" Gillian pressed his well-manicured hands against his hips, careful not to crease the fabric of the chinos he knew he looked fabulous wearing.

"I've decided to go into physical training, and sleep is one of the things I'm doing less of. I'm practicing, so keep up or move over," Allie threw back at him.

Training? Gil strained to pick up the slight nuance in Allie's voice that pricked his ears, different from a normal Monday morning. What was she babbling about? Allie and training, error message cannot compute, sorry. She hated breaking out in a sweat. Gil's face wrinkled in concentration for two seconds.

He walked with a natural grace into the cubby section of the office they used for a kitchen. The coffee aroma surrounded him in a cloak of deliciousness and he nearly forgot all about Allie's mysterious tone of voice. Gillian poured the stimulating dark liquid into an oversized cup.

"Don't mess with my hairdo this early in the morning, dear. Since when have you had to train for anything? That figure is one most women would die for, you know that." The first hot sip of heaven went down his throat. Just a hint of vanilla came through the rich flavor. Allie knew how to make a perfect pot of coffee to satisfy his finicky tastes. They had enjoyed a mutual challenge over the years in perfecting different blends of gourmet coffee.

"I can't help what body parts God decided to give me. She has a strange sense of humor sometimes. I have two arms to slap you silly if you don't get going on those latest additions I put on your desk." The manic clicking of Allie's keyboard kept a staccato beat in the background.

"Yes, sir. Buddha knows expensive sod doesn't grow under feet of dragon boss lady's feet. No matter how puny they might be." Gillian would have a tough time shoving his size twelve-and-a-halfs into her stiletto heels. But the thought had crossed his mind a time or two during his years of employment with Allie. Well, not exactly hers. Gillian couldn't break her away from the sales at Payless shoe stores. Heaven forbid some chemically created shoe should touch his tender tootsies.

Gillian picked up the first page of the changes on his desk. Allie had told him about building the software company, Novel Software, Inc., out of a scheme she cooked up in college. Each program and concept had been written out, screens sketched in designs and rewritten on pads of legal size paper. His boss had a strange bond with computers, yet admitted to a love affair with a blank sheet of paper and a Number 2 pencil, a rather successful one, Gil admitted to himself. Gil wanted to be half the woman she was, and would follow Allie's lead to whatever prosperous roads it took the company.

Allie excelled at both her chosen fields, computer programming and marketing, thought Gillian. Able to leap tall buildings between the left side of her brain and the right in a single bound. Her clientele grew at a sensible rate for a small business and his boss seemed content. She carved a niche for herself in the volatile children's software market and was quite comfortable with her slice of the consumer pie over the years. She was as busy as she wanted to be, some periods more hurried than others, but never hysterical. Gillian liked that in a woman CEO.

He took another sip of coffee.

Gillian was a twenty-something model, with the ink still wet on his computer science degree and an ungodly amount owed in student loans, when he applied for a job at Novel Software. Allie's initial questions during a phone interview were standard, and she inquired about his hands-on experience with programming other than in college. They discussed their both being native Southern Californians, born into the culture and climate of the envied sunshine.

In a crowded field, Gillian realized he was competing against not only a wave of fresh pocket protectors out of universities each year, but the legions of experienced, laid-off dot-commers joining a lower-paying technology merry-go-round with network certifications plus working credentials. He wasn't worried about getting on the fast track straight out of college, he just wanted to stay in the stadium. Allie's company seemed perfect.

Then he'd been hit broadside with her off-the-wall interview questions.

"So, what do you know about Oliver Wendall Douglas?"

He paused, surprised. "He's a Supreme Court Justice?"

Her second question seemed just as quirky: "What does na-noo, na-noo mean?" Who are these people, and what do they have to do with computers, Gil fussed to himself. "I'm sorry, I haven't a clue."

He heard a brief snort over the phone, and then the rest of the questions became recognizable as professional.

After he was hired, Allie explained the questions about television from the sixties had tipped her off to how young he was without asking any politically incorrect questions regarding age. It became the first of many trivia questions he would endure over the years from his boss. She thrived on the details of television and movies in the sixties and seventies and drove him insane with her relentless challenges.

Gillian asked for the address. "We're at 99 Haven Avenue on the fourth floor," her voice pitch never varied as she continued, "in Rancho Cucamon-ga."

Gillian's Anaheim snobbishness showed through in his voice. "You're kidding, right? Cucamonga? I thought that was an old comedian's joke. What was his name? Jack something," he said indifferently. No wonder the area code for the company on the job flyer hadn't seemed familiar; she was outside the real world of Orange County.

"Keep driving east, young man," she said, blithely ignoring his prejudice, "and before you reach barren desert, turn left off I-10. We have a cultural mecca out here, I might add. We're not just wineries and vineyards any more. North of here is the old Virginia Dare Winery they used for some of the scenes in *Combat.*"

"What kind of combat?"

"A weekly television drama, sort of an *NYPD Blues* about World War II, only filmed in black and white—before I was born, of course. Vic Morrow was the lead character."

"Didn't he get killed on a movie set years ago?"

"That's the guy. Anyway, we're about an hour northeast of you. Is the commute going to be a problem should you be hired?"

"Hardly. The parking lot commuters will be on the other side of the freeway going west toward civilization. There's no difficulty reaching Rancho Cucamonga at any reasonable hour in the morning."

Sales for Novel Software had tripled last quarter. The new Web page Gillian set up brought mountains of new orders and requests. Though Grandmama had left him financially secure two years ago, Gillian enjoyed his work with such a visionary leader, despite her polyester tendencies. He enjoyed riding the caboose of her energy and talent, and Allie had no reservations in keeping him abreast of her ideas. She depended on his perfectionist talent. Gillian liked being a big fish in a little successful pond, even in Rancho Cucamonga.

Another sip of coffee fortified the minimal adrenaline creeping into his system. Nothing like working for the queen of dawn, disgustingly punctual, such a dull habit for a person. Gil usually dragged his bare muscular frame out of bed at the time he knew she was already pulling into her preferred parking place outside the main doors.

Setting down the cup and seriously reading her latest changes, he raised his perfectly shaped eyebrows. "Damn, she's good," he mumbled under his breath. She'd mapped out the answer to a bug that had been bothering them for over a week. He called out, "Al, you got it! This is the magic key. Why didn't I know this?"

"Next time I'll let you spill catsup all over the kitchen table. I grabbed a dishrag to mop up the mess, and the numbers simply played themselves out," Allie yelled back from her office.

"Oh, right, the old spilt-catsup-in-the-kitchen routine. Didn't I read about that in *PC World* last month? Girl, you are insane." He reached over and turned on the portable CD player behind his desk. Sounds of Mozart faintly pervaded the office from a pair of expensive miniature speakers.

Immediately Her Highness bounced out of the back office.

"Do you have to play snoring sonatas first thing in the morning? Don't you own anything livelier than some dead guy for a Monday? Gillian, this will drop your blood pressure, and I don't think the strongest coffee available could make a difference."

"Okay, okay. Don't get your hormones in a crisis. Here, will this do, Ms. Audio Sensitive? If you ever get your boy to do a *Buffett Does Broadway* CD, I'd play it just for you, darling." Gillian slipped a new disc into the player and strains of *West Side Story*'s opening bars began.

"Get those fancy fingers of yours flying over that keyboard, anti-Buffett boy. We've got a meeting with Metro at ten o'clock this morning, and I'd like to see the results of my changes at the meeting." Allie ducked back into her inner sanctum. Her sharp words hung in the air behind her.

"Whoa, where'd PMS come from?" Gil wondered about the look he saw around her eyes. Something's going on in that marvelous mussed-up head of hers, and I don't think it has to do with the meeting. Something is brewing besides coffee. Could it be? Nah. Could she have had a real live date this weekend? Hardly possible. Allie confided everything to him—well, until now obviously. Gillian sniffed.

She'd better come out with it by lunchtime, or he'd…or he'd what? Well, he'd think of it as soon as he made these program changes, before she bounced out of her cave again for a fresh attack.

An hour passed productively. Gillian clicked his mouse to print the seven transparencies for the meeting. Waiting for the color copies, he had the chance to question Allie's aura this morning. She hadn't come out of her office once since the outburst, even for a coffee refill. Gillian took the initiative and walked over to her doorway.

The mighty Allie sat inert, staring at her computer screen with just a hint of a smile pulling at the corner of her mouth. Gil watched and without thinking held his breath. It's Monday morning, moments before a big meeting and his boss is in la-la land. Lights are on and nobody's home. This is not like her at all. A slightly ominous shiver slid down his back.

Gillian cleared his throat, shifting his weight from one Italian leather-shoed foot to the other as he stood in the doorway.

Allie jumped imperceptibly, trying to cover up her sudden lack of focus. "Have you finished everything I gave you? We need it for the presentation." She saved her document and swiveled around in her office chair.

"Oui, mon cheri dictator. The graphs are printing, the dog and pony show will be ready to unveil by ten o'clock, and that leaves us more than enough time for you to explain what happened this weekend."

Allie looked down at her desk as a rose-colored blush crept over her face.

"Hold that thought. Obviously, this is going to be good, and I want to be ready." Gillian dashed over and grabbed the pot of coffee out of the cubby. Refilling their cups, he settled into the upholstered chair across from her desk. He crossed his legs, which stretched the fabric of his pants tight against his muscular thighs. "Okay, what's his name, where did you meet him, and do not leave out any of the details, pull-eeze."

"What?" Allie smiled mysteriously back at her enthusiastic assistant as she sipped the fresh coffee. "Sorry to disappoint you, my gay Romeo, there's no new guy."

"Get out of here. You can't tell me a man's not involved when a workaholic comes to a complete stop on a hectic Monday with big bucks knocking on our door in a few hours. It has to be sex, great sex. I stood at the door and saw the most incredible, satisfied look on your face. It was Madonna-like."

"Gil, I haven't been on a date since you-know-who flew in from Seattle. Get serious. You know what my love life has or hasn't been like. I'm not sure I even remember what sex is like anymore. Doesn't it have something to do with naked fun, and sweating, and 'I'll call you tomorrow' between two con-senting adults? I couldn't tell you, 'cause it's not something that has been near this body or my bed in a long while."

"Beds are overrated." Gillian gently pulled at his collar and straightened the front of his shirt. "I'm not being critical about your chastity problem, though God knows, I don't have a clue as to why you have a problem. You're not bad-looking for a woman." Gillian smoothed back a strand of hair. "But I saw you, just a minute ago. You were practically glowing, all the signs of fulfilled lust and longing, my dear. A schoolgirl with her elbow on her desk daydreaming about the boy sitting three rows over in history class."

"I want to have a baby."

"And do I know about the cute boy sitting three rows over. Lord have mercy! He had the most darling dimple in his left—" Gillian stopped in mid-sentence with his mouth still open. "What did you say?"

"I want to have a baby. A non-adult that eats and wets in random order, and crushes your heart and sanity with love and worry."

"Baby?"

The word traveled up toward the stucco ceiling, echoed faintly, and hung in the air for a second until Allie claimed it back. "Yes. A pre-aged adult. A short, immature Democrat of my very own."

Gillian smiled a wry, pained smile at his boss. "You?"

"Who else has biological plumbing in this room? I know it's a shock. Okay, I'm still working out the details myself. Yet, I can't get rid of these feelings saturating my very thoughts, my goals, my instincts."

Allie slapped her hands on top of the desk. "Do you know the names of the seven dwarfs in *Snow White*?"

"Huh? Oh, uh, Grumpy, Doc, Happy, and Dopey. Um, a couple with very small speaking parts, and one that needed a good plastic surgeon. I don't know, and I know you do. What has that got to do with having a…a baby?" Gillian had trouble even saying the word. His heroine, his mentor, pregnant? The physical concept made him nauseous.

"The other three were Sleepy, Sneezy, and Bashful. Don't you see? I want to share the magic of Disney with my child, pass down the trivia and delight I adore to one of my own. My parents were so wrapped up in work, success, and winning, they never took the time to savor any of the animated classics with me. Just dropped me off in front of the local movie theater and had someone taxi me home when it was over.

"Shit, look at the time." Allie flew out of her chair toward a closet in the back of her office. She kept an extra power wardrobe ready on a moment's notice. Unbuttoning her cotton blouse in front of her assistant, she continued her conversation without hesitation. Sexual harassment or politically incorrect concepts didn't impact their relationship at Novel Software.

"Gillian, it's a really weird feeling, a rush, like my hormones have all cashed in their lotto tickets and are demanding payment. I've tried ignoring them and stuffing any maternity concept in a drawer but it keeps coming back at me full force at the oddest times. I have to follow this through." Allie hung her blouse on a padded hanger and flipped through the selections.

Gillian nodded, still in shock. Nothing was ever going to be the same again.

Allie, a mother. This did not compute. He knew his boss quite well, once she made up her mind on an idea she had the tenacity of paparazzi.

"No, not the beige polyester, girl, the champagne silk blouse," Gillian kibitzed at her without thinking. He didn't bother to cover his eyes; he adored his boss with not a lustful bone in his body.

Gillian created a new responsibility when hired, dressing Allie in a more professional fashion. Her pathetic sense of clothing style didn't extend beyond comfortable and machine washable. Gillian took it upon himself to remedy her pitiful wardrobe as she screamed poverty. He found she could sew a great seam and the two of them spent many a weekend ferreting out material and patterns from pages of his *Vogue* magazines. Together, they created business ensembles for her that were modeled after some of the latest designs out of Los Angeles.

Professional, yet polyester. Some faults she refused to change, and he was forced to compromise. Many an in-house business meeting between the two of them included him on his knees pinning a hem to a new creation she modeled while they talked shop.

"Okay, let's continue this discussion later. Maybe this afternoon, how about an early dinner if you're not busy tonight. I'll give you a chance to tell me all the rational why-this-is-not-a-good-idea theories—I know you'll have a list. As for the Metro meeting, it looks like we have the vice president and an assistant to the CEO attending. You take the VP and I'll work on the assistant." Allie slipped a jacket over her ensemble and stepped out of her black ballet slippers. Padding around barefoot, she looked for an elusive second high heel.

"Behind your chair. Honestly, can't you keep your shoes together? How old is the assistant?" Gillian asked.

"Ooh, are we being picky? He's thirty-something and the VP is fifty-something. It's my turn to have the young one, Gil. You know you're good schmoozing the older crowd. I need your talent, this could mean a great revenue source for us. The guy is looking for commitment."

Gillian raised his perfectly matched eyebrows.

"Don't look at me with those shocked baby blues, those were his words. I flattered the hell out of him as best I could in the first meeting, which is nothing compared to your, uh, natural abilities."

"Whatever you desire, my queen. It's all for the good of the company. I think you're going into this with your fingers crossed. Are you sure *you'll* be free for dinner tonight?" Gillian shook a finger in her direction as she slipped into her pumps.

"Don't start with me, prima donna. I had a date this year. I think. Maybe."

"This is only July, Allie." Gillian headed out, grabbed his jacket and the printed transparencies. "Whatever happened to that gorgeous sex-starved fishmonger from Seattle?"

"Et tu, Brutus?"

Chapter 3

After a long day of jousting and bargaining with the two suits from Metro Scholastic, Gillian followed Allie to a table in the back patio of their favorite restaurant not far up the boulevard from the office. Convincing Gillian when he first started in the company that any city called Rancho Cucamonga could serve decent food had taken Allie months of wheedling and whining.

Allie tried to ignore Gillian's blowing quick kisses to the waiters as they passed through the dining area. She knew many were close friends; ex-Disneyland compatriots Gillian had encouraged to explore the slower-paced Inland Empire for work. Lower housing costs convinced his toned and tanned friends to migrate east from the Orange County mecca.

"Does the Wicked Witch of the West know about this maternal decision of yours?" Gillian pounced on the morning's neonatal topic after ordering their first round of drinks. Allie noticed he did nothing to disguise the sarcasm. His face looked twisted as if he'd just bit into something disgusting.

"Yes, Soozi knows. We were at the mall this weekend when it spilled out. And I don't want competitive lip about who found out first between you two. Sheesh! You're like two starving alley cats fighting over a dead fish." Allie smiled across the table, trying to placate her temperamental assistant as she steeled herself for the battle ahead.

Gillian sniffed with scorn. "Some of us are pedigreed, my dear. Never mind, I don't want to ruin my appetite over Miss Martyrdom tonight." Gillian studied the perfect manicure on his right hand. "Let's go over a few minor details regarding these maternal intentions of yours. One glaring deficiency I see in this concept is of a paternal nature," Gillian upturned his hand, "or lack of paternity, if you will. Just how do you expect this pregnancy to happen when your bedroom is totally barren of male testosterone? Immaculate conception, my dear?"

"Thank heavens, that trick's been done." Allie faked wiping her brow and then snapped the same hand across the table as if flicking the perspiration. "And let's not use the word barren to describe my pathetic social calendar. I do have one, you know."

Allie leaned toward the table. "I'm looking into artificial insemination for the daddy. I've done quite a bit of research on the Internet for information, details, numbers, and found all kinds of support. I want to be able to pick out my baby's possible paternal characteristics. I want some control over the body type, eye color, hobbies, that sort of thing. And, of course, he has to have a maximum ph factor."

The drinks arrived and Gillian slowly stirred the thin plastic straw in his pink lemonade. The ice tinkled against the glass. "Okay, I'll bite on this one, just because it's you, and I expect a paycheck next week. What is a maximum ph factor? We can't be talking about acidity levels—yours borders on the level of kryptonite. I give up. What must this paternal donor have?"

"Ph factor is for Parrot Head. He's got to be a Jimmy Buffett fan."

Gillian groaned and laid his head daintily against his fingers. "This woman is insane. I should have known. You think the clinic is going to have a special box for guys to check if they love Jimmy Buffett? Get real, girlfriend." He took a sip from his drink. "Ph factor, that's quite hilarious. I must remember to tell the girls when I get back to reality. I don't know how you're expecting to find that out. No pun intended, darling." Gillian flashed his brilliant smile.

"None taken—too lame, especially by your standards. I will find out, though, somehow. I'm not having my child be a hip-hop, rap, or heavy metal connoisseur." Allie twisted her mouth into a wicked grin, "Look how long I've worked on your musical tastes without success. Like this morning, for instance. Classical put-you-to-sleep music first thing is not how you start out a decent workday. Now *Last Mango in Paris* will ease you right into a Monday better than an injection of B_{12} vitamin. Jimmy knows his Caribbean rock and roll." Allie laughed at the shocked look on Gillian's face.

"You're a sick woman. Order something to eat, darling; it's been a traumatic day. I think my blood sugar is dropping off the scale." Gillian picked up his menu, scanning the pages quickly. "Pitifully obvious options," he sighed.

"You whine about this every time we go out. Hello? You chose the restaurant."

"This whole valley is limited in epicurean delicacies," he said, turning a page of the menu. "If you're truly serious about this motherhood deal, and I'm not the slightest bit convinced mind you, order something with broccoli. It's important to increase your folic acid levels before you conceive." Gillian looked up over the top of the menu. "Don't squint your face muscles like that, you're ruining your makeup, darling. Yes, I know all about folic acid and its correlation to droll little healthy fetuses."

Allie snapped her napkin and laid it across her lap.

"By the way, the more current phrase is alternative insemination. You did say you've done your homework? Raphael and Andrew became parents last year, using AI and a surrogate mother. Raphael I can see as a nurturing maternal figure. I never dreamed *you'd* want Santa to bring you a layette for Christmas." Gillian leaned slightly forward. "Do you know the health risks involved when you spread yourself open, so to speak?"

Allie moved in and lowered her voice. "If you are trying to delicately talk about diseases, why don't you just say it? The articles about insemination having some problems with HIV infection all date before 1986. Ancient history."

Allie watched her gorgeous hunk of an assistant sip on his drink with the finesse of a dancer, each move choreographed. "I'm going for a young, fertile college guy with fresh, healthy genes, not some 1960 baby boomer who wandered in years ago without a clue about vulnerability and thought beer was one of the four basic food groups."

"Hmm, not unlike the bohemians you've dated in the past?"

"Meow. Do I pick on your bed partners?"

Allie watched a bored look come over his face. "My stable of delicious stallions is untouchable. Expensive perfection. Your once-a-year grabfest on the couch with some reject from an Eddie Bauer Outlet store is scandalous. My dog wouldn't date some of the guys you've gone out with."

"You don't have a dog."

"Of course not. I'm too selfish to own such a thing." Gillian flipped his blonde mane over his shoulder.

"I could have sex if I wanted to." Allie dropped her face over her drink.

"Can't look me in the eyes and say that, can you?"

"Hmpf."

"So, I know you're dying to tell me details. I'll pretend to listen while I check out the scenery. Go right ahead." Gillian flipped his fingers around.

Allie recited from memory some of the statistics she'd found. "Alternative insemination is safer than receiving blood donations. The normal routine is test the donors when they first apply, freeze their specimens, and retest again in six months before the sperm's accepted."

As her emotion for the subject grew, Allie spoke faster. "I'm not going into this blind, you semi-maleness, you. Did you know there are seventy-five thousand women in this country using the process each year? This is not a fly-by-night scheme set up in a vacant strip mall. Concerned medical practitioners are making dreams come true for women not able to get pregnant the old-fashioned way." Allie straightened her shoulders and snapped her head back, flipping the ends of her hair over her shoulders.

"Bravo, teacher's pet. I'm only worried about your body, and what this outrageous idea of yours may actually produce. You're not allowed to see photos of the donors, you know. With your face and body, you could have absolutely gorgeous children given the right companion DNA. I don't want that dulled with some aardvark from a community college," Gillian said. "I'm merely inquiring if you realized the importance of a good, quality-assurance laboratory."

Allie watched him focus on the backside of the waiter at the next table. Disapproval of the tight derriere immediately spread over Gillian's face. "Ken needs to make an appointment with the health spa, posthaste. Pant seams were not meant to take that kind of strain. Remind me to speak to him after dessert," Gillian said in a low voice.

"I want a donor who is young, energetic, and healthy. Imagine the possibility of sitting at the Rose Bowl, screaming myself hoarse for my son, the wide receiver down on the field in USC colors, heading for the end zone with the winning touchdown tucked under his arm."

Allie stared off with a faraway look. "Or maybe I'll be standing in the back of a local bookstore as my daughter signs her seventh best seller for hundreds of people waiting in line to see her." She sighed.

"What if this gamble gives you something quite different? A special child out of the toy store?" Gillian asked in quiet tones. "Be realistic in your pre-parental daydreams."

"I would hope God knows I could handle it. She, in all her wisdom, may think I'm not cut out to be a mother at all, I don't know." Her seriousness matched the man across from her. "I want to try and satisfy this ache, fill this absence deep in my soul. There's a nurturing hunger inside begging for satisfaction. All I can do is try, Gillian. Whatever the fates deal me after that, I'll be up to the challenge." Allie tried to sound convincing.

"Have you thought whether you want to do it at the doctor's office or get 'take-out' and do it at home?" Gillian switched subjects and voiced the question matter-of-factly, his arm raised to catch the attention of their waiter.

Allie choked on her drink. "Excuse me? Take-out and do what at home? Am I missing something? I thought you lay on a table in some freezing examination room, in a ridiculous paper gown, and endured the unromantic syringed deposit?" Allie's mouth remained slightly opened.

"I'm sorry, could you give us just one more minute?" Gillian excused the waiter from their table with a flick of his wrist, then leaned across the table. "I thought you completed your research. You do not have to 'endure' anything. Self-inseminate in the privacy of your own home, that's the new way. Set the ultimate fertility mood, darling, with candlelight and soft lullabies on the stereo. Surround yourself with your dearest friends. Make it a blessed event begetting a blessed event."

Allie's face paled. "Yuck. You had me until I was surrounded by a bunch of women playing doctor." Grabbing her drink, she downed the liquid, slamming the glass on the table. Anything to wash away the image in her mind.

"Okay, forget the bovine gossips, just you and the guy's donation on your own bed. No Comedy Central jokes will pass my lips about the turkey-baster." Gillian smiled at her shocked expression.

He signaled for another round of drinks, pointing his perfectly buffed nails toward their table and nodding to the waiter. "I know of some wonderful sperm clinics in California. A few will FedEx directly to your home. Or, go ahead with the paper gown on some doctor's table."

"Since when did you become a practicing midwife? How do you know about this do-it-yourself home option?" Allie sipped her second Perrier with lime.

"I told you, Raphael is a parental unit. I happen to be godfather to the toddler man. What a charmer and only three years old. Deion Sanders better get his tight butt ready for retirement, this one is a definite Hall of Famer."

The waiter took their orders and disappeared into the crowded restaurant. The evening sun dipped behind a carrotwood tree, leaving patterns of delicate shadows across the tables. The patio purred with conversations wrapped in early summer heat.

"What about health insurance?" Ever practical, Gillian turned the conversation to important details. "AI can be fairly expensive. I hope our HMO will pick up the costs."

Allie wiggled in her seat. "Actually, they cover the majority of it. Can you believe it? As a So Cal Medical baby/alumni myself, I'm going to have my baby in their new and improved maternity wing. I have to supply the sperm but they cover ultrasounds, lab tests, the prenatal exams, and everything else. What are you laughing at?"

"You, supplying the sperm. Do not wrap the precious specimen tube in a Hawaiian shirt, my Parrot Head goddess." Gillian stamped his expensive shoes under the table. "You'll frighten the masculine tadpoles into immobility." Gillian started laughing harder. People turned in their chairs. The crystal tone of his infectious laughter brought smiles to the stiffest faces around them.

Allie pointed her finger across the table. "Cute. Pull yourself together or we're cutting you off from pink lemonades right now. Embarrass me and I'll reduce your visitation rights to zero. Do you want this embryo raised by Auntie Soozi alone?"

"That's not funny," he sobered immediately. "Don't threaten the baby with evil witches. Uncle Gillian will make sure it is pampered in Beverly Hills culture and Rodeo Drive classics."

"More like Uncle Gillian and *Fractured Fairy Tales* for this egg, with your sense of humor. Oh, I forgot, you're too young to remember *Rocky and Bullwinkle*."

"Oh, gag me with a silver spoon. I've seen your precious R & B toons on DVD. Get over it. Really, just because the graying generation has seen the originals, syndication management bowed and the whole series is available on DVD. Mature humor, I admit, but rather infantile animation. Straighten up, darling. Here comes dinner."

Later, Gillian slid into his teal-colored Mercedes convertible, a scrumptious reward to himself for enduring the commute to Allie's office. Turning the key, he looked up into a perfect Southern California night. He drove the miles of endless freeways home with the top down, his blonde hair dancing in the air. Heading west, Gillian hit the play button on the CD player. Chopin's music surrounded him. For the next hour of his trans-county drive, the *Concerto in D Minor* would help him unwind and shake loose the dust of the local yokels.

So Allie wants a baby. Gillian felt like an Osterizer blender on slow as a range of emotions swirled through him. Shock, irritation, confusion, and a touch of happiness flashed like laser beams through his mind. *How could his boss consider such a drastic change? I thought she was different, a rare form of female genesis, capable of escaping those touchy-feely moods of longing for diaper rash and spit-up milk.*

However, the flipside of the estrogen argument meant he'd be in charge of Novel Software while Allie was out on maternity leave. Could be rather interesting. How many glorious weeks would she take off, leaving him the freedom to rule? Probably none, knowing her. She'll be one of those dedicated divas who drop the baby between meetings and continue to snap the proverbial whip.

Gillian reached down toward his car phone console and grabbed the headset. He delicately punched the buttons and waited for the ringing to stop. "Tyrone? Set up the massage table, love, and call Eric so he's ready when I get there. I'm leaving the uncultured now, and you can't imagine the day I've endured. I'll need the vanilla oils, and put something sweet and bubbly on ice for me. I should be there in an hour or so."

Chapter 4

"Do you want me to come with you?" Soozi volunteered, with what sounded like maniacal energy to Allie over the phone. "I'm sure I can find a sitter for these two."

Allie noted that small talk was not on Soozi's agenda this evening. Setting her briefcase down to pick up the ringing cordless phone in the kitchen, she had known it was Soozi, who wanted to remind Allie about the appointment. Tomorrow morning, she thought to herself, my first ob/gyn visit since making the baby decision. Ten o'clock was the magic hour.

To Allie's amazement, Soozi had instantly raised her hand to participate once the appointment had been made. Is this one of those women things I don't always understand, like you can't go to a public restroom alone? Do I want to go to Dr. Adams' office by myself or with support surrogate Sooz at my side? A tough decision, and now Soozi waited for her answer.

I've made the majority of life's important decisions by myself. I started a business, bought this house and more, unaccompanied, à la carte, solo. But I don't want to hurt her feelings either by denying her pleasure from something as simple as the first physical, do I? The pout queen could make life miserable. The three-second argument ping-ponged inside of Allie's head as she stood in the empty kitchen.

"Sure, sweetie. Come with me, and we'll go shopping afterward at the mall." Allie relaxed the muscles of her neck and face with the decision. Don't sweat the small stuff between girlfriends. Soozi'd been Allie's shadow since grammar school, and this was not a time for disappointing her eager compatriot. If she wanted to sit in the doctor's waiting room like a blooming cheerleader, what was the harm.

"Great! I'll be the chauffeur and be at your office by nine-thirty sharp."

"Do not, I repeat, do not harass Gillian when you come in," Allie stated in stern tones, as she reached into the refrigerator for a Diet Coke. "Do not flaunt the fact you're going to the doctor's with me." Why these two halfway reasonable adults couldn't get along was beyond Allie's comprehension. Years of targeting each other with nasty, vicious verbal snipes and attacks that practically drew blood from the soul had left Allie defensive.

"Who me?" Soozi asked in a slow Southern drawl.

What was the old saying Aunt Kitty used, "Butter wouldn't melt in her mouth if it were a hundred degrees outside"? Allie could almost see Soozi sharpening her claws like a calculating cat, twitching her tail at the anticipation of taunting Gillian. Allie shook her head and popped open the soda can. "Girl, behave yourself, or I'm locking the office front door and I'll meet you outside in the parking lot."

"Oh, please."

"I mean it, behave when you come in, or I'll go alone to this and all other appointments down the road. And Auntie Soozi can wait for the test results like everyone else."

"Cold blow. I'll ignore the tanned bitch, party pooper." The phone clicked dead.

I swear I'm dealing with Samantha's wicked twin cousin from *Bewitched*. If Sooz could, she would twitch her nose and zap Gillian far away from Allie and this whole valley. Allie took a deep breath and ran upstairs to take a shower. Getting pregnant might be more difficult than she thought. Oh, not the AI process, but keeping the two friends she depended upon most in life from killing each other for her attention.

Soozi pointed the car into an empty parking space in the crowded lot and applied the brakes. "So, now will you tell me? What did the doctor say?"

Allie had kept the conversation deliberately casual until they were at the mall, enjoying Soozi's strained patience.

"Probably the same speech you got before you were pregnant with Lenny or Zoe, about cutting out caffeine and alcohol. Keep up a good exercise routine, as if I had one, and create a good incubator for the baby. Gillian was right, they strongly recommend you begin taking folic acid, ideally before inception." Allie watched the muscles in Soozi's face tighten with the mention of Gillian. "I have to start taking a multi-vitamin every day."

Allie climbed out of the car, noticing the change from the air-conditioned car interior to the outside air was unusually temperate. "I'll be taking a prescription for Clomid over the next couple of days, and then I switch to an estrogen pill for a few more days. That's about all there is to it." Allie closed the car door. "Oh, and I take my temperature before getting out of bed each morning to pinpoint ovulation of those all-important eggs. And Dr. Adams had the nerve to say I have good birthing hips." Allie linked her arm inside Soozi's and headed toward the mall. "It's nice to know oversized has a reason."

Allie smiled. "Come on, let's buy something for the baby before you take me back to the office."

"Girl, you don't have a clue. You'll be buying 'something for the baby' forever." Soozi made quote marks in the air with her fingers. "For the next eighteen years you'll be in stores and malls for this child. Oops, scratch that, only about fourteen years, then they wouldn't be caught dead in anything you'd like." Soozi pushed the heavy glass door open as they entered the air-conditioned store.

Soozi continued, "You buy the darling layette with nightgowns and play sets, and the little ankle-biters grow whenever and however they want to. The clothes you bought for cold weather will be too small by the time the season actually changes. That's the rule."

"Why not just buy the clothes as you need them?" Allie directed their path toward the baby department at the back of the store.

"Since when do we ever shop by necessity? We are impulse- and emotion-driven. Get real! You buy the adorable newborn two-piece outfit 'cause it's too choice to leave behind, but the nine-pound bowling ball that shows up at the hospital couldn't squeeze its left leg into a newborn-sized anything." Soozi stopped to press a flowered-print miniskirt up against her thighs. The plastic hanger clicked against her belt buckle.

"Lenny came out a size three to six months. I'm not kidding. The moose spent maybe a week in newborn Pampers and went directly into extra large." She snapped the hanger back on the rack.

"I don't think so," Allie said, laughing at Soozi's selective maternal memory. "I remember you being panicky over the tiny mound of receiving blanket they handed you at the hospital. Especially when they shoved you out the door a few hours later and said 'Have a nice day.'"

"What did I know back then? Compared to Zoe, he was King Kong at birth. She pops out a month early at a whopping five pounds, and had absolutely nothing to wear. Everything hung on her like a sack. She'll probably grow up paranoid about loose-fitting clothes. I traumatized any sense of style she may have carried in her genes."

"Jeans? She's too tiny for jeans. Levi can't stitch denim that small." Allie's voice faded off as they entered the infant section.

"Genes, not jeans. Are you inhaling baby powder? You didn't hear a word I said," Soozi pouted, crossing her arms in front of her. "I can be ignored at home, you know."

"Sorry. Aren't these just the cutest things?" Allie held up a one-piece outfit with colorful bunnies printed everywhere.

"What theme are you going with in the nursery? Are you going traditional or commercial? Teddy bears or Disney?" Soozi flipped through the rack of toddler dresses. "Do you want pastel for calming imagery or primary colors for stimulation? Are you going with oak furniture or painted wood?"

"What are you babbling about?"

"Hey, your baby's first environment after the hospital is the nursery. You want to make a good impression. Remember the little darlings will check out their baby albums during those nasty adolescent years, and you don't want to give them any more ammunition to hate you than they'll already have."

Allie stopped and stared at her best friend with her mouth open. "Stop it. Lenny isn't anywhere near puberty. Unwrinkle that face I love, and help me pick out something cute."

"Your fan mail, maven of the office," Gillian said. "Evil warlocks demanding payments are at the bottom of the stack and a few new orders are on top." A thick manila envelope, slightly worn from its trip through the postal service, balanced the rest of the mail from underneath.

Allie gave a cursory glance over her shoulder to the day's stack and went back to work on her computer.

"You may want to look through this."

"Why?" Allie kept typing her report.

"Daddy's here."

She swung her chair around and grabbed the edge of her desk with both hands. So soon? No way. The list of donor details? Already? Allie's hand shook slightly as she reached for the padded envelope.

Allie watched Gillian curl his gorgeous frame into the guest chair across from her desk, practically purring from delivering the good news.

Sliding the rest of the mail onto her desk, Allie's fingers clutched the heavy packet. The mailing label bore the styled logo of the sperm bank, the application for Allie's artificial insemination process. "So it begins," she muttered out loud. "Some tree gave its life for me to have a baby."

She ripped the top of the envelope with her mother's antique letter opener, a gift from Aunt Kitty when she first opened Novel Software. Allie videotaped this moment in her mind for posterity. The handle of the brass letter opener weighed heavy in her hand. Would her mother have been happy for her? Would she have approved of the process, a baby by donation?

Allie had worked hard to avoid connections to her parents in the ten years since their fatal car accident. Neither of them lent any moral support or guidance when she began Novel Software. Before that they'd been too busy even to show up for her college graduation. No whining on the phone to her mother about the hardships of being a young woman entrepreneur. No fatherly advice regarding car repairs when her cherished clunker stalled in the middle of Euclid Avenue. Before or after the accident didn't seem much different.

Allie fought her grownup battles alone. But then, she always had. Preoccupied with their professional work in geriatric research during her childhood, her parents rarely came out of their offices, let alone home to their only child. Her parents' professional success had the three of them traveling around the country with one or the other speaking at seminars and conferences. Allie grew up thinking most kids spent their summer vacations in different parts of the world at a variety of four-star hotels with room service and swimming pools.

Dear Aunt Kitty had been Allie's strength and nurturing force, whether the family traveled or stayed close to home. Her mom's younger sister, Kitty, became Allie's nanny and best friend. Would the possibility of being grandparents have distracted her parents from their precious work? Allie frowned, and a twist of pain shot through her chest.

"Maternity ward to Allie."

Allie blinked at Gillian. "I didn't expect such a quick response."

"They're in the business of making babies, dear. The process takes enough time without holding things up dribbling the paperwork. This part they can rush along." Gillian moved his chair closer to the desk for a better view.

Allie stuck her hand in the envelope and pulled out multiple stacks of papers, some stapled, some paper-clipped. "Good grief! Look at all this."

"Uh, Allie, the dad part is rather important to the process. They don't want you taking the first frozen vial you see." Gillian took a tissue and dabbed at his nose. "This is a serious business. You want quality sperm. Understand the biz—most labs will not deal with just any old chromosomes. You want the best you can buy." Allie surrendered part of the papers to his outstretched hand.

"'*Dear Ms. Thompson: Our laboratory's goal is to provide traditional and pioneering cryopreserved human semen products of unsurpassed quality.*'" Allie read out loud. "Thank God, they specify human semen."

"Mere testosterone overachievers."

"'*Enclosed please find information about our facility, the standards for donor selection, and the procedure for obtaining donor specimens…*' yadda, yadda, yadda. Sounds so clinical, no flowers, no dinner, just Muzak in a doctor's office and a vial of frozen male by-product." Allie's nervousness showed. They were talking about a possible daddy for her child.

"And it's that precious liquid that will give you the seed of your dreams."

Gillian didn't look up from reading the paper in his hands.

"No, I'm the seed, this is the fertilizer. A frozen Popsicle of life-forming goo."

"Hey, here's an application for a private donor. I could volunteer a few samples for you. I'm set up at another agency, but I wouldn't mind changing cryobanks if you wanted."

"Thank you, Gillian, but that's too weird. Working together is one thing, creating a baby together sounds messy and complicated. We don't need to be a program idea for the *Oprah* show. You stay Uncle Gillian and all will be easier," Allie said. "Besides we had this discussion earlier, remember? You are Parrot Head deficient, not a Jimmy Buffett gene in your whole body. That's no way for my child to start out."

My child. A wave of ticklish chills washed against her skin. These papers start the making of a baby process, the pre-signed and delivered product of lullabies and formula. Allie leaned back in her office chair and quietly rocked back and forth, using her tiptoes to push against the plush carpet.

Page after page of data, questions, and details. Did she want whole frozen semen in vials, or pre-washed frozen semen in straws? Did she want to throw the dice or try for better odds with a pre-washed, pre-sex-selected female straw or male straw? "Can they do that? Is it possible to screen the semen down if you want a boy or a girl?" Allie overwhelmed herself with the advertised concept.

"Omigod, look. Here it is, the list of donors." Allie held up a set of papers with rows of information on potential fathers, shaking it toward Gillian's face.

"Allie, be respectful. Each one is a man who donated a part of himself so women like you can have whatever." Gillian looked through the pages. "Nice selection, I must say. Do you know what you want for Daddy Dearest?" He looked up at his boss.

"I want someone over six feet tall. Long legs run in my family and I'd like to keep the tradition going. Other than that and Buffettness…I didn't know how much they would tell me."

Allie and Gillian spread the list over the desktop. The ethnic origins covered most of the European countries in various combinations: Irish/Polish, German/French, Swedish/German, Scots/Irish. The religion column, too, covered a wide range from agnostic to Zen Buddhist.

"Gil, I'm giving you an assignment. All these heights and weights don't mean diddly to me. I don't have a clue what a six-foot-two guy weighing one-seventy-five looks like. Is that a flautist or a baseball player? So get hold of something on the Internet and give me a breakdown of Mel Gibson, Tiger Woods, Derek Jeeter, and a few others' stats for reference."

"Right, boss. No problem." Gillian pulled himself out of the chair and headed for his desk out front.

"You even get their grade point averages and hobbies. This is more than most girls get after dating a guy for a year," Allie said loudly, flipping the printed pages back and forth. "Hey, how come football jocks are not volunteering for this cushy money? Look at this, a lot of basketball players and a few nature freaks, but where are my tailbacks and wide receivers? The list is sorely lacking an NFL quality."

Gil tucked his head back in. "Excuse me, football freak in pantyhose. What if you have a baby girl? Aren't you being the tiniest bit discriminatory? How would you feel about your little NFL player dressing in Donna Versace and Anne Klein?"

"Not a pretty picture. I'd rather she didn't have her heart broken from Y chromosome desires, but nothing would stop her from owning a NFL team some day."

"We lost one football team out of Southern California because of a woman owner. Teach your female child about ethics and pleasures of the game and less about the almighty dollar, would you?"

"Gillian, I'm shocked. I didn't think you knew the Rams left California, let alone you had an opinion about it. 'Course they've gone to the Super Bowl since they left here. Oh, gawd, don't tell me you dated one of the players?" Allie enjoyed watching Gillian blush.

"Mind your manners. I live near the stadium and am well aware of what drastic changes took place in the nineties. The team's desertion affected taxes and economics all through the area." Gillian said. "My dating habits do not color everything about my personal life." He fussed with the top button on his shirt, while leaning against the doorjamb.

"Sorry, it's the estrogen. Lately I'm mouthier from these pills I take every morning. I thought I would become hysterical during Hallmark commercials, but the waterworks don't seem bad. I'm more argumentative though."

"Some of those commercials are fabulous; they make anyone cry."

"Yeah, gotta love 'em. I seem to have more…energy, I guess. I thought I'd be comatose cutting out caffeine—thank goodness Diet Coke comes caffeine free or I'd be out of my mind. Chocolate's one thing, but cut off my Diet Coke? Close call." Allie turned around and stuck one of the forms in a small typewriter she kept behind her desk. "The estrogen seems to lift my spirits. Days are brighter and colors more vivid."

"We had Santa Ana winds on Saturday, girl. I love when they clear the smog away and everything is rainbow land. Maybe you should just take the pills and skip the baby. You won't see much of anything but exhaustion after having a baby," Gil badgered. "Isn't this better?"

"Cute. Get your opinionated butt back to your desk and make us some money." Allie flipped her hand toward the door. "I put this company together with passion and a bank loan. I may lead with my heart in certain decisions, but I don't lose any details along the way. A change in attitude, whether maternal or material, doesn't mean you can sit around fantasizing about a corporate takeover in my high heels. These precious little vials are expensive."

"Uh, first I need you to sign the Miller contract, Mommy Dearest." Gil handed a stack of papers to her.

"Thanks, Cruella," Allie grumbled as she swiped a pen across the bottom of the contract.

Gillian reached for the contract. "Now you can go back to deciding whether you want a *Full House* Jesse specimen or a *MacGyver* sort."

"Ooh, doing late night cable again? Allie's smile faded. "The donor probably grew up on MTV and Pop Rocks. I'm almost old enough to be the donor's mother, for gawd's sake, and I'm going to have his baby?" Allie's voice went into a squeak and she sank back against her chair like a deflated balloon. She brought a shaking hand up to her mouth. Old enough to be his mother. I'm going to be sick, she thought.

"You're not sleeping with them, darling. You're just using specific biological parts. Parts are parts. Sperm doesn't care how old your uterus is, they're after the new egg. Don't stress over something trivial. The guys are of age, they've signed the consent forms, and this isn't statutory rape in the back seat of a Chrysler. Now, I have to get this contract out. Are you going to be all right?" Gillian hesitated by the office door.

"Yeah, sure, you're right. There's an age requirement, isn't there? I'm fine, really, mail off the contract." Allie waved him away with lackluster energy and turned her chair toward the window.

Chapter 5

Allie sat on the carpeted floor of her family room with a half-moon of scattered white papers circling her. She propped her face on her bent knees and stared at the information chaos. Post-it notes in various sizes and colors dotted different pages. Highlighter colors in rainbow hues marked individual human characteristics listed on the pages in lines, squiggles, and blotches. Allie picked up a purple marker and popped the cap.

"Okay—I've got height, eyes, and possible great physique over here. I've got a football player of unknown position or skills with blue eyes there. I have brains and Scottish bloodlines over here." Allie gaped at the strewn papers, tapping the pen in the air against an invisible drum.

"Nobody has Jimmy Buffett or Parrot Head listed under interests. Surely one of you has a ph factor. Where did the lab find you guys?" Allie clicked the top back on the pen, dropping it into a pile of discarded highlighters. "Well, if I can't tell whether you like Jimmy, I guess I can pick physical factors that look like him. How 'bout naturally curly blond hair and a great Southern twang that makes me smile just listening to it?" She shuffled papers and stacks, separating out a few. "There, that's *this* pile of pressed wood.

"Do I want a man from a big family?" Allie picked up a sheet of paper with a few random colored marks. "This one has a lot of brothers and sisters."

She sighed and put the paper back into the ring of choices on the floor.

"I'm going nuts talking to these forms," Allie called out to the empty house.

How do you pick a father for your child when you're not blinded by love, when lust and heat for his body don't prejudice your choice? Or the "oops" factor isn't even a viable excuse to becoming pregnant? This is incredibly tough.

Allie pushed with her hands against the carpet, standing up. She stretched her long frame toward the cathedral ceiling. She'd been on the floor with the daddy donor papers for hours. She walked around the stacks, every now and then carefully bending at the waist to touch her toes and get the kinks out of her system. The silent house echoed her pacing and her creaking joints. With a tired sigh, she grabbed the portable phone off its cradle and punched in a number.

"Hello?"

"Sooz—help me," she whined. "I'm overwhelmed with this whole pick-and-choose-a-daddy thing. You've got to help me; it's too much." Allie held the slim cordless with both hands, her knuckles pale from the pressure.

"Don't beg, it's not feminine. Take a deep cleansing breath, two-three-four. Now, what are you doing to yourself over there in your pleasure palace?"

"How do I justify my choices to myself, let alone to a future child? These daddy decisions are giving me a ferocious maternal headache." Allie walked the length of the room. "Do I want brains or brawn, Catholic or atheist? Am I being too picky in the wacky world of fetus fate?" Allie chewed on her little fingernail as she stared back at the mess on the floor.

"Girl, I told you, pick the best five of the bunch, tape them in a clump on the wall, then throw a dart at 'em. You don't actually know what you're going to get from the gene pool of these donations. The donor's grandfather could have a stronger DNA than his grandson's. The great-grandmother may be ready to come back in the next generation. Your relative's genes may override Mr. Perfect's portfolio. It's a biological crapshoot, Allie, with Mother Nature's sense of humor ruling the outcome."

Allie heard Soozi sip something before going on. "Don't take this part too seriously. If you'd had a brother or a sister growing up, you'd understand better.

It's a game of baby roulette. Three kids from the same set of parents may not be anything alike. There's no rhyme or reason to the makeup of the children. Just choose," Soozi said flatly, finishing her speech.

"But what if I'm wrong?" Allie croaked back to her, hating the fear in her voice.

"Wrong? There *is* no right or wrong answer to the mommy game. When you hear that first incredible newborn cry or you hold the wet sticky bundle fresh from your womb, you won't remember any of this stress and bother tonight."

"Thanks, I needed the pep talk." Allie smiled as she scratched her head, and bent over one more time from the waist, her hair brushing the carpet.

"Now, go away. I'm trying to seduce Randy, if I can remember how the carnal act goes."

"Sooz! Why didn't you say something sooner? I'm so embarrassed. I'll hang up. Warn me about these things."

"Whoa, girl. He's still in the bathroom," Soozi laughed. "You kept me from falling asleep waiting for him to come out. I swear he's reading *War and Peace* in there. Why do they spend so much time on the john?"

"Beats me. I don't have to worry about toilet seats being left up. Start the fun without him—that'll get his attention when he finally comes out." Soozi would do it, too, Allie mused. "Okay, so I just draw a guy out of a hat, huh?"

"G'night. Whatever you decide will work. It's not all biological, this parenting thing. Your love will color this baby's world. Doesn't matter if it has brown eyes or blue, it'll look at you as Mom."

Allie caught her breath. Mom. She cleared her throat. "Give Randy a squeeze for me if he ever comes out of the bathroom." She hung the phone up. Sex. Do I remember what that is? Allie complained. I'll bet Gillian's not alone in his bed tonight either.

Allie stood over the well-handled papers on the floor. "You don't know me, but I want to be a mom, and I know you all volunteered to be biologically paternal."

Allie reached down and picked up three pages with the most colorful markings and Post-its on them from off the floor. She shuffled them behind her back, and then very carefully let two of them fall to the ground, holding her breath. The single page in her shaking hands held the identification of her newly designated donor, the father of her future child.

She brought the paper around front and stared at the printing: Number 45, brown hair, brown eyes, tall, smart, and Catholic. "Okay, guy. We have an important date coming up. Don't trouble yourself about bringing flowers. Though I love getting 'em, I'll understand if they don't arrive at the clinic."

Allie laid the chosen single page on the dining table, caressing her fingers over the ink markings and circles. Number 45. Quickly she gathered the rest of the mess on the floor into a sloppy pile. No second thoughts, don't look at them any more, she mumbled to herself. Decision made, fellows. Better luck next time. Keep trying, I'm sure there's a uterus out there for you somewhere.

She stuffed the profiles of the rejected donors into the trash. With shaking fingers Allie touched the page describing the father she selected. Leaning both hands on the edge of the table in a semi-pushup she said, "Number 45, are you excited about being a father? Do you want to know if your son goes to the Super Bowl someday, or if your daughter sits on the U.S. Senate? I promise to make the little one warm, safe, and happy. You do your part for me and help make it healthy."

Allie's voice bounced off the painted walls in a sing-song voice. "Num-ber for-ty-five. I made a choice, I made a choice." She twirled in a perfect circle on one foot, and wrapped her arms around herself. "I'm going to be a mommy." A mommy of a brand-new baby.

"What time does the man usually get here?" Allie paced outside her office door between the drinking fountain and Gillian's desk, her arms tightly crossed in front of her. The smooth leather of her high heels made the turns quiet and sharp.

"I know it's before lunch. I don't pay close attention to deliveries coming into the office, especially in those uniforms. Pull-eeze, like I would give a second glance to someone in polyester. Get a grip, woman." Gillian tapped his manicured fingernails on the desk. "I can't believe how nervous I am. I'm flushing," Gillian fanned his face with a sheaf of papers as they watched the glass doors for any movement.

"He should be here, shouldn't he? Come on, FedEx, I'm counting on you." Allie pressed her face against the glass and looked out by the elevators. "Where is he?" Her breath left a slight fogged mist on the surface.

The phone rang, breaking the tension. "Omigod, they lost the package," Allie gasped. She twisted around, staring at her assistant for support.

"Novel Software. May I help you?" Gillian answered, with a worried face turned toward Allie. They locked stares.

"Let me talk to Allie, office boy," came the order both of them heard.

"It's the bag lady," Gillian said with disgust before handing the receiver to Allie, holding it like hazardous waste material.

"Sooz, don't antagonize my help. What's up?"

"Sorry, it's an enjoyable habit. Has it come yet?"

"Soozi," Allie gasped. "That's a horrible pun, especially from you."

"What? I just asked—oh, I'm good, and I didn't even catch it. You know what I meant. Is the FedEx guy there yet with your magic potion?"

"No. It's not quite ten by my clock. We're getting way too pushy over this. They have their scheduled stops to make..." The glass office doors creaked behind her. Allie turned the upper part of her body and saw a uniform coming through the door.

"He's here," she whispered into the phone.

"Go, before Gillian asks him out and he runs away screaming. Go, go. Call me back later." Soozi hung up.

A small Styrofoam box, decorated in bright red and blue labels, sat on the corner of Gillian's desk. "Would you sign here, please?" The man handed Allie his electronic clipboard.

Allie glanced at Gillian then back to the machine. "Gladly. Uh, would you like something cold, a Diet Coke to go?" Allie's hand shook as she picked up the stylus. "We're kind of celebrating."

Gillian gingerly picked up the small package with something close to awe.

"Sure, thanks." He shifted his weight from one leg to the other. "This is my first delivery from a lab since I've worked this job. Is this a good thing? I'm not sure what to say."

"It's my first time, too." Allie laughed, leaving a jittery signature across the device.

"Okay, you two, enough already. Shake hands or hug, but, Allie, you have an appointment with this precious package at the doctor's office." The three looked at each other. Gillian broke the tension and went to get a Diet Coke from the office refrigerator. Allie opened her arms after handing the uniformed man back his machine and gave the startled man a quick embrace. The man raised his can of soda and left.

"Doctor Adams, if nature wrote the rules that the man shoots his entire…uh, deposit, to put it in crude terms, into the woman during sex, and she ends up pregnant, why do they 'wash' the semen before insemination?" Allie asked, lying flat on her back with her bare feet up in the icy cold stirrups. Now was as good a time as any to go over the last few nagging questions, Allie thought.

Dr. Adams' voice was patient and calm from the end of the examination table. "Sperm washing removes things called prostaglandins that if placed directly into the uterus can cause cramping. Nature put them there to help them swim upstream through the cervix. Because we're going to be doing an intra-uterine procedure, we want to use the most concentrated form of sperm to give it the highest possibility of being effective and by not making them travel as far.

"I'm inserting a speculum, Allie. It's going to feel slightly cold. This will open the vagina a bit for me. It's the same thing I use for your pap-smear exam." Dr. Adams reached to her side and selected more tools from the instrument tray.

"Now I'm inserting a narrow plastic catheter. It's going to go pass the cervix and into the uterus. There may be some discomfort. The sperm is injected through this tubing. If you're ready, go ahead and take a deep breath for me. Thatta girl. Now, exhale slowly through your mouth to the count of three. Relax."

Allie realized she had reached for the nurse's hand during this process and was now squeezing it roughly. "I'm sorry," she mumbled, easing back in her death grip.

"That's okay, you're doing great. Nervousness is normal," the nurse said with compassion.

"By placing the sperm into the uterus through the catheter, we're saving the sperm from long distance swimming. More survivors along the way make you more likely to conceive. There, all finished." Dr. Adams pushed her stool away from the examining table, pulling off the latex gloves with a snap, and turning off the overhead lamp.

The nurse stepped around quickly and began to clean up the area. She dropped the metal stirrups and pulled out an extension to the table, breadboard style. "Scoot yourself back, and lay here for a while. I'll get you a warm blanket."

The doctor patted Allie on the foot. "I want you to rest for a few minutes. Let's give the little guys a chance to wake up and check out their new home before you get up." Then she left the room.

The nurse opened a thin flannel blanket and laid it across Allie. Allie melted under the delicious heat of the blanket, fresh from a warming oven. The nurse slipped quietly out, leaving Allie alone.

"Okay, body, let's make a deal." After staring at the ceiling through the process, Allie closed her eyes. "You don't throw out the new neighbors, and I'll treat you to a whole carton of Häagen-Dazs Vanilla Almond Swiss. It's not like you've never seen critters like these before, it's just been a long time." Allie almost giggled.

"I know I've begged you not to get attached to wiggly guys in the past. I remember a few panicky nights where I promised you the moon if nothing happened. Look, we grow up. We change our minds. Then it was, 'don't take seriously what's poked at you in fun.' Now it's okay. Dr. Adams put them there because I asked her to. See? It's different."

Allie laid her hands with fingers wide on her flat stomach under the blanket. She kept her eyes closed and listened to the taped music piped through the office. She hummed a strain of "One Particular Harbor," her hands massaging the area of deposit.

Fifteen minutes later a short knock at the door startled a sleeping Allie as the nurse let herself in. "Miss Thompson? Go ahead and get dressed. Meet me at the appointment desk and we'll set up your next visit." She held Allie's chart in her hands and looked at the forms. "The doctor will see you in a month. If you have signs of pregnancy before then, we want you to call and she'll start you on a regime of prenatal vitamins. If you don't become pregnant this time, we will arrange for another process. Be good to yourself today." She left Allie to get up and dress.

Allie hugged the thin blanket, and then draped it on the table, missing its warmth as she slipped out of the cotton gown. She picked up her clothes from the metal chair and slowly dressed. She waited for something wet to slip out between her legs, that miserable, irritating drip that happened when she got out of bed heading for the bathroom after sex. Nothing. Number 45 seemed content to stay and do the job.

Chapter 6

"Allie, over here." Soozi waved her newly manicured hand above the heads of the others at the table, trying to get her friend's attention. The pastel fingertips fluttered.

Allie swept across the length of the crowded café in a veil of preoccupation. Quick brushes of lips to powdered cheeks, she made her way around the circle of women. Soft murmurs and glances of feline appraisal followed.

Allie seemed flustered as she settled into the padded chair pulled out for her at the table. Maybe she should be lying down at home right now with her feet propped up. Maybe this wasn't such a good idea, having a celebration with all her girlfriends right after her first appointment.

The familiar faces around the table stared expectantly at Allie. "Well?"

"I didn't have an orgasm, if that's what you're waiting to hear. I'm not craving a cigarette or anything."

"Sounds like sex at my house," someone spoke out, and laughter exploded. With the ice broken, everyone started talking at once.

"This is incredible!"

"Who would have thought you'd join the ranks of the diaper brigade?"

"Allie, how terrific for you."

"I'm surprised you want to clutter up such a perfect life with pediatricians and strollers."

All her friends chipped in their immediate two cents' worth of friendly advice and emotions.

"So, what was it like?" Soozi laid a protective hand over Allie's on the table. The group quieted down for the juicy details from their guest of honor.

"I lay like a virgin on a cold cement slab waiting to be sacrificed." Allie laughed with a slight catch in her throat, looking at the amicable faces around her. "I can't tell you how nervous I was. Dr. Adams kept reassuring me everything would be fine and that it was perfectly normal to be anxious. She informed me it may take months before a process takes, not that I have my hopes up for an instant pregnancy or anything." She twisted and fiddled with the cloth napkin in front of her.

"Artificial insemination is not guaranteed results. Especially in my age group, the statistics are high for failure." Allie squared her shoulders. "But right now, I feel absolutely famished. Any chance I can use the excuse I'm eating for a possible two now?" Laughter went around the table.

"Allie, you have a glass of Perrier with lemon as our expecting-to-be-expecting guest of honor. The rest of you raise your wineglasses to the latest of our group to fall prey to the maternal hormones of our generation. Allie, we salute your dream." Soozi raised her zinfandel and clinked glasses with the women around them. She swallowed half the glass before putting it down.

There were twelve offspring among the six women around the table, each having one to three children being cared for at home with fathers or babysitters, making the afternoon celebration possible. Two were recent single mothers due to divorce or separation papers. Never married, Allie would be the first of their circle to venture into motherhood solo.

Allie had taken a lot of flak over the years from this ensemble for not being married. They used to lunch together, fresh out of college, at least once a month on paydays to share a laugh and a piece of gossip. Now the lunch gabfests were sporadic as their lives splintered in other directions.

Allie broke the matrimonial daisy chain in her group when she followed a career as a single woman, but she rarely regretted the lack of a husband. "Okay, so my little bundle won't be growing up with a Desi as well as Lucy at the house." Allie leaned into the edge of the table, closer to her friends. "Why is it single fathers got all the prime-time television while we were growing up? *Bonanza* and *Gunsmoke* prove my point. Buffy and Jody even had Mr. French as well as Brian what's-his-name in their New York apartment. Where were my role models growing up, equal prime-time examples of single mothers?" Allie threw this out to the group with a smile, sitting back in her chair.

"What about *One Day at a Time* with Ms. Romano? That broke a few manly rules, I must say."

"God, I loved that show."

"Allie, I thought your role models were going to be Ann Marie and Mary Richards? You were supposed to be the single, successful career celebrity in our group. We love to fantasize about your personal affairs as we're wiping up the dried cereal off the floor from under the highchair. Another fantasy hero bites the dust." Cindy tucked a loose bobby pin back into her dark hair, noticing bits of baby food under her nails.

"And part of you is jealous that Allie doesn't have to endure the same guy for years to get a baby. She can keep the passion and excitement of sex alive with whomever she pleases, and still have the joys of a baby."

"What's sex?" Janelle downed the last of her wine. "I'm beginning to think sex is truly overrated."

"Ooh, is Santa bringing you lots of batteries for Christmas this year?"

"You know, I never could get into the mechanical wonders for women. I, uh, use a stuffed animal when the, uh, need arises."

The screams stopped most everyone in the restaurant for a moment. "Get over it! I'm sure I'm not the only one."

Cindy blushed over the intimate turn the conversation was heading. "So, Allie, give us the scoop on this phantom father. What did you go for?"

"Youth and physical stamina," Allie kidded. She wouldn't describe the mental picture she had painted for herself of the donor's physique. Some fantasies are better left unsaid with this group. "We know he's over six feet tall, with an excellent 4.0 grade point average. He's British Isles' lineage mixed with the spiciness of South America, a little milk toast with a dash of red pepper."

"Doesn't it sound fun that you can try and choose some of your child's characteristics? You want a Shaquille O'Neill, you don't use a five-foot-two librarian. Janie's got Carl's long legs and she struts them every chance she gets. Can you believe miniskirts come back when I have a twelve-year-old in junior high." Katherine picked up her wineglass and killed the rest of the pale liquid. "I need a refill."

"Isn't it 'what goes around, comes around?' You gave your mom gray hair with your adolescent weekend hijinks," Janelle twittered.

"Sheesh, I was a junior in high school before I started crushing mere male spirits! This heartbreaker is in middle school, for heaven's sake. You ought to hear the encounter stories she brings home. I'm terrified her homeroom friends are going on the pill, if they haven't already." Someone reached over and patted Katherine's shoulder in mock sympathy.

"The pill's rather out of style, isn't it? I thought everyone was into shots or patches of something now." Soozi bit into a pickle from the plate in front of her.

"Not at the free health clinics the kids are populating. I think cheap is the main concern of the federal government and those plastic discs of tablets are still the standard handout. Just like the ones we used."

"Speak for yourself."

"What else do you know about this donor guy, Allie? I mean what if his brother is a serial killer?" Everyone at the table stopped for a split second to stare at Janelle's tasteless remark.

"Or his siblings could be the Baldwin brothers. Janelle, chill that gruesome imagination of yours. They don't tell you if he likes ketchup on his scrambled eggs or sourdough bread with his caviar in the profiles," Soozi said drolly, rescuing the moment. "Some things are environmental; not everything is DNA."

"Thank God. Lou used to drive me crazy with his economically tight obsessions. I swear if we were on a picnic, he tore the paper napkins in half! Use only what you need, he'd say. I swear I would have screamed if the kids had followed that road. Give me a break." Janelle took another bite of her salad, trying to be forgiven for her last remark. She didn't mean to hurt Allie.

"Are you supposed to rest this afternoon, Allie, or anything?" Cindy leaned toward her, resting her shoulder against Allie's.

"The doc says carry on as normal. No bungee jumping or skydiving, as if I would ever be caught that far off the ground without being in first class. Not many rules to this AI maternal game after this point. The hard part is over, and now it becomes more of a waiting game. Though I continue my vitamins and exercise routines."

"Don't expect miracles, though. Rod and I had a tough time getting pregnant," Jill sniffed. "Two years of doctor appointments and fertility drugs. Rod kept a beeper handy to make love when my thermometer said, 'Ta da, you're ready' a couple days a month. It was torture."

"Jill, no one is arguing you endured the worst of us to have a baby. Surprisingly, most of us didn't go through the rigors of infertility to get pregnant. After so many years on the pill a lot of our generation's bodies are shutting down the ol' fallopian tubes. By the time they're ready for a family, their bodies are pushing for retirement."

Soozi frowned at the negative turn of the conversation. "Not that this is the case for you, Allie. I swear you probably have the same diaphragm from when we graduated from college." She paused as the group squealed, then added, "I'm kidding, I'm kidding."

"At least you have home pregnancy tests to cut some of the waiting," Janelle spoke up.

"Are you going to do Lamaze training, Allie?"

"I will for the knowledge of what to expect during labor, but I'm reserving my drugs with Dr. Adams already, and she knows to keep them coming until an hour after it's born." Another glass of Perrier was placed in front of her.

Allie lifted her glass. "Okay, my turn—a toast to the tremendous support and caring you've all given me. To lullabies yet to be." The women smiled and clinked their glasses with Allie's. "Okay, go ahead and spill your guts. Get all your labor horror stories on the table now and out of your systems. I want every gruesome detail, and then I want a vow of silence not to speak of them again until after my baby's born. I will have forgotten most of the pain and gore tales from you guys by then."

The noise level crescendoed as they all started to talk at once. Soozi squeezed Allie's hand briefly then joined into the labored fray.

"My first took no less than thirty hours of labor. I didn't think the damn thing was ever coming out of my body. And you know what, he still doesn't come out. That kid stays locked up in his room for days."

"I had an epidural so I don't remember much about the actual birth. God, but my water broke while I was on the phone with some salesman and it freaked him out royally when I screamed. What a puddled mess on the kitchen floor! I thought the baby was going to fall out right then and there. What did I know about birthing babies?"

"Carl refused to stay at the hospital. He was out jogging when I delivered, can you believe it? I remember the nurse telling the doctor the father was out of reach for the birth information and someone would page him. What a joke."

"Don't start male-bashing. Allie has conveniently eliminated that sore point of the process. Besides you don't want me going down that road, girl. You don't even want to hear what I'd have to say."

"Richard behind in child support again?"

"Behind? Has he ever started? The DA has him on the Ten Most Disgusting list," Cindy snorted, putting one hand on her hip while the other waggled a finger at them all. "Allie has the right idea, use the good part, and don't get suckered in with the rest of the package."

"Check it out. Did anyone see the latest goings on with John and Marlena?"

"Excuse me?" Allie brought her head up from the bowl of soup in front of her. "Who?"

"Sorry. *Days* talk." Cindy giggled with a quick wave at Allie's ignorance of the popular soap opera.

"That made it clear, care to try again?" Allie frowned at everyone smiling around her. "What?"

"*Days of Our Lives*, of course. John and Marlena are my favorites, but Bo and Hope are hot and heavy right now in an ugly triangle with Billy. Again."

"Girls, you don't really follow daily television candy, do you?" Allie looked around the table in shock. "'Fess up right now. How many soap opera junkies do we have here?" Five hands went up. "I thought I knew you people. All these years together—I'm shocked."

"Carl flips out at the time I spend on the computer catching up on all the soaps. Like his obsessions aren't annoying." The girls burst out laughing at Katherine's serious face.

"Al, you never leave your PC screen anymore for television. I tape the shows for delayed viewing in the evening after the kids are asleep."

"Seriously, everyone, back to baby talk." Cindy took another sip of her wine. "No matter how drastic the pain in labor or how exhausted you feel after the incredible number of hours, nothing compares to that wrinkled, wet bundle they hand you when it's all over." Cindy practically had tears in her eyes. "Your heart almost breaks at the sight of the blotchy-skinned prune in a blanket. And then it starts yelling about how cold the room is, how bright the lights are, and how rude the doctor was, grabbing it out of the birth canal, and it's all downhill from there." A burst of laughter went around the table.

"She's kidding. Maybe, sort of. Nothing a little Prozac in her drink wouldn't suffice to calm her down. What are you drinking over there?" Jill leaned closer to Cindy's glass for closer inspection.

"To the fall of the last of our group to be bitten by the baby bug. Allie, may those slimy sperms traveling inside bring you nothing but happiness."

"Hear, hear," they all agreed.

Allie nibbled slowly on her salad after finishing her soup. She looked around the table at her assortment of friends, a delicatessen of female hormones. How many times had they gathered like this for critical turns in their lives? First were the bachelorette parties as, one by one, each member fell victim to the fragrant perfume of orange blossoms and wedding bells except Allie, who seemed immune. Later came separation support lunches, where anger and tears were the condiments to lunch when the orange blossoms for some had withered and died from neglect and fear.

Only crumbs and a few wilted lettuce leaves were left on most of the plates around the table. The conversation and disagreements continued strong, along the course of diaper services versus disposables.

"Who would have time to wash a load of cotton yuckies all the time for two years?" Janelle whined, waving her hand at the group. "I worked eighty hours a week between my job and the first kid. There was no way I could avoid using disposables."

"Ditto for most of us, but my mother believed in doing it all the hard way. Experiencing the thrill of urine-soaked material, by hand," Jill chuckled.

"What do our mothers know? They grew up in a different culture altogether. Their generation was regular coffee to the cappuccino of now," Cindy sniffed. She brushed at non-existent crumbs on the table in front of her.

Allie threw out one last television challenge to the group, leaning into the table of women. "Name your favorite TV mother."

"Mrs. Cunningham, no doubt about it, on *Happy Days*. One part traditional, one part ditzy, made the best combination to survive motherhood ever." The women nodded their heads around the group.

"But wouldn't we all have liked Samantha Stevens as our mom? She could twitch her nose and have your PE clothes ready Monday morning no matter where you hid them."

"You just wanted to be fussed over and spoiled by Grrrand-mama," Allie stretched the name out with a dramatic flourish, waving her arms above her head. "Agnes Moorhead doted on Tabitha."

That woke up the estrogen. Everyone spoke at once about grandmothers and levels of spoiling. The squeals and hoots echoed in the restaurant when Soozi sat up straight in her chair. "Warning, danger, Will Robinson!" Soozi snarled under her breath.

Allie noticed the abrupt change in mood for Soozi. Only one person could rile her friend this quickly. "Gillian, what's up? You know everyone here, don't you?" Allie threw the questions over her shoulder as he came up behind her chair.

"Excuse me, elegant ladies, I do hate to intrude, but I need the guest of honor back at the office." Gillian bowed slightly at the waist. "I've been calling your cell phone every five minutes for the last half hour." Allie leaned over and rummaged through her purse. "Mr. Simple wants revisions to his edition of the Ice Cream Dream 5.3 program. We'll have to FedEx it by three-thirty." He leaned on the back of Allie's chair and spoke directly to his boss, trying to avoid Soozi's daggered stares.

"Dang, I forgot to turn it back on after the doctor appointment," Allie said as she flipped the phone open and pressed a button.

"Couldn't this have waited a few minutes more? Can't you stay out of her shadow for more than an hour at a time?" Soozi sniped at the male intruder. "Or does sunlight bother you?"

"Allie, Mr. Simple was insistent over the phone." Gil ignored the bitter attack.

Allie patted her friend on the hand. "Down, girl. It's okay. I was going to skip dessert any way. I have to watch my maternal figure, you know. It's been great, guys. Thank you all for the support and a great lunch." Allie pushed her chair back and bent down to kiss the cheeks of her nearest neighbors.

A chorus of good-byes followed Allie and Gillian out of the room. The waitress passed them going toward the door. "Good luck to you," she called.

"Thanks." Allie let Gillian open the restaurant door for them and squinted as she stepped out into the brilliant sunlight.

"Why does monster mother hate me so?" Gil asked as they walked to the car. "Every time I appear, she gets out verbal whips and chains."

Allie sighed. "I don't know. You're my right-hand person, causing a jealous streak a half-mile wide down her back. She likes being my main squeeze. Sharing me with you sticks in her throat, yet she knows the rules: daylight hours are yours and nights and weekends are hers." Allie fluffed her hair with her fingers.

"I feel like I have child visitation issues with you two. One of these days, you're going to have to learn to tolerate each other. This has been going on for too many years."

"Whenever she's ready to let go of her crown as Miss Bitch."

"See, that doesn't help. You want her to give in, and she wants you to find another job, preferably in another state. Enough. Let's get back to the office. Mr. Simple has rights to me, too. And he's paid a dear price for them."

"You are expensive, my dear, I must say." Gillian laughed and waved his hand in the air as if to blow the distasteful matter of Soozi out of the atmosphere. "How are you doing after your session?" Gil opened the passenger door of his car for her with concern painted across his face.

"Like my ovum wants to be a zygote when it grows up," she sighed, settling into the passenger seat. "Right now the mass of male by-product is probably lying around looking for the remote control and not paying attention to what they're supposed to be doing. I actually feel pretty good. It's hard to comprehend I've taken the first giant leap of motherhood."

"Remember all the literature says it probably won't take the first couple of go-arounds. Don't start buying the crib and layette already. I don't want to burst your bubble, but I don't want you to crash and burn early in this pediatric idea of yours, either." Gil pulled out into late lunchtime traffic.

"Shoot!"

"What? Are you okay?" Gillian panicked and slammed on the brakes. The car behind him slammed on his brakes, too, avoiding a collision but hitting his horn loudly.

Allie started to giggle at his overreaction. "Sorry. It's just that I left my car at the restaurant. We need to turn around." She covered her mouth lightly with her fingers, shaking her head. "I got flustered with you two catfighting in the café. Could you go around the block and take me back? Duh."

The next morning dawned hot and still, a sunny Saturday. Allie's bravado during the group lunch had ebbed considerably. Sitting up with a shock during the middle of the night, she wondered if she had done the right thing. No one answered her questions in the empty bedroom.

Even now, in the clear light of morning, hundreds of doubts pricked her brain as she lay still in her queen-size bed. She slid her foot across the mattress to a cooler spot on the sheet. A kaleidoscope of thoughts danced in her mind, justifying her actions, reaffirming her decision. Would she be a good mother?

Allie quickly changed the focus to Soozi. No one could set a better example than her best friend, could she? Sooz was maternal occupation personified, a font of practicality, of calm good sense when needed, and a splash of insanity to balance the pain with the pleasure. Soozi didn't think it was totally out of the question for Allie to be a mom.

"Besides," Allie continued, driving the point home to no one in the room, "the baby's not here yet."

A baby. Allie rolled over, snuggling deeper into the covers, enjoying the no-work morning. Someone of my own to play dolls with or build me a private jet from Legos. "Someone to share Santa Claus, the Easter Bunny, and the tooth fairy. Or camp out in the backyard under the trees telling spooky stories to each other, lying on our sleeping bags in a tent we put up ourselves. They'll bring out their personal DVD player and twenty flashlights, probably. Maybe I should get on the Internet and start buying stock in Duracell."

Chapter 7

Perched on the edge of a barstool in Soozi's bright fiesta-colored kitchen, Allie nursed a caffeine-free Diet Coke. Low rumbling of television cartoons in the family room made continuous background noise. Occasional ear-piercing screams and shouts from Soozi's children accented their close proximity to the grownups. Typical high-rocking Saturday afternoon in this middle-class household, Allie thought as she turned to watch her friend dig through a cupboard gathering ingredients for a batch of cupcakes.

"Sooz, I had the weirdest dream last night." Soozi looked up from her search. "A bunch of us were on a vacation in the Caribbean; I guess there were six or seven of us. Had to be an odd number because you all were in couples and I traveled solo. Anyway, the islands and the scenery were crystal clear in this thing. I mean vivid, drop-dead Technicolor. I can remember each outline on the horizon and these emerald-green hills in the background. And the lush smells of damp earth and incredible spices or flowers or something." She took a sip of Coke, savoring the memory. "Freaky, girl. Remember I was just telling you last week I've never been to the Caribbean?

"So, we all piled out of this huge rental car and were cruising a small village for some serious tourist shopping. I wandered away from the pack of you and found a used book store."

"Oh, there's a surprise. Even in your dreams? Girl, you'd find a bookstore at the North Pole," Soozi snorted, measuring out a cup of flour.

"Well, I would expect Santa Claus to have at least one store up there. Where do you think all the Christmas books go after children are through with them?" Allie asked as her friend rolled her eyes heavenward and let out a groan.

Allie shifted on the stool. Her sandaled foot tapped against the back of the counter. "Anyway, I walk into this book shop. It's kinda dark inside because palm trees and flowered bushes grew against most of the windows so it gives the room a green sort of underwater look. Rows of books are on these crude hand-made shelves, nothing manufactured or store-bought-looking, with the books mainly leaning against each other every which way.

"I found what looked like the children's section and picked up an old white hardback, with a brown ink illustration of Christopher Robin and Pooh on the cover. I can't tell you how clear this whole dream felt, every detail was like right there. I remember thinking that I had never seen an A. A. Milne book about Pooh with a white cover, so it truly caught my attention. The price of twenty-eight dollars was penciled on the inside cover. Soozi, it gives me chills. I can feel the book in my hands, I can smell the musty pages of print, and I know I'm going to buy it for the baby." Allie stared at her friend across the near-spotless kitchen.

Soozi snapped the Tupperware lid on the flour container. "This is going to be the only baby born with its own library already stocked in alphabetical order, with separate sections of classics and modern literature. And probably a separate sports category thrown in for good measure, if I know you. God, I hope the baby's not dyslexic." Soozi slammed the wooden pantry door with her hip after emptying her arms of the matching pink-topped Tupperware containers of sugar and baking soda on the kitchen countertop.

"What are you doing with that stuff?" Allie almost choked on her drink. "Haven't you heard of Duncan Hines?"

"I make a gazillion cupcakes for the under-legal-height club that lives here. Once in a while, I like to make 'em from scratch. It's a Susie Homemaker thing—you wouldn't get it, office queen. I freeze most of them for future rainy days. Continue with the dream, girl, I'm listening."

Allie shook her head slowly. "I leave the bookstore and I can't see any of you guys around anywhere. I walk off and it's like I'm on a hill or a second-level kind of thing. I find these narrow, crude stairs you have to climb down single file. People below are waiting for me to come down first before they can go up. Get this, the first stair was a weather-beaten wood slab thing, the next one seemed kind of the same, but smaller, and then the next three were these tiny round spots of steel that you were supposed to balance on as you went down, then a three- or four-foot drop to the bottom that was now covered in clear water. The people below are standing ankle-deep in a slow-moving river." Allie slowly shook her head, still puzzled over the changing scenes in the dream. Her heart pounded harder against her chest. The dream still affected her.

"So I climb down, make my way up this pristine river back to where the rental car should be, and it's not there. You've all taken off for dinner and left me. Sooz, it freaked me out, I kid you not. I'm stranded in this forsaken village on an island somewhere in the Atlantic, and you've all boogied without me. In one hand I'm clutching this huge oversized purse, I swear it looked like a black canvas diaper bag, and in the other hand I've got the plastic store bag with the Pooh book in it." Allie gripped the sides of her Diet Coke till the white showed in her knuckles.

"I never felt so alone, like just because I'm into this baby thing now, the rest of you take off and become free adults to do as you please." Her voice cracked with the memory. "My stomach felt like it had been hit by a truck, and the sad thing was, when I looked down, I wasn't pregnant. My blouse was tucked neatly into these khaki shorts with nothing there, not one extra ounce. God, I hurt. I woke up as you were all piling out of the rental car with everyone talking at once, 'Gee, you missed a great dinner,' 'We couldn't wait for you any longer.' Talk about an abandonment issue. Whoa. Probably stressing because once a baby comes, I won't be dining out anytime soon, let alone flying off to an island. Sooz, what a rough nocturnal experience!" Wrapping her arms across her flat stomach, Allie rocked back in the stool.

Soozi stopped stirring the batter and looked up at her friend. "Take a deep breath, girl. It's over, it's daylight." Soozi put her hands on her hips. "It was only a dream, well, maybe more like a nightmare. Your mind and body got into a release session last night without your permission. It happens. Artificial insemination is a huge decision."

"But what if it's the wrong one? What if I'm not supposed to start having a family at this late date?" Allie nervously played with the empty gold can. Maybe she needed to schedule a good massage, some relaxation therapy for herself. She hadn't done an all-day pampering treatment at the Total Look Salon in a long time.

"Allie, I never, ever thought you'd be a mom," Soozi said with a short laugh. "When we were kids, I had to loan you one of my dolls to play house together. Before two minutes were up, you rejected the doll and wanted to be the old spinster schoolmarm from Laura Ingalls Wilder books, or a surgical doctor. You avoided all contact with changing diapers and making formula." Soozi wiped her hands on a kitchen towel and leaned against the counter.

"You spent your childhood typing up plays for us kids to perform in the backyard for the grown-ups. You were in love with keyboarding on an old Smith and Corona before we even knew what keyboarding was. That typewriter held your attention and the loving touch of your fingers more than any peeing plastic doll with painted on hair."

Allie laughed. "You owned every doll ever made, I swear. Walking into your room was scary, seeing all these eyes staring back at you. Yeah, dolls were never my thing."

Soozi handed Allie a wooden spoon smothered in batter. "That was then, this is now. You still love striking magic with your words on ordinary plain pieces of paper, yet there's room in your heart for more. If you want to be a mom, if that maternal ache or need is there, go for it. You've never hesitated before on any of your harebrained ideas—don't be cowed by a few hormone shots and a sample of sperm." Soozi deftly finished filling up the paper cupcake holders in the tray.

"You do know it's the shots throwing you for a loop. Your X and Y chromies are all confused and disorientated. It's not status quo in your body anymore. Flow with it." Soozi reached into the refrigerator for an opened bottle of white zinfandel and another Diet Coke can. Setting these down, she reached for two crystal glasses from the overhead cupboard.

"Here, pour your Diet Coke in this. None of my luscious juice from the grapes for you, lady." Soozi filled her glass and raised it up. "To the future. Whatever happens, I'll be there for you. With diapers or without, we're a hell of a team." The glasses clinked lightly.

A crash and an ear-splitting scream stopped them in mid-swallow. A young male body came flying through the kitchen doorway.

"I didn't do it—she made me," Lenny shouted out fast, grabbing his mother's legs.

Soozi picked up the filled baking pans and turned her back on Lenny. "Okay, Auntie Al is going to do the honors today and handle this. Mommy is busy. Go plead your pathetic case with her."

Allie covered her mouth with her hand, hiding her smile. Her blood pressure may never come down today, first reliving the dream and now the arguments from the "I didn't do it" squad. She took an extra sip of her drink and placed both hands on Lenny's shoulders.

"Come show me what you didn't do. Then show me where Mommy keeps her books. I want to borrow one." Auntie Allie pointed him out of the kitchen.

"It's on the bottom shelf, big thick red thing. You can't miss it."

"You're spooky. Stop reading my mind." Allie watched Soozi down the glass of wine and pour herself another glassful.

"Ooh, we're going to an-a-lyse Allie," Soozi said in a sing-song tone. "This ought to be fun."

Allie placated Lenny with sympathy, helped scoop up the fallen toys, then followed the leader to the bookshelf. Allie grabbed the worn red book from where Soozi said it would be on the bottom shelf—*10000 Dreams Interpreted* by Gustavus Hindman Miller. How many times had the two of them poured over these pages back in high school, trying to interpret each other's night dramas? The thin, brittle pages crinkled as she opened it randomly, walking back to the kitchen.

"What do I look up first?" Allie settled back on the upholstered barstool.

"Let's start with the big picture and work our way down to details. What about Caribbean?" Soozi splashed water into the empty mixing bowls at the kitchen sink.

"Nothing. What about islands? Maybe an island's an island when you're dreaming." Allie flipped through pages, strands of hair falling in front of her face. "Here it is: *'For women to dream of islands omens a happy marriage.'* Great—I'm trying to go down the baby aisle and my dreams are trying to make it the matrimony aisle." Allie chewed on a strand of hair before flipping it away, an old high school habit. "Ooh, under shallow or clear ocean, which is a perfect Caribbean-type description, don't you think, it says *'signifies prosperity and pleasure.'* That's a little better. What else should I look up?"

"How about the being on vacation part?" Soozi took a swallow of wine.

"Nada. Seems strange there wouldn't be a huge section on weekend excursions, or…oh, passengers! Okay, look, what about this: *'To dream of being a passenger leaving home'*—duh, they couldn't just call that a vacation—*'a passenger leaving home means you are dissatisfied with your present living conditions and will seek to change them.'* Right on, book, just as powerful as ever." Allie laughed. "Change is an understatement for a baby. I'll take it."

"Okay, what about daylight? The dream happened only during the day. Seems night or day was a big factor, if I remember." Soozi washed the utensils, wrist-deep in soapsuds.

"*'To dream of day denotes improvement in your situation.'* And in the back of the book, sun. Here: *'Sun at noontide denotes the maturity of ambitions.'* Both rather positive signs, I must say. 'Maturity of my ambition' sounds like I should get pregnant from this, don't you think?" Allie tucked her hair behind her ear. The worn yellowed pages of the book felt like an old friend. Many a teenage crisis had been resolved by patiently researching every nuance of a dream to make it fit into whatever situation they had gotten themselves into back then.

"Almost two for two, the marriage thing is still bizarre. What about the bookstore part? You seemed to spend a lot of time in there."

"Mom, I gotta go peepee," Lenny yelled from the living room.

"Go by yourself. Just call me if you need me," Soozi hollered back, filling a new set of cupcake papers in a second tray.

"What was that all about? I thought Lenny was housebroken?" Allie questioned in a stage whisper.

"He is. The warning around here is 'pause before you pee.' Sometimes I leave Zoe's dirty diapers soaking in the toilet. You don't want to know the mess it makes when Lenny has flushed them after his business."

"Yew. Plumbers must love you. Another plus for disposable diapers."

Soozi sniffed, "Now, where were we?"

"Hmm, books. They don't talk about children's books, or old, antique books. Stretch it out, Sooz, brainstorm for me," Allie encouraged her friend. Soozi killed at dream interpretations.

Soozi swallowed more wine. "Bookstore, books, what about bookcases, those weird bookshelves they were on? Didn't you say they were wooden, in the middle of the store?"

"Bingo! '*Full shelves of books foretell happy contentment through the attainment of hope.*' Girl, we're just as good at this as we always were. Isn't it incredible? Keep going—what else? You were the best at picking apart the details out of a dream." Allie's eyes twinkled, the daring duo riding again into the sunset of sacred silliness.

"What about going down those stairs into the clear river part. Let me get a piece of paper and break down the particulars."

"Just like Nancy Drew and Honey," Allie giggled.

"You must be kidding. Look at these bodies, we are not teenage snoops anymore, maybe matronly meddlers. Okay, start with the railing, because I don't know how you're going to find those tiny spot things you walked down to the bottom." Soozi leaned against the bar counter with a pencil to write on a sheet of construction paper grabbed from the front of the refrigerator.

"'*To dream of holding onto a railing foretells that some desperate chance will be taken by you to obtain some object upon which you have set your heart.*'" Allie's voice dropped to a whisper as she read the last part. She stared at the page of the book with the tip of her finger just under the sentence. A desperate chance will be taken on an object upon which you have set your heart. The words blurred as her eyes filled and overflowed.

"Dang. There it is there. Close the book; don't mess this up with any other details. Always leave them wanting more, you know." Soozi fussed around, putting the construction-papered artwork back on the refrigerator. She quickly finished her glass of wine. "It's just a book, Al, and we're lousy fortune-tellers, but wouldn't it be great if we're not."

Allie wiped at her wet face with the back of her hand. "Sooz, I want a baby. I don't know why, but the emotions are here and I can't shake 'em loose. A messy, poopy, soft, cuddly bundle to call mine is what I want, with or without colic, hair, or diaper rash." Allie finished her glass of Diet Coke. The empty crystal pinged as she set it on the counter.

The next moment Lenny chased his sister screaming and shouting into the kitchen. So much for getting mushy on the baby subject; reality barged in again with its own ideas and energy force.

"Look at that face. What have you two been doing? Your sister is green!" Soozi grabbed a wet dishrag.

"I drawed on her like the clown did to me, 'member?" Lenny puffed his chest out.

"Face painting is for clowns only, you self-made harlequin. Don't try to be Picasso on your sister again," Soozi rubbed dish soap against the tiny cheeks. The toddler started screaming in anger and tried to wrench free of her mother's clean-up operation. "Zoe, hold still or you'll get soap in your eyes."

Allie walked around the melee and reached in the refrigerator for another Diet Coke. Lenny's bottom lip protruded far beyond his face while watching his mother destroy his morning's work. "Hey," Allie said as she put the gold can back on the chilled shelf, "It's almost time for lunch. How 'bout I treat us all to McDonald's?"

Zoe's face bounced up and down in Soozi's hand. "Mic-Don-oh's, Mic-Don-oh's!" Allie winced. How can such a tiny body make such loud cries?

Soozi looked up at her friend. "Nice save, pal. Let me get these two in the bathroom for some major reconstruction work with soap and water. Maybe even a hairbrush, if I'm lucky. Keep an eye on the cupcakes, and when the timer dings, take 'em out to cool. This will be fun."

Sooz needs to get out more, acting like a visit to McDonald's is the high point of her week. Allie shook her head, tossing the empty wine bottle into the recycle glass bin.

Allie clicked on Save, swung her office chair around with a sigh, and grabbed the ringing phone. "This is Allie," *and I don't have time for interruptions right now. I'm in the middle of a deadline, go away,* she finished in her mind.

"Hello there," said the deep, silky male voice.

All present motion stopped for Allie. Those two words melted across her ears by phone maybe twice a year and never failed to raise her blood pressure a few notches with a pounding heart. Seattle was back in town, well, not the whole city, just one particular gorgeous male fishing boat owner, who managed to make Allie weak in the knees after years of their long distance sexual interludes.

Brief but passionate weekends of minimum food and maximum physically attentive exercise were enjoyed when he traveled south on business to California or she scheduled a meeting up in the Northwest.

Allie remembered hotel female staff watching enviously as she disappeared behind whatever numbered door he'd been given for what they correctly dreamed would be hours of fantastic sex. If the elevator was empty, Allie emerged half-undressed, shoes and pantyhose in one hand.

Flashes of noise and color passed through Allie's mind, sheets and bedspread crumpled on the floor after the first round of lovemaking. Round two began as they moved their damp bodies to the shower, never taking both hands off each other, and started all over again under the cool spray of water. His muscles rippled under snowy white mounds of soapsuds. Large, workworn hands slid down her back, cupping her wet backside, and pressed her up against his nakedness. He gently nibbled her ear, and Allie shivered as his hot breath blew against her neck. Time and again similar hot, wet scenarios played at either end of the West Coast. Neither seemed serious about stretching their union any further than fly-by sex, though once or twice the subject of going steady had teasingly been broached and rejected.

Allie envisioned him on the other end of the line, stretched out, his long legs crossed at the ankles and barefoot on the hotel bed. The phone would be cradled against the dark salt-and-pepper beard that Allie loved to feel against her cheek and other parts of her body. His intense blue eyes would be staring out the room's sliding patio door or window at the hazy outline of mountains now so close to both of them.

Seattle? Here? Now?

"Hello, yourself," she finally whispered, then cleared her throat. "What brings you down here, stranger? A sale on fishing reels, or are you stocking up on sunshine for a while?" Allie flushed as her hormone level skyrocketed with each word. Her heart pounded against her chest.

"What if I told you I missed you terribly and came down only to ravish your body for a couple of incredible days and nights?"

Allie fidgeted in her chair. "I believe the body part, the first part is skeptical. Loneliness is not something I associate with you. I expect there's a girl in every port, Don Juan." She tried to make her voice serious but her face muscles kept pulling into a silly grin.

"I'm crushed." Allie smiled at his dramatics. "How can you think that way after all our years together? You are my only love."

"Finish the sentence, Michael. My only love in the Inland Empire, maybe even Southern California, but I seriously doubt it. I would think there are one or two women near the John Wayne Airport and maybe a young flirty thing based out of LAX. Could be twins down in San Diego. Okay, I'm the Ontario Airport pin-up girl." Allie laughingly challenged at him. She ran her fingers through the top of her hair a couple times, leaning way back in her chair.

"Allie," the voice purred.

Looking toward the ceiling, trying to breathe, she said, "Don't pout. You are totally irresistible when that darling bottom lip is sticking out, begging to be kissed. And you know it." She played the phone cord with her nervous fingers. Oh, my gawd; oh, my gawd. Seattle's here.

"When are you going to come kiss it and make it better, then, if you know me so well? Can you get away, right now? Tell ol' Gillian to hold down the fort and come meet me at the Hilton. I have something special for you."

"Something more than just you? Hmm, a personal present from some faraway land, or smoked salmon from a great fishing season I have to share with everyone?" Allie squeezed her eyes shut.

"Something just for you, Al, but you have to come to my room to get it. Come on, put me on hold and buzz the drag queen out front. I can't wait to see you and hold you in my arms."

"Gillian is not a drag queen, Michael. Sheesh, hold on." Allie pushed the hold button and walked with a little skip out to Gillian's desk.

"What's up, boss? You're looking flushed, should I call the doctor? Are you okay?" Gillian's forehead creased in concern.

"Michael is on the phone. He's in town for the weekend."

"The nerve of that man showing up at a time like this." Gillian stared at her guilt-laced face and his eyes widened. "Doesn't he know what you've been up to?"

"No. I hadn't thought about him, actually. I guess I'll have to tell him tonight. I didn't expect him to pop into town so soon, you know?" Allie complained, twisting her fingers in front of her.

"Soon? It's been six months since you've seen him, if not more. Allie, you can't go messing around with some overgrown stud poodle right now. You're ten days into your first AI deposit. Sex is a no-no. Are you sure you're going to be able to explain this to the love machine at arm's length—not between some hotel sheets?"

"I don't know. We've never been in the same room for very long without being naked. Sometimes, if the service was slow at a restaurant, we'd be ready to clear off the dishes ourselves and go at it on the table. I don't know how I'm going to get a serious discussion in before he starts unsnapping things," Allie said.

"Correction. No unsnapping things. You can't get naked with this guy. Don't even take your shoes off in front of him. You might be pregnant right now. Sex is out of the question." Gillian pursed his lips and folded his hands together. "I suppose you came to ask for the rest of the afternoon off."

"He's holding on line one, cooling his heels and the rest of his naked self at the Hilton."

"Allie," Gil sighed. "You have to meet him somewhere in public, preferably crowded, and break the baby news as soon as possible. Promise me, if I excuse you right now, you will meet him where you'd be arrested for exposing your breasts."

"Gillian!"

"Promise me, or I'll tell salmon-lover to take the next plane back to Seattle." Gillian reached for the phone on his desk.

"Okay. All right, I thought you weren't too keen on this baby thing. I didn't expect a mad dog routine from you when I came in here."

"You'll thank me tomorrow."

Allie walked back into her office with a numb expression on her face and closed the door. What am I supposed to say?

"Michael? Sorry that took so long. Uh, yeah, I can leave now," Allie stuttered.

"Great. I'm on the ninth floor, just for you. I'll have the wine chilled and the bed warm."

He remembered my favorite number. Allie sighed and continued with difficulty, "Uh, I was wondering if we could meet at the Panda Inn first. I haven't eaten anything today, yet, and I, uh, don't want to faint from hunger in the middle of our…visit. Would you mind, Michael?" Allie struggled for something to say. This was nuts. How do you turn down great sex? "Could you get a table for us, in a corner maybe? Be a love and order me a Perrier with lime." Allie kept her voice light over the pounding of her heart.

"This is different," he said. Allie winced at the questioning sound in his voice. "I don't know that I can share you with others tonight. It's been forever, Allie, since we've been together. We can do room service, if you get hungry for something other than me…is something wrong?" His voice had a concerned quality and Allie melted against the receiver.

"Yes, uh, no, it's just…I can't wait to see you either, but, uh, the doctor says I have to be careful with my eating and all." Allie twisted the phone cord in a knot.

"The doctor? Is everything okay?" Michael's voice rose slightly, no mistaking the concern this time, Allie thought.

What do I say? "Uh, yeah, she's pleased with the test results so far." Allie stared up at the ceiling. Somebody help me. Her palms were sweaty from skirting a fine line of truth in the conversation.

"Test results? That doesn't sound good." Allie could hear rustling in the background as he moved around. "Okay, sure, let's meet at the Panda Inn. That's fine, darling. I'll get a table for the two of us. I can't wait to hold you in my arms and kiss that sweet mouth of yours. It's been too long, and I'm hungry, hungry only for you. Hurry to me." And Michael hung up.

Allie sat and stared at her hand holding the dead receiver. Her female juices had already acknowledged the phone caller. I'm worse than Pavlov's dog. A phone call from Michael and I'm dripping all over my chair. What am I going to do? She slammed the receiver down.

Gillian tapped on the door jam before he stepped inside. "I saw the light go out on your line. Are you okay? What did he say?"

"I told him I'd meet him at the Panda Inn for dinner. I don't think he believed me at first, but I told him I had doctor's orders to clean up my health. That caused some misgivings, so he's falling all over himself to get there."

"Are you going to be strong enough to pull this off?"

"I really don't know," Allie whispered, closing her eyes.

"Do you want me to come with you?"

Allie stared at Gillian. "He's getting a table for two," she stated tentatively.

"Like we couldn't pull up a third chair? I don't know that we'd be staying for all courses, do you? Once you let the cat out of the bag about what you're doing to have a baby, I don't think Mr. Seattle will stay. I don't mean to be crude, but sex is the biggest thing you two have in common. Once you eliminate sweat, what would he hang around for?"

"Ouch, that hurt. You're saying he's shallow?"

"I've seen terriers with more compassion and human kindness. He adores your body but in all the years, I've never heard where you two come out of the hotel room for more than a couple hours at a time. You either go to a restaurant for nourishment, or take a walk along the beach to refuel your oxygen levels. A marathon love machine is all you are to him."

"What's wrong with that?" Allie snapped.

"Down, girl. Bad timing on his part does not constitute harming the messenger. I know things are emotionally sensitive for you, but don't bite me because of your carnal cravings." Gillian held out his arms, and Allie slowly walked in for a hug.

"Look, let me come along. I might be able to ease the awkwardness or provide an ice bucket if needed, or at a minimum save you from ruining the AI process. You've come so far with this, don't screw it up." Allie knew a smug smile tugged at Gillian's lips over the pun.

"Thank you," Allie mumbled against his shirt. "Someone has to protect me from myself. He's got a great body, Gillian. We care about each other, in our own way," she groaned.

"I know, girl. I've had my own fantasies about your manly hunk from the fishing docks. He does make a person's mouth water just walking into a room." Gillian sighed. "Be strong, girl. Think about the baby, not his biceps."

Allie wiped a single tear from her eye. She pulled away from Gillian and reached for a Kleenex. "Okay, let's shut things down here and get ready to go. He's saving a table at the restaurant."

Allie walked in front of Gillian as they entered the restaurant. A young girl at the front desk looked up. "We're, uh, I'm expecting someone to be saving a table already. His name's Michael."

"Ah, yes. Will there be three of you now?" The woman stared at Allie with obvious surprise, looking over at Gillian.

"Yes, please."

Gillian leaned in to whisper. "She can't believe you have two gorgeous lovers. What is your secret, girl?"

Allie laughed, despite the situation. "Stop it. Behave yourself." The woman looked up and beckoned them to follow her.

The restaurant was almost empty. The Friday night social scene hadn't begun as most people were at their desks counting down the minutes. Allie sucked in her breath as she spotted him across the room. Michael caught her gaze behind the hostess and pushed back his chair to stand. Instantly he realized she had company, and a slight frown crossed his face.

"Michael," Allie said as she came into his arms. She was immediately enveloped in an enormous bear hug against his expensive jacket and the smell of hotel soap. Michael never wore cologne, and his manly scent could drive Allie wild all by itself. How warm and safe it felt inside his embrace.

After a long moment, Gillian cleared his throat behind her.

"Michael, you remember Gillian, my assistant? He's joining us this evening, uh, for a while." Allie reluctantly brought her face up and away from Michael's broad chest, but with her arms still wrapped around him. She searched his eyes and saw the confusion in them, a split second before his lips crashed down on hers.

"Good to see you again too," Gillian said, moving over to the extra chair the hostess had brought up to the table. A water boy quietly came and added a set of silverware. "Too petite for my taste," Gillian sighed under his breath.

"This is going to be a tough night for everyone."

Allie's lips felt bruised from the pressure of Michael's kiss. His tongue slowly forced its way into her mouth and they stayed locked together for seconds. Allie melted into his body and drank deeply from his kiss. His soft beard rubbed against the side of her face. A quiet groan escaped from him that only Allie heard. Her legs became weak, as she forced herself to pull away from the man.

He let her move a few inches and then locked his arms, still holding her. His piercing gaze tried to see into her, to answer the questions of why a restaurant and why a chaperon.

She stiffened her shoulders against the stare and forced a smile from her numb lips. She dragged up a professional appearance. "It's good to see you again, Michael. Let's sit down—I think we're making the hostess anxious." Allie put her hands on his arms and unwillingly moved them away from her. Michael came around a step and pulled her chair out for her, which she gladly sank into. Her legs were not going to hold her up much longer on their own. He brushed his lips against her hair and set his strong hands on her shoulders before he moved away. She felt the lingering warmth.

Michael stretched his hand out to Gillian. "Good to see you, Gil. Looks like Allie's treating you well," he said, moving his own chair closer to the table.

"She's a hardened taskmaster, but worth the effort. How are the delicious salmon? I hope you brought a few smoked samples with you."

"Yes, a successful season. So good, in fact, I needed a break and came down for a little R and R with Allie." He reached next to him for Allie's hand, and kissed her fingers with his lips lingering longer than was necessary. "I've missed you."

Allie blushed a soft rose color, as hormonal heat pulsed through her body. She tried not to squirm in front of Gillian. She picked up her water glass with her other hand and found it shaky. She took a small sip and returned the glass to the table before she spilled the contents.

"So, what's been happening?" Michael threw out the question, but his eyes never left Allie's face for a moment.

"Oh, the usual," Gillian started. "A few stage-one smog alerts, a few tremblers. Nothing drastic. We're looking forward to a good Santa Ana season, cleaning up the sky quality, though I hear it may be a very wet winter." Gillian signaled for the waiter while gibbering to himself. "The sex-starved couple can't hear anything but their lust. I need a drink, this is going to get messy before it's over."

A young man appeared in a soft pale jacket with a leather order pad in his hands. "May I help you?"

"A martini, very dry, please," Gillian patted his forehead with the napkin. "How am I supposed to break them apart without a hose?" Gillian tilted his head at the waiter who stared blankly back. "Never mind," he said and twisted his wrist dismissing the man.

Gillian checked his perfect cuticles, one at a time, while the staring duo practically sucked the air from the room.

When the waiter placed the drink in front of Gillian, he raised his glass. "A toast, to Michael's return, and to the expectant future ahead of us."

Michael and Allie both turned their heads sharply toward Gillian, startled to find him still at their table. Allie picked up her Perrier and goaded Michael to pick up his beer. "Yes, to, uh, the future."

Michael's glass froze at his lips an extra second. Gillian watched him closely as he took a large sip from his drink. This was it.

"Is something going on I should know about? Am I missing a connection here? Allie, talk to me." Michael leaned closer toward her, across the edge of the table. "What gives with this restaurant meeting plus bringing Gay-zilla along? I don't understand—don't you want to be with me tonight?"

Allie moved toward the sexual pull, feeling his warm breath on her face. She jerked back in her chair just an inch away from his lips. "I do want to be with you, so much it hurts. It's just that," Allie turned to Gillian for support, with pleading in her eyes, then back to Michael, "it's just I can't. I can't go to the hotel with you tonight."

"What do you mean you can't? You're telling me you want to be with me, right here, right now, but you can't? What on earth are you talking about?"

"If I may," Gillian interjected, playing with the olive in his glass. "The woman might be pregnant and can't take the chance of physical contact right now."

Allie ducked her head. Well, that's one way to blurt it out, thank you very much. Crawling under the table sounded like a great idea about now, but her skirt was too tight for a lady-like exit. She couldn't breathe.

"You might be what?" Michael reached over quickly and put his hand under Allie's chin. He raised her face until their eyes met. "You might be pregnant? Is he joking, or insane?"

"Yes, and no," Allie eventually squeaked out, staring at the gorgeous familiar face so close to hers. "Yes, I might be pregnant; and no, he's not insane."

"I thought you told me he was gay. What have you two been working on, pornographic software?" Michael spat out his words. He released her face then picked up his beer and downed the rest of the liquid, slamming the glass back on the table.

"Michael!" Allie couldn't believe the possibility of jealousy. "It's not Gillian. He's only here to help me explain the situation to you. He didn't think I could do this alone, and he was right. I wouldn't have been able to, to say no to you by myself. I'm glad he came."

"I thought you didn't want children. You've always told me there wasn't any danger of you getting pregnant because you were on birth control all these years. I don't understand." Michael slumped back in his chair looking like a deflated balloon.

"If someone had told me I might be pregnant by autumn a few months ago, I wouldn't have understood either. Michael, I truly thought I didn't want children, ever. But things have changed, I've changed. I'm seeing a specialist, Dr. Adams, who is working with me to get pregnant through artificial insemination."

Michael stared at Allie with first a blank expression, then his eyes widened as if he'd just seen her head fall off. Allie rubbed her hands together and broke from Michael's stare. They both turned to Gillian.

"What?" Gillian threw his hands up. "I didn't talk her into this. It's not my idea of a terrific time, though I vow to run the company with style and success while she's out on maternity leave." Gillian sipped at his martini, regaining his composure.

"Artificial insemination?" Michael spoke the words like they were something dirty. His nose crinkled as if from a bad smell in the room. "Why didn't you call me about such an asinine idea? We could have discussed this."

"Discuss? Discussed what?" Allie stared back at Michael's anger. "We don't talk to each other, we screw around a couple times a year. Granted, it's magnificent screwing, but that doesn't change the fact we don't talk seriously about anything of significance when we're together. And I wasn't asking for volunteer sperm donors."

"I did raise my hand as a possibility, you know. I've had some experience with this sort of thing," Gillian reminded her.

Allie laid her head in her hand. Michael looked like he was going to explode from high blood pressure. His cheeks were flushed, and Allie could just imagine how fast the hamster was cranking the wheel inside his mind. Gillian's crack about being a donor did not help the volatile situation at all.

"Look, Michael, I'm sorry I didn't call you. It didn't seem appropriate to call up one day and say, 'Hey, I'm thinking about having a baby, want to put your two cents worth in?' I love you for your body and the fun we have together. Not some kind of potential father material."

"So, I'm not good enough to be a father?" Michael spat at her. "Is that it?"

"That's not what I'm saying. I'm sure you'd make a wonderful father someday, if that's what you want to do. But it would be real awkward with all we've done together, to take our relationship into the baby section of Sears. The Kamasutra could learn things from us, but parenting skills are a whole other thing."

Allie's comment eased some of the pain in Michael's face. "Yeah, we are pretty hot together, aren't we? Look, this baby thing has just caught me by surprise." His face flushed. "Oh, shit, your surprise I got for you." He rubbed his hand on his forehead.

"Well, the box is out in the car. I might as well bring it in, since you obviously aren't coming back with me to the hotel. Can you wait a minute?" Michael pushed his chair back and walked toward the front of the restaurant. His shoulders drooped, and his pace across the room was erratic.

"Gillian, thank you. I'm not sure I liked the way you threw the subject out on the table, but then I might not have had the courage to go through with telling him, either." As Allie looked away from his face, her eyes began to well up with tears.

"Hey, it's going to be okay. He didn't put a hole in the wall, and you still get a present for being a good girl." Gillian tried to be flippant. "I don't think it's something for the baby, so enjoy the hell out of it. This may be your last personal gift for a long time. I hear babies tend to get all the glory and attention once they're here." Allie knew he hated to see her cry, said it ruined her coloring, as she struggled to maintain control. Gillian finished his drink and quickly signaled the waiter for another.

Michael came back with a medium-sized department store gift box and handed it to Allie. He dropped into his chair, without touching her, and leaned his arms on the table. Never before had they passed without a gentle squeeze on the shoulder or a sinful brush of the hand.

"Would you care for another beer, sir?" the waiter interrupted. Michael handed him the empty bottle and nodded, not trusting his voice.

Allie carefully lifted the tape at one end of the box. Under the pastel blue flowered paper was the typical white cardboard box. The wrapping fell to the floor under the table, and Allie gently shook the box, to separate the lid, avoiding Michael's eyes. She broke the stickered seal on the white tissue paper, and gasped at the beautiful silk material folded neatly inside. As she lifted it up, the folds of red silk revealed a robe of luxurious glamour, the embroidered design taking shape as she turned the robe around. Allie realized a brightly colored parrot was outlined on the back, with tail feathers that wrapped around to the front.

Allie gasped, "Oh, it's beautiful! It's perfect. I, uh, maybe I can model it for you someday." Allie dropped her face into the soft material.

"Don't cry on that, you'll stain the fabric!" Gillian insisted across the table, starting to rise from his chair. "Use your napkin." Then, to Michael, "You'll have to excuse her, she's been crying during dog food commercials lately. It seems her hormones are already working overtime."

Allie started to chuckle through her tears. "I have not."

Michael looked like a fish out of water. "You always talked about being a Parrot Head. You're the most beautiful Parrot Head I know. What can I say, Allie? Good luck, I guess." He took a large swallow of the new beer. "I never thought diapers were in your future. I'm sorry those dreams aren't the same as mine. Tiny bed wetters tend to fall overboard in my line of work. Men joke about using them for fish bait. I can't share in your happiness, Allie, I'm sorry. But I hope it's what you want."

Michael stood up and took a thin wallet from inside his suit jacket. He pulled out a couple of twenty-dollar bills and laid them on the table. Allie put the box and robe down and stood up next to him.

"I'll miss you tonight," he started, but his voice cracked. The intensity of his eyes bored right through Allie, searching for an answer, a shred of possibility that this was a joke, but found none. He reached for her, pulling her close for the last time. Before he kissed her, he squeezed his eyes closed, and a single tear trickled down his cheek. "Hell, I'm going to miss you forever," he whispered.

Gillian pulled a monogrammed handkerchief out of his pocket and dabbed it under his nose as he sniffed. The loss of a good lay, especially on purpose, was always worth crying over.

Michael tenderly pressed his lips against Allie's, pulling her tightly to his body, until she felt her chest being flattened in a vice grip. She was going to remember this farewell in the morning with bruised ribs. She returned his kiss with fervor, her hands around his neck, pressing with a need of her own. Her tears crossed their lips, mingling a salty taste with the kiss.

Damn, life isn't fair. Date drought for months, and now it's offered on a silver platter by a great looking guy with incredible hip action, and all she can say is no? Allie let her arms fall to her sides. Her lips felt swollen, and fresh tears trickled down her cheeks.

"I guess this is it, Allie. I can't imagine trying to set up our weekends with you scrambling for a babysitter. The kid would be teething or have a cold. There'll always be some kind of an excuse. I'm really going to miss you, babe." Michael gathered what restraint he had left and reached over and offered his hand to Gillian. "Take good care of her, guy." The next moment he was gone.

Allie sank heavily into her chair. Gillian quickly moved over to Michael's vacant seat and offered his handkerchief to help mop up the tears. Thank goodness the restaurant was fairly empty.

"I'll never see him again, Gillian," she sobbed into the soft cotton. "I can't believe it's over."

"Let's just wait a few minutes," Gillian said, lifting his hand for the check. "Nothing worse than seeing your lover's car drive away without you inside."

Chapter 8

"Look who's here. What will it be tonight for you? Full dinner or just single entree, Allie?" The slight Asian gentleman behind the glass counter smiled.

"Let me be part-owner of this establishment, Chen, or adopt me. You make most of my meals anyway, and I am eternally grateful. You're my favorite stop on the way home." Allie brushed a strand of hair away from her eyes as she teased Chen. "Tonight let's have a quart of the beef and broccoli and a pint of steamed rice…um, and a cup of wonton soup, to go."

Allie knew the menu by heart and had worked her way through every succulent dish at least once since the store opened six months ago. What a great invention, Chinese fast food. Is there anything more delicious than eating it straight from the cardboard carton with wooden chopsticks? Leftovers make the perfect breakfast and clean up is painless, though it's too bad I can't recycle the printed cartons. Hmm, there's a thought, she mused, considering how many I collect over the months.

The corner restaurant in the strip mall was quite busy for an early Friday night, most of the tables filled with families and young couples.

"How is business for you?" Chen said as he scooped the dark-colored mixture expertly into a quart-size container without spilling a drop.

"Better than ever, thanks. Two new packages finished their beta testing last week, and I think we'll be able to hit the markets with them by Christmas. How's your Web site doing?" Allie had convinced Chen to get online with his homemade recipes of herbal medicinal potions.

"I think we over twenty-five thousand hits this summer. You right about market out there. People looking for natural cures for most ailment, my mailbox now crammed with questions from 'round the world. My typing much improved because I answer e-mail each night. I getting a strong following, thanks to you." Chen put a fortune cookie and chopsticks in a paper bag for her.

"I may need your magical herbs myself soon," Allie said, nodding to the man. The barest flush spread across her face as she picked up the offered sack.

"You need something special, you tell me. I fix for you, make you feel healthy, strong. You tell me, anytime. No problem."

"I will. Soon." Hopefully very soon, Allie thought. "Thanks for dinner, Chen." Allie lifted the paper sack in acknowledgment. "Put it on my tab and I'll probably see you Monday, same time." The man smiled and waved her away.

As soon as she turned on her street Allie pushed the garage door opener clipped to the sun visor. She braked the car and waited for the slow-moving obstacle to lift. The houses in her tract had very short driveways, leaving half of her four-door car hogging the sidewalk while she waited for the garage to open. Fortunately, no evening parades of tricycles or pedestrians made her feel guilty for the obstruction.

The house itself was comfortable, a two-story dollhouse with postage-stamp lawns, front and back. Created in the eighties, with minimal ground space, the tracts of miniature neighborhoods were built for the upwardly mobile crowd who worked overtime at careers all week and didn't want to spend the elusive weekend hours pulling weeds or mowing grass. Thank you, city planners and greedy developers—a little green without the insanity. She believed in free enterprise and hired Timothy, a young neighbor, to mow the grass.

Each weekend the kid complained under his breath while doing his work, though Allie paid well for his troubles. A mini-forest of trees grew in Allie's backyard, with more in the front. Edging around the base of each tree took almost as long as mowing both patches of grass.

Her first home out of college comprised a single story condo in a maze of identical units. Efficient and stylish, Aunt Kitty had told her. Practical and dull, thought Allie. She couldn't get used to having neighbors on the other side of her main walls all the time. Her green thumb had to be content with a few measly plants on the domino-sized patio. Allie pretended it was the California equivalent to *That Girl's* New York abode. The condo's usefulness came in establishing credit and a tax write-off. Claustrophobia set in and Allie moved out.

Allie had always wanted to live on a tree-lined street, the kind she read about in her favorite novels growing up. Donna Parker, Nancy Drew, all enjoyed a suburban lifestyle. Maybe she didn't need as many as she'd planted over the last few years; there could be too much of a good thing, she supposed. Each one represented a symbolic date or event, such as her first big sale of software.

"You are the only person I know who celebrates the sun coming up in the morning by planting another tree. Are you campaigning for a Tree USA contest or something?" Soozi continually teased her.

"Hey, you notch your life's calendar your way, and I'll do mine. I like trees; there's no law against how many I can have in the yard."

"Don't count on it. The rate you're going, Rancho will come up with some ordinance about growing forests in a residential area."

Trees represented security and longevity to Allie. She thought of them as roots to the house, to the neighborhood, to the earth. Solid and living creatures, she could lean against the bark of a tree and feel its strength and the sap moving through the wood. The gentle murmurs of the leaves as breezes stirred the branches provided conversations around her in the backyard.

A colorful rope hammock she bought in Mexico and tied between two of the trees provided a perfect resting place for Allie on hot Saturday evenings. She could lie there staring at the green leafy patterns against the sky and let her mind brainstorm ideas for the company. The gentle rocking of the hammock more recently had awakened a longing inside her to push a baby's cradle. A carved oak cradle with a soft quilt of creamy eyelet keeping the infant warm at night.

Allie relished taking off her shoes and moving through the mini-forest at the end of a busy day. The cool grass tickled between her toes. She pretended to be Briar Rose of *Sleeping Beauty,* her favorite Disney animated film. She wished three fairy godmothers would keep an eye on her, too. Being single and independent had its high points, but it would be nice to come back to a home-cooked meal some nights or just the twittering of concern by the motherly fairies of the movie.

Allie didn't believe she'd bump into a prince among her trees, but no harm daydreaming about Prince Charming walking along the way from her side gate. Of course with her luck and dating history, the pampered prince would probably be highly allergic to tree pollen. Nope, no prince among the trees, at least not these trees.

Allie wondered if her astrological chart had a dual major sign involved somewhere in one of the houses. Whether barefoot and sassy as an earth mother in the backyard or a techie in three-inch high heels, she was a paradox. Garden freak on weekends and power techno-guru during the week.

Allie sorted through her mail and made a beeline for the couch with her delicious treasures from Chen. A quick swipe through the evening news brought her up-to-date with the rest of the world before she happily cocooned herself away for the night. It had been a productive and exhausting week, with Gillian discovering another avenue of online selling that should bump their revenues quite nicely next quarter.

Allie clicked off the television. Only the hum of the central air conditioning broke the stillness.

"Hear ye! Hear ye! Lend me your ears, good people of the Valley of Goldfish," sounded a young female voice loudly across the yard.

"What the hell is that supposed to mean?" The disgusted tone matched the look in a pair of washed-out blue eyes, squinting from the brightness of the afternoon sun, looking up toward Allie's young voice. Tough talk for an eight-year-old.

Alissa's own eight-year-old arms waved around, wildly flapping the dangling sleeves of her father's favorite plaid shirt in the air. "For your information, you doorknob, it's the town crier getting everyone's attention. He has something important to say and he yells at the people on the street, making them stop and listen to the news of the kingdom. This is supposed to be from hundreds of years ago—they didn't have radios or nothing back then."

"Who says?"

"I do, smartypants, because I listen in class to Mrs. Ferguson. You should try it sometime. And if Aunt Kitty hears you use the H-word again, we're both in major trouble. She won't let us put on the play at all." How mighty one could feel standing on a broken kitchen chair in the middle of the backyard, high above the lowly stagehand slaving over painting the backdrop.

Hell yourself, young Alissa, she thought. Allie tried to throw away the memory as she threw the remains of her takeout in the kitchen trash. What *good* had it done to stay out of trouble all those many years, the adult Alissa nagged herself. Two young kids jerking around in a 1960s tract-styled backyard, who didn't know the meaning of anything about life, nor care. No, correction, not just jerking around for young dreamer Alissa, nothing could be further from the truth. That was to be my finest backyard play ever presented to the adult world, she thought. She smiled to herself as she walked up the carpeted stairs of her home and into the master bedroom.

Allie leaned her hip into her painted bedroom door to close it, a maple serving tray balanced in her hands. Pampering for a princess, the tray included an ice bucket with a pair of clear plastic tongs, a crystal wineglass, and a twenty-ounce bottle of caffeine-free Diet Coke. Closing the door of her bedroom with a definite click in an empty house may have seemed absurd. Who would notice or care? Yet old needs of privacy never die.

Allie walked into the adjoining bathroom through a short archway off the master bedroom, past matching walk-in closets that lined the left wall. She had loved this part of the house when the realtor first walked her through. These two rooms alone made up a fourth of the square footage of the house. She carefully set the tray on the counter, placed two ice cubes into the glass and filled it, watching the dark carbonation swirl down the ice.

Reaching down, she turned the brass handle marked with a scrolled *H* on the bathtub. Water gushed in a torrent, splashing the sides of the peach porcelain with a vengeance. "My finest play ever," still whispered in Allie's mind.

As steam began to rise from the tub she twisted both knobs back and forth, sticking a bare wrist under the water now and again to find the elusive "just right" temperature. Why couldn't she push a button for 99-degree water and be done with it? Not too hot, not too cold. Simple. God, something simple in her life, what a concept.

"Al, you cannot start a play by yelling 'Hear ye, hear ye, lend me your ears.'"

The childhood argument between the two girlfriends continued in her mind. A half-hearted grin stretched Allie's dry, lipstick-caked lips.

"And why not?" Young Allie glared down from her vantage point on top of the chair at her soon-to-be-ex very best friend. Soozi had just finished outlining a fluffy white cloud above the painted buildings on the piece of old cardboard being used for scenery in act one.

Surrounding the miniature stagehand were jars of paint with brushes sticking up, pointing in odd directions. Completed sets of countryside views, drying in the warm spring sun, leaned against a young fruit tree a few feet away. Allie wanted no chance of smearing the artwork.

"Because it's really stupid." Soozi did not miss a stroke with the paintbrush, working on another cloud while she made this final statement. White drops of paint were splattered across her freckled nose and cheek.

Alissa jumped off the chair, landing with both feet hard on the ground. Her hands curled into fists at her sides as she threatened Soozi, "Take that back."

Soozi still held the paintbrush in her hand, sitting on her knees. "I won't. That's the stupidest thing I ever heard, and I'm tired of doing your stupid plays."

There it is. Life had been so easy at the ripe old age of eight. You told it like it was. No compromises, no exceptions, no prisoners. How had it managed to get away and become so complicated over the years?

Stripping off the day's outfit, Allie watched the reflections of her tanned body in the many mirrors hanging along the back wall of the spacious bathroom. Allie collected unusual mirrors. The wall above the double sinks was made entirely of mirror, which reflected back the peach and blue wallpaper of geometric blocks between the assorted smaller framed mirrors she had hung. She had gathered them from different antique markets during shopping sprees in coastal towns of the Pacific states. Painted wooden frames of peach and ivory decorated two of the larger mirrors. One of her favorites had a nasty crack in the lower right corner. Who suffered the chilling seven years of bad luck for the broken mirror? And where was the person now?

Although her expressionless face looked toward the reflective surfaces of glass, Allie's stare saw nothing of the flowing rivulets of auburn hair, a color not unlike a newly minted penny, cascading past her shoulders. Even her eyes of darkest brown saw nothing gazing back, no woman standing naked in the room with a deep, golden tan and sharp contrasting bikini lines as her panties fell silently to the gray carpet in a crumpled pile. Her vision dulled from the sharp thoughts and short film clips in her mind.

Allie slowly shut the bathwater off. The silence was deafening after the constant roar against her eardrums. An occasional drip from the faucet broke the stillness in the room. The multiple reflections of Allie slowly stepped into the warm water as she sank into it with a heavy sigh of end-of-the-week re-lief. Can you feel alone in a crowd of yourself? She reached up and brought down the glass of Diet Coke. Taking a small amount of the chilling liquid in her mouth, the bite of carbonation surged through her.

All the frantic madness of the past week melted away. Allie sank lower into the heated bath until she could rest her head against the cool rim of the tub, stretching her long legs out along the bottom. A second breathy sigh escaped from her soul, pulling with it the negative emotions buried inside. Beads of condensation trickled down the glass she held in her hand. Icy droplets fell into the bathwater.

"Come get your sweater on before you catch your death of cold. What are you doing out there?" Aunt Kitty yelled out the back door. "You haven't got a lick of sense God gave you, crawling around in the backyard all day. What happened to Soozi? She practically ran out of the backyard, slamming the gate behind her. Did you have another fight? I told you about arguing with the neighborhood, young lady, didn't I? You better not be fighting with that sweet girl. Will you get over here and get a sweater on? Or do I have to interrupt your parents?" With that Aunt Kitty shut the back door with force, rattling the plate glass window.

"A dumb old sweater. And if I get paint on it, I'll get spanked for sure." Her wet paintbrush continued in short, angry strokes against the cardboard as tears welled up in her eyes. "Why do they always take stupid Soozi's side? Every time. The whole family likes her better than they like me. It's my show, it's my play. Grownups never think about that. Soozi this and Soozi that." Another tear crept out of the corner of her eye and Alissa let it fall on the white paint. She struggled to push the pain away, imagining the tear as a single raindrop, ignoring its origin.

It rained in England quite often, didn't it? The Crystal Prince would have servants to protect him from the rain. A butler holding his umbrella...hmm, did they call them umbrellas in England? She finished painting the cloud as the running chatter in her mind blocked out the hurt and frustration.

"I'm warning you for the last time, Alissa. Don't make me come out there after you."

I will not be the kind of parent that screams out a back door at her child. What I'd give to have my mother back, though, even if only to hear her sigh as I interrupt her work once more. Work kept her away from Allie, out of the house or locked away in the study for hours, so Aunt Kitty's outbursts and threats in keeping her niece in line came often. You missed a lot, Mom. You were a great audience member, though. I always heard your applause over everyone else. Did you know I'm trying to make you a grandmother? Wouldn't you be surprised!

Friday night soaks in a hot bath had been a high school ritual. After that, the long soaks functioned as a private think tank for her projects with Novel Software. Tonight the process developed to another level, a deserved pampering for the expecting-to-be expectant Allie. Writing plays as a pre-adult had been the creative foundation for the software she designed now. Tweaking parts of *The Crystal Prince* became *Hear Ye, Hear Ye,* a best-selling game of international sights and sounds for elementary school kids. For Novel Software, *Hear Ye* was a great money-maker.

Over the last five years, Allie had dabbled off and on at serious playwriting, an unrequited passion. A full script for *The Crystal Prince* sat in the bottom drawer of her desk at work. Allie loved the main character, perfect on the outside but fragile and pure on the inside. No hidden agendas, you could see right through the man.

Soozi, you don't know how much you inspired me. Everyone adored your long, dark curls and soft, demure personality back then. "Be like Soozi"; "Behave like Soozi." How Mom would raise her eyebrows if she could see you now, the wild-colored mama-butterfly blossomed from a meek little cocoon. You are more like Aunt Kitty, loud and loving with a bite. Look what having a couple of kids has done to you.

What will this one do to me?

Allie dropped her hands under the warm water and tenderly stroked her flat stomach. Could she feel any changes going on inside? She closed her eyes and sank deeper into the bath. Steam from the surface whispered across her face. She inhaled the wetness. As she exhaled, layers of tension blew away from her. No brainstorming tonight, no anticipation of a Friday night date with pimples, just Allie and a few million male microns tonight.

She reached out of the hot water for the glass of Diet Coke. Suddenly, a sharp pain stabbed through her midsection. She dropped the goblet, shattering glass and spilling soda everywhere. She took a stuttering breath, and let it out quickly. She lay deathly still in the water. *Maybe I'm just low on potassium.*

Fear began to radiate deep inside. *Oh, no.* A second pain spiked across her pelvic area, tightening the muscles across her belly, and she clenched her arms around her midsection. *No, not now,* Allie thought she was screaming in the silent bathroom. No noise echoed back to her. *Maybe I worked too long hunched over the keyboard.*

A third, stronger contraction hit as a thin sliver of red trickled in the bathwater, immediately swirling and breaking up. Her period. No baby. Allie squeezed her arms tighter and her hip brushed against a shard of glass, cutting the skin. *I'm becoming shark bait in my own bathtub.* Allie almost enjoyed the physical pain as she tried to avoid the emotional anguish forcing its way into her heart.

"Shit!" This time Allie did scream. "Shit all to hell!" Tears flowed down her face, mixing with droplets of sweat from her forehead. Her hair framed her face in damp ringlets. Tears ran freely, breaking down the walls of strength, and Allie sobbed. Letting out the pain, Al flashed back to her powerless young self in the backyard, whose best friend had just abandoned the play and her.

After all the ridicule she had taken from her aunt about being a crybaby in those early years, Allie vowed no one would ever see her cry again, and she had kept that vow until the restaurant fiasco with Michael. Her abdominal muscles cramped again with a vicious stab. Her strength had become her façade; her strength saw her through anything, including the horribly sudden death of her parents.

Older, but maybe not wiser, Allie let the little girl in the backyard cry. Her first attempt at maternity about to slip down the drain, the accumulated disappointment of the past and the present rocked her back and forth in the bathwater. A loud moan wrenched from her soul as Allie sobbed. "Oh, Mama, I wish you were here," she whispered into her hands covering her face.

Get hold of yourself. Allie took a deep, shuddering breath. The doctor had explained over and over it probably wouldn't happen the first time. You've got a mess to clean up, and I'm not just talking about your pitiful existence. You don't need a trip to Emergency to get glass out of your butt by some gorgeous male nurse. Get up, and clean up.

Allie viciously kicked the lever with her big toe, letting the now lukewarm bathwater begin to drain. The rest of the process of getting out of the tub had to be handled more delicately with shards of glass, nearly invisible in the tub, surrounding her like a minefield. This kept her focused for a moment as she reached for the towel near the sink. Another menstrual cramp doubled her over.

"Give me a chance to get out of the water at least," Allie growled through clenched teeth. She pressed the towel against the gash in her hip, wiping off the small trickle of blood as water dripped off her body.

Monday morning Gillian stopped with surprise in front of the glass doors to a dark office. He fumbled in his pants' pocket for the rarely used door key. He glanced at his watch—a quarter to eight, not early for him but definitely late for Allie. A sense of saddened doom painted over him as he entered the unlit office. The blank stare of his PC monitor gave no clues, only reflecting the florescent lights from the hall.

"This is not good," Gillian whispered. This was not good at all. He flipped the light switches and hit the power button for his computer as he set his briefcase on the desk. Maybe it's just car trouble, but no reassuring message light flickered on his phone. No note, nothing. Gillian automatically headed for the kitchen to start the coffee. Would she be in or not? His cappuccino talents were blocked by concerns and worries of his boss, and robbed of any pleasure in the process, he took robotic swipes at the machine, filling it with water and grounds.

The company door creaked closed as Allie made her way to her office. Not a word spoken as she passed the kitchen. Gillian stared at his cold, empty coffee cup. Only one miserable thing could have drained Allie this deeply. The insemination didn't take. Damn. What do you say? Better luck next time? Does Miss Manners have a chapter on what to say when there's nothing you can say to make it better?

"Morning."

He jumped in place, shaken from his reverie by her soft greeting. "Yes, it is morning, and it will be again tomorrow." Gillian turned to her, noticing the dark circles under her eyes, then the wrinkled disaster of a T-shirt below. "Ah, casual Monday, I see," was his pitiful attempt to lighten the mood. He opened his arms and Allie stepped in.

"I promised myself I wouldn't cry," she sniveled into his shoulder.

"Cry all you like, this jacket was ready for the dry cleaners anyway." Her muffled sobs added to the shaking body he held in his stiff arms. How do you hold a sobbing woman? They're all angles. "It's just the first time, Allie." How many office assistant job descriptions included Kleenex monitor? No Monday morning grousing over a bad golf score or some disastrous blind date.

"Girl, it's time to party," he spoke into her hair.

Allie sniffled and snorted into the Kleenex as she raised her head from his shoulder. "What? I'm not up for a party."

"Pity-party time. You get that cute rumpled bod into your office and make out an invitation to yourself, scheduled for whenever, today or this evening, for one hellacious pity party."

"Gillian." Allie almost giggled.

"You deserve it. Order the best of whatever you're up to, a whole cake with ice cream? Caviar and vodka? I'll even endure your grotesque concoction of potato chips and pork and beans, so disgustingly middle class. You decide." Gillian leaned away from her a little; his jacket could handle only so much saltwater. "Give yourself time to get past this unfortunate baby delay."

He reached over and gave her a handful of fresh Kleenex. "You know the pity-party routine, princess, it's just been a while since you've had one. Cloth napkins, stemmed glasses, do yourself proud. Pick up some gorgeous flowers at Suzanne's, too. Something glorious, like lilies, or what are those long-stemmed things you like?" Gillian cocked his head at her.

"Gladiolus."

"Phallic symbols." Gillian drug out the words, raising his eyebrows. "Or you've got a woman warrior thing, those stems are thick. Do this party, just for you."

He placed his manicured hands on her shoulders, flipping his ponytail with a snap of his head. "Get going, I've got real work to do today, and you're cramping my naturally positive aura. I'll bring you in a cup of java decaf when it's ready. Go on." He turned her limp frame around and, with tenderness, pushed her out of the kitchen cubicle, wriggling his fingers as he watched the pitiful sight walk away. He felt flushed from the exertion of keeping a positive front. This is dreadful. The poor dear, he mused.

Allie blew her nose on the Kleenex as she headed for her office, her shoes dragging against the carpet. Gillian was annoyingly right, as usual. The odds against insemination taking the first time were high. She would try again next month. It's not the end of the world, just a minor postponement in the maternity department. I'll call Dr. Adams' office when they open this morning and let them know.

Allie slumped into her chair, staring out the window at Cucamonga Peak in the distance. She hadn't bothered to turn on the overhead lights. The dim sunshine from the window was enough to light her immediate area, surrounding her in the comfort of shadows. Pushing her toe against the floor, she softly rocked back and forth.

"My body is saturated with artificial sweeteners and preservatives. I'm a walking chemical storage plant," Allie whined into the phone. "I'll never get pregnant." She tucked her legs under her on the couch, hugging an embroidered pillow over her stomach. Protection? Sympathy? Comfort? She twisted the ends of her hair with her fingers. Allie didn't notice the hair felt oily and limp from neglect.

"Would you like a truckload of cheese with that whine? Girl, you're getting on my nerves. It didn't take, get over it. You're not perfect; it's not a perfect world. What can I tell you?" Allie listened to the clatter of Soozi emptying the dishwasher in the background.

"Well, aren't we Miss Sympathetic tonight," Allie snapped. She squeezed the corner of the pillow with her fist in frustration.

"Al, this is your third call today. That's not counting yesterday or the GTE reach-out sessions from last week. Get a grip. You're a hormonal hurricane. Lock yourself in the bathroom till the hysterics pass. Take a long, hot shower, and stuff a washrag in your mouth. Scream and cry until you can't anymore. Works for me. Besides which, you gave me the idea last year during the post-partum blues from Zoe."

"Sounds like me."

Soozi made a noise against the mouthpiece of her phone.

"Thank you," came back in a whisper, fresh tears trickling down Allie's face.

"You're welcome. Go soak your head and go to bed. I'll call you tomorrow and check on you."

Allie wiped her wet face and stared at the phone receiver, too tired to sigh.

Soozi hung the cordless phone back in the station with a sense of sadness. A single tear ran a course down her cheek. Sometimes being a best friend sucked. She drained her glass of wine, feeling helpless. This was not something Soozi Homemaker could fix. If Randy even looked at her funny, she got pregnant.

Rain poured down around his dented two-door car as Randy gripped the cold steering wheel with white knuckles. "Are you sure?" His voice sounded lifeless as he stared out the cracked windshield, blinded by the downpour outside.

"Yes," Soozi whispered, her hair creating a veil with her head down. "The doctor called the dorm this morning."

Randy slammed his fist against the black plastic wheel. He ran shaky fingers through his long, stringy hair, leaving it in chaos. "I can't...we can't do this, babe. A baby would mess up everything right now. We still have two more years left in school, and then I have graduate school. Shit."

"I know," was all she could answer.

The curtain of rain isolated them from the rest of the world, creating a cold, damp island in the middle of nowhere on a Southern California campus.

"Sooz?"

"I know, I know."

"You sure?"

"No, not really. Don't look at me." Soozi curled up into a tight ball in her seat. "I know what I have to do. That's all there is right now, no more. I have to do it."

"Do you want me to come with you?"

"Just hold me, Randy. Just hold me." Her tears fell as fast as the rain outside as she buried her face in his chest with shame and loss.

"I'll go with you, Sooz," he choked out, his own tears falling against her hair. "I'm sorry, I'm sorry."

The sobs lessened, and the last wave hardened inside her. "I have to make an appointment, and I'll let you know."

It's so easy to get pregnant, thought Soozi, wiping a tear with the back of her hand. When you don't want to—when it's the worst possible timing, and you're too young—it's easy to get knocked up. Soozi let go a painful sigh for herself. Allie had no clue how easy it could be. The hurt never fully goes away.

Chapter 9

Allie entered a shoe store in the mall, swinging her purse back and forth. What's the old saying? You can never be too rich, too thin, or have too many shoes, mused Allie, as she walked down the display of women's shoes. Sounds like something from an old Lucy show, though. But wasn't it hats instead of shoes for her? Ricky yelling about another hatbox in the closet. Having left Dr. Adams' office, once again on her quest for motherhood, Allie wanted to cross her legs for the rest of the day with a new pair of shoes on her feet for good luck.

What to choose, evening or casual? Low heeled or sexy? Comfortable or alluring? Manufacturers of women's shoes do this on purpose. Men have about three decisions to make, black, brown, or casual while women have a hundred. Oh, and I feel Gillian bristling back at the office for that thought. She smiled. Gillian's footwear collection could make a cover article for *Shoe Weekly,* if such a magazine existed.

Out of the corner of her eye, Allie caught a flash of blonde curls. Over the row of neatly arranged chairs bobbed a small head haloed in ringlets, ducking underneath a padded maroon-colored seat, and then springing up again.

"Carrie, please. Mommy needs you to sit still while she's trying on shoes. You're going to fall. Just sit here on the floor for Mommy, okay? Play with your toy." The woman sounded harried, and her plea set off a small siren of protest from the toddler. The cry became insistently louder in the confined store.

The baby defiantly hung on to the chair and caught Allie's stare. A single tear glistened on the baby's cheek, and spiked eyelashes surrounded eyes of fire. The bright pink cheeks darkened as the child took a deep breath.

Allie walked quickly around the chairs. "May I help?" Allie touched the mother lightly on the shoulder.

The woman looked up, her blonde hair tucked into a loose bun, and Allie noticed the eyes register a slight hint of fear, mixed with exhaustion and suspicion at a stranger approaching unsolicited.

"I'm sorry. I'd like to help. Can I distract her, keep her company while you try on shoes?" Allie kept her voice friendly and light. "I could stay right here so you could keep an eye on her. I'm trying to have a baby myself."

How sad the first reaction anymore to an offer of help between people is doubt and mistrust. We've let others take too much away with despairing news at five o'clock that damages peace of mind and comradeship. We're left vulnerable to thoughts of kidnapping and Amber Alerts. You can't take your eyes off your child for a moment, let alone have a perfect stranger offer to assist, without panicking that they will abscond with the child as soon as you blink.

"Well, I guess so; yes, that would be nice," the mother decided straightening up in her chair. "She's just learning to walk. All you need to do is hold out your hand, she'll walk toward you eventually." Carrie's mom smiled at the towheaded angel at her side.

Allie squatted down in front of the mother, off to one side, and held her hands out. The round cherubic face looked up to her mother's face, and then to the strange woman in front of her, a tennis match of back and forth head-bobbing. Allie watched the chubby legs stiffen in anticipation. Tiny white Nikes began to scuff across the shoe store carpet as the baby stretched her arms toward Allie and struggled with her newly acquired balance. Every other step, toddler Carrie discoed through a routine, bringing her left leg up high and stomping it down, without having gained a fraction of an inch in direction, and moving her arms to regain her precious balance. Allie choked back a laugh.

Two full minutes passed as the toddler traveled the short distance from the seat of the chair to Allie, giving the mother time to finish. Carrie squealed in delight when her plump, stocky fingers grasped Allie's, completing the daunting adventure across the floor.

Paying the clerk for the shoes, she turned toward Allie. "Thank you so much," the wearied mother expressed. "You have the same look I had about two years ago." The woman set her package down. "My name's Becky."

"Allie," she said, turning the baby around slowly and pointing her back to the row of chairs. Allie let go a giggle and the baby echoed the laughter back to her. How quickly their minuscule moods change. "Someday, she'll be hard to catch." Allie watched the difficult journey back to Becky, again the left leg making wild high movements without any forward success.

"My husband and I struggled a long time to have a baby."

"I've only started the last few months. The stork and I are trying to negotiate a deal."

Both watched Carrie stuff a handful of fingers in her mouth until the mother reached down and dislodged them. "I'd almost given up. We did three in vitros."

Allie watching the mother gather the sacks and bags around her in one hand and lift the toddler onto her hip with the other, a maternal ballet. "I'm doing artificial insemination," Allie said.

"Good for you. I hope all goes well," Becky said with a friendly nod. "Thank you again. We weren't going to be very long at the mall, so I didn't bring her stroller. She spends most of her time trying to climb out of it anyway." The fatigued mother smiled her appreciation. "She's my in vitro miracle, I must say. Draining and exhaustive, but a miracle."

Allie watched the pair leave the store and started a mental notebook. Keep shopping trips short and sweet. Maybe hire a babysitter so the tiny tot doesn't get tired and cranky. How do women do this? Motherhood creates a lot of questions. Where is the instructional manual? Where is the bachelor's degree in parental studies?

Carrie's kaleidoscope of faces stayed with Allie, those incredible eyes tugging at the strings of her heart. She couldn't wait for the day she could hold her baby and stare at similar windows to a soul, whole minutes of locking gazes with miniature eyes of the future. Allie sighed. Someday.

Allie didn't notice she'd protectively laid a hand on her flat stomach, looking over the selection of shoes. She grabbed her cell phone.

"Novel Software, Gillian speaking."

"Guess what?" Allie didn't wait for his response. "I'm seeing babies everywhere. And they like me."

Allie heard him tapping on the keyboard. "Allie, of course tiny targets of drool are all over the place, it's an epidemic of Gerber proportions out there. So are bad haircuts, but it doesn't mean everyone should have one. I thought you were buying shoes."

"I am. Can't I check in to see how the office is doing?"

"Right. By the way, don't get those awful fuchsia slingbacks you've been hinting about. I know you, you'll trip and hurt yourself or me or the baby, and I'll die of embarrassment when the paramedics see your feet."

Allie swung by Blockbuster and stocked up on DVD rentals for a sedentary weekend, a movie marathon weekend. She picked up a half dozen classics from MGM and Universal. Enjoying rest and fantasy, stretched out on the couch with her legs propped up on a mountain of pillows, Allie hoped to give the swimming chromosomes a chance at romance.

"Are you behaving yourself?" Soozi asked when she called later.

"Oh, sure. Just let me empty the champagne from the bathtub, and chase the Baldwin brothers out of here." Allie snuggled down and stopped the machine, muting the TV. "What's up with you?"

"Same ol', same ol' here. How did the appointment with Doc Adams go yesterday?" Soozi had to shout above the background din of washing machine, televised football, and children communicating at higher decibels than all the above.

"Don't yell in my ear—I can hear you around the squall. Well, number forty-five felt pretty much the same as last time, he's so consistent. Don't you just love that in a man?" Allie fluffed a pillow behind her head. "I'm treating myself to nonstop classics with my feet up. The guys of Semen Avenue better pay attention and swim their hearts out."

Soozi screamed into the phone.

"Are you okay?" Allie bolted upright on the couch, knocking off pillows in her haste. "What happened, is it one of the kids?"

Soozi tried to catch her breath, laughing. "You won't believe this. Oh, my gosh."

"Will you tell me already? You gave me a heart attack. Are you playing in the oven cleaner again?" Allie picked up the pillows from the floor and piled them on the couch once more. Sometimes she questioned Soozi's sanity switch.

"The Florida Gators just scored a touchdown by a young, tight-butt thing with a huge number forty-five on his back!"

They both squealed at each other. "No kidding? It's a sign, Sooz!" Goose bumps traveled up her arms. "A real honest-to-goodness Parrot Head sign. A touchdown by number forty-five from a Florida team, can you believe it? Go, forty-five," Allie hooted at her pelvic area, patting it lightly with the palm of her hand.

"What's the matter, Mama?" Allie heard in the background.

"Nothing, Lenny, it's okay. I'm talking to Auntie Allie."

"I wanna talk to Auntie Allie," he pleaded. Allie pictured him impatiently bouncing on one rubbery leg.

Grabbing the phone Lenny talked with the speed of an avalanche. "Daddy says Mama's nuts. Mama yelled and scared Zoe real bad. Did she scare you, Auntie?"

"Yes, Lenny, a little bit. Tell your daddy it's okay. Girls are like that sometimes. We get excited and it comes out kind of loud."

"Zoe does all the time. She yells a lot, Auntie. I tell her 'shut up.' I gotta go, Mama wants the phone. 'Bye." Lenny handed the phone back.

"See what you have to look forward to? Never a dull moment with a kid around," Soozi said.

"I'm ready already."

Putting the second movie in a row back into its plastic case, Allie stood up from the couch and stretched. Her muscles ached from being prone for hours, and she walked into the kitchen stretching her calf muscles. Opening the refrigerator door, Allie stared at the brightly lit shelves of condiments. Nothing exciting in there, she thought. Road trip. She turned around and dug her shoes out from under the coffee table. Finding her car keys would be another matter. Grocery shopping will get me out of the house for a while.

Either the sperm guys have fulfilled their mission by now or they haven't. Allie was far away with thoughts of reproductive processes in the juice aisle, when a tiny hand reached over and grabbed the sleeve of her blouse. Startled, Allie turned and looked down at a young chocolate-smeared face in sailor whites, sitting in the front seat of a neighboring shopping cart, grinning at his capture, not about to let go of Allie's shirt.

"Hi, big boy. Come to the big city often?"

The miniature sailor wiggled against the safety strap in response to her attention, cooing his satisfaction at his successful catch.

The mother of Baby Popeye stepped closer and made eye contact with Allie. Allie watched her shoulders relax. "Jared, let go of the nice lady." She started to pry his clenched fingers from the material.

"It's all right." Allie stretched her arm out as Jared's fingers moved jerkily down her sleeve. The buttons on the cuff fascinated him, and he picked at their edges. Allie watched his captivation of the buttons, the tiny fingers strong as they pulled on the buttons. The two women smiled at his determination and absorption.

"How old is he?" Allie asked.

"Eleven months and growing," she beamed back.

"He's a charmer, that's for sure." Allie smiled at the concentration on his face.

"Thank you."

Allie reached over to straighten the stained red tie of the sailor suit caught under Jared's chin and brushed her hand against his cheek in the release. Jared giggled from the tickle and ducked his head, letting go of her blouse. Both women laughed with his infectious sounds.

The tiny sailor continued flirting, batting his eyes, and Allie melted at his unconditional affection. Before the conversation between the women was through, Allie gave the mother a business card from Novel Software and invited her to call anytime about their preschool software. "You'd be surprised how quickly they grasp the different concepts. He'll be ready for his own track ball in a few months."

As the mother pushed the cart down the refrigerated aisle, Allie felt her heart yanked for the second time by an invisible maternal thread. Jared flapped his whole arm up and down, encouraged by his mother's hand under his elbow to wave bye-bye.

"'Bye, sailor. Safe voyage home," she said quietly to herself.

As she turned the corner a cart came out of nowhere and rammed her front wheels. "Hey!" Allie looked up to a man talking on a cell phone.

"No, Sherry, I don't understand," he shrugged his shoulders in "I'm sorry" sign language.

Big strong shoulders, Allie noticed as she caught her breath when his brown eyes locked on to hers. Dark brown eyes, fringed in thick, black lashes. A tingle raced through her body as the man ran his other hand through his hair. Allie watched his movements as if in slow motion.

"Okay. Later. Yeah, I love you, too." He flipped his phone closed.

His arm muscles rippled as he reached behind and shoved the phone in his back pocket. Allie shook her head, breaking the spell. Whoa, too many chick flicks, girlfriend, this one's married. Allie grabbed her cart and walked away. Why are all the cute ones taken?

Soozi reached over and picked up the kitchen phone on the second ring. "Hello?" A phone call after nine at night had to be Allie.

"Hey, you shoulda seen the cute sailor trying to pick me up at the grocery store," Allie said.

"Cute?" Soozi picked up her second glass of wine and took a large swallow, not in the mood to hear about cute single guys after a long day of domestic madness.

"Incredibly cute. Literally grabbed me in the orange juice section and wouldn't let go."

Soozi grimaced at the perkiness. "Okay, give me a break, it's been a long day around here. He did what?"

"Grabbed my shirt and started playing with the buttons."

Soozi drained the rest of the pale pink liquid. "What's the gimmick?" She looked at the empty glass in her hand. "Since when do you let a strange man molest you in public? Under florescent lights, no less." Soozi's mood darkened the more Allie's bubbled over. *What was she supposed to do, applaud Allie's social life? What about those of us who don't have one?*

"I didn't say it was a man, just a sailor, an adorable eleven-month-old wearing dress whites in a passing cart. Soozi, kids are so neat. You should have seen the determination on his face, working the button on my sleeve."

"Hello? Earth to Allie. I have two rug-crawlers of my own, remember? Been there, done that." Soozi walked to the refrigerator and grabbed the open wine bottle. "Nature's wonderful at making humans cute and cuddly in the beginning. Don't tell me you're going to morph into one of *those* mothers?"

"Huh?"

"The first time yours spits up all over you, you'll frame the shirt." Soozi filled the glass from the cold bottle, watching the tiny waves against the sides. *As if it's never happened before in all of maternal history,* she finished in her mind.

Allie said. "Gotta go back to the couch. Ciao."

"Good thing," Soozi mumbled back as she hung up the phone, staring at the instrument an extra moment. Another large gulp of wine did nothing to drown her miserable mood. Damn Allie anyway. Soozi started to put the rest of the wine back in the refrigerator and changed her mind. Guilt crashed over her, standing alone in the kitchen, for thinking such vicious thoughts of her best friend. Soozi emptied the rest of the bottle into her glass. *What is the matter with me?* Soozi dropped the bottle into the glass recycle bin, clinking against two other discarded bottles. She took another large swallow. *Maybe life'll be better tomorrow.*

"Sooz, how do I know if one of these tests works better than the others?" Allie paced in front of a shelf of home pregnancy testing kits at the drugstore.

"Am I jinxing the whole thing by looking at this stuff early?" Her backless shoes clicked in rhythm on the tile flooring.

"Look at the instructions on the box. Is it quick and easy, pee on a plastic stick, or are you supposed to fill a ridiculous dinky cup first and pour a few drops of the disgusting stuff on a tester? I'd love to meet the man who thought that one up. Then, if you want to be really superstitious about the whole process, do you want a blue or a pink result?"

"Hey, I'm the one obsessing about all this. Don't get color-coded weird on me and make it worse."

"I'm not kidding. Look, this one has blue indicators and this one has pink. Give me some credit, I've used these before, you know."

"Totally true. I think maybe I want a pink response. Is that too bizarre a notion? Pink sounds warm and fuzzy to me right now." Allie picked up a box and turned it over. "Should I buy two of them? Maybe take one and then wait a couple days and try another one just to be sure?"

Soozi draped her arm around her friend's shoulders. "Couldn't hurt. You have to pee every morning anyway. Whether you do it on litmus paper or not is up to you. This is the one I used after Zoe was conceived. It's my personal choice, but you decide what you want to do. Two tests should confirm whether your purchased male friends did their job or not."

"I am so nervous. It's just a test, I keep telling myself. I'm not used to flunking tests, Sooz. I've been straight A's all my life, an over-achiever of the royal order of nerds." Allie chewed on her bottom lip, then shook herself gently. "So what if I'm not pregnant this time? I can go back to Doc Adams and do it over again. This is only my second try. She said there was plenty of number forty-five product on hand. He seemed more than generous with his by-product." Allie held the plastic-wrapped box close to her chest. She leaned against her best friend. "You've got two cute kids. I'm going with the one you used."

They both laughed. Soozi reached over and hugged Allie. A few customers down the aisle smiled. One woman gave Allie a thumbs-up sign. Allie blushed with pleasure that complete strangers would root for her.

"Come on. Let's go check out and take ourselves to lunch. You need some positive distractions right now. Besides, it's not often I get Randy to babysit a whole afternoon now that football is back in full swing. You'd think his pension depended on the final scores of the college and pro games. He gets insane."

"Where should we go?" Allie gave the cashier her money and waited for the change.

"It is gorgeous out there. Let's have a super view while we eat—I want a window table wherever we go. You can almost count the trees on those mountains over there. I love when the Santa Ana winds blow the smog away, it reminds you this truly is a valley where you're surrounded by mountains and foothills."

"Are you staying at the same house in Cambria?" Soozi bit into her pastrami sandwich.

"Yep. This year life at Cambria will be sand, sea, and semen for this girl."

Soozi nearly choked. "You're awfully frisky with this hormonal stuff inside you. You have to call as soon as you find out anything from the test." Soozi broke off a piece of her sandwich. "Part of me is furious you're going hundreds of miles away from me."

Allie stared at her best friend across the wooden table. The stare went on for a minute or two as she thought about what Soozi had confessed.

"What? Do I have mayonnaise on my face?"

Allie carefully laid her sandwich back on the plate and wiped her hands on her napkin, making a decision. "You know, you're right."

"Right about what?"

"I can't do the test in Cambria. You've been there for me since we were two little maidens in school. You let me in the delivery room with Zoe's birth where the maternal dam broke for me." Allie's voice softened as she said, "How can I run away to Cambria and do this? That's not fair to you, to us."

Soozi ducked her head, avoiding her friend's gaze. "Al, I'm not going to stop being your best friend if you do this a million miles away. It's a test, for gawd's sake—what's a little urine sample between friends?"

"That settles it. When you can't look me in the face, I know you're lying through your perfectly white teeth." Allie smacked the edge of the table.

"What if I just go on vacation for the week and forget this whole baby-making process for a while? A little rest and relaxation, fresh air, and sea spray. I'll do the tell-me-if-I'm-pregnant test when I get back home."

Soozi kept studying the tablecloth, nodding her head slightly, and a tear dropped to her plate.

Allie passed her crumpled napkin to Soozi. "I'm sorry, I know it's my life and someday my baby, blah, blah, blah. Doesn't mean I don't want to share the big moments of it with you." Allie watched her friend dab the napkin in the corners of her eyes, not a smudge of makeup out of place. "Thanks for the great acting job at the store, by the way, of not caring one way or the other." Allie raised her water glass in a toast. "Here's to a week off for good behavior, for both of us."

Soozi clinked her wineglass with Allie's.

Driving up Haven Avenue toward home, Allie gazed at the glorious sight of the San Gabriel Mountains peaking into the robin's egg blue sky. Majestic palm trees lined the center of the street, giving a paradise quality to the area. The spiked fronds fanned over her car, making a dappled canopy of shadows in the sunlight. A great place to raise children, Allie mused. She laid her arm maternally across her waist. If you like it here, guys, with mountains and palm trees, you're gonna love Cambria.

Chapter 10

"Is it September already, Allie?" the older woman asked from behind the counter. "Welcome back. I can't believe it's been a year since we last had you up here in Cambria." The first stop for Allie on the way to the beach house each year was the local grocery store to stock up on fresh produce and edibles for the week.

"What *I* can't believe are all the changes going on around here. What is the matter with developers? You have new buildings on every other corner and housing additions going up everywhere. This isn't the quaint and peaceful place we all love anymore," Alissa stated as she took a few twenty-dollar bills out of her wallet to cover the costs.

Making change, the old woman sighed. "I know. The transition is hard to understand or endure sometimes. You need tourists to survive, but they come for a visit, and then they want to stay permanently. With them come bigger houses and more tourists. The charm of the pines has to be squeezed in between buildings, I guess. I don't know. I just don't know. Well, welcome back anyway. Looks like a gorgeous day out there for your return." The woman had already begun ringing up the next order. Even in paradise, it's business as usual.

The downtown streets were filled and chaotic with cars competing with pedestrians for available space. The Friday night scramble of the tourists to find their motels and cash in a few dollars of shopping before nightfall had begun. Normally, Alissa avoided the town on the weekends; her rental was on the other side of the hill, away from the hustle of the almighty dollar. The house keys, secure in her purse, unlocked a small haven of sanity across the street from the mighty Pacific Ocean.

The sun felt good through the window as she headed the car along Burton Drive beyond Highway One. The familiar canopy of trees played shadows on the windshield. Alissa turned off the air conditioner and rolled down the windows. Fresh sweet air immediately filled the car and cries from the birds drifted through the open windows as she headed for the house. Her foot on the gas pedal wasn't used to the slow pace as she drove. The normal rushed tempo down south didn't work up here. You want to savor each curve of the road, each overhanging branch and secluded home, not speed by in a blur of chrome and metal.

Block after block took her further away from the stress and strain of reality and closer to rhythmic ocean breakers and relaxation. Alissa reached up and hit the garage door opener as she rounded the last curve. Okay, some modern conveniences make for a happy vacation home. Camping for Alissa meant room service and fresh towels each morning from a smiling maid. The beach house came equipped with a microwave, washer and dryer, and a gas fireplace in the main room. Two-story home, two bedrooms, two baths; a slice of heaven to be sure. Alissa couldn't wait to unpack and begin her time off. Walking into the kitchen from the garage, she felt as if she had never left this place. Could it really have been a year?

First order of business, open the windows. Running through the rooms in the different levels of the house, Alissa unlashed window after window, letting a rush of sea air blow away the stuffiness of the closed-up house. This set-up would last until sundown, when the majority of windows would be closed against the damp chill of ocean night. A few strategic ones would remain open all night, allowing the sounds of the crashing waves throughout the house.

Stepping out on the sundeck of the second floor, the expansive miles of ocean peacefully welcomed her back. Out a ways, the kelp beds marked the blue waters in pockets of brown. Nothing had changed, nature couldn't be bothered with something as infinitesimal as a passing year. Even during a year as charged with change as Allie's, the ocean's rhythm stayed its course. The peaks from underwater rocks marked the boundaries of the tide pools uncovered at low tide. The kelp beds scented the air with their salty smells. The cliffs down the street held back the power of the Pacific, beckoning Alissa to come walk the miles of ranch land solitude.

The front doorbell broke through her daydreaming. Alissa hadn't noticed the minivan pull into the driveway while soaking in the nautical scenery. Dashing down the carpeted stairs, a vision of roses greeted her through the etched glass in the front door.

"Mom said you were back in town." Jimmy handed Alissa a dozen long-stemmed white roses. The crystal vase had beads of condensation on the chilled glass. Alissa inhaled their perfume, then put the vase on the kitchen counter as Jimmy came back up the walkway with a second dozen. "We saved the best just for you, Alissa. They came out right pretty this year, I must say."

"It may be an exceptional year for me, Jimmy. Maybe the flowers know something we don't." She smiled as she signed his delivery clipboard and slipped a tip under the fastener. The fragrance from the roses already filled the small kitchen.

"Have you got another new game for those computers?" Jimmy shyly kicked his toe into the porch step. He had been delivering flowers to the vacationing Allie at this house for the last four or five years. His innocent crush on Alissa bloomed richer over the years.

More than one hot selling software product had germinated in Cambrian fashion for Alissa during these visits. "No, something much more important. I'll be sure and let you know if things work out. Give my best to your mom for me, Jimmy. I must say the flowers are extra beautiful this time." Folks are like family around here, Alissa thought.

"Take right care of yourself. Call us if you need anything, anything at all." And Jimmy walked back to the van.

One vase of flowers went upstairs in the living room area. The cool sea breeze would keep them fresh most of the week, brightening the open room a touch more with their natural splendor. The second vase decorated the master bedroom. Alissa wrapped her arms around her waist as she gazed at the roses reflecting off the mirror in the bedroom. Yes, they were uncommonly perfect this year, the creamy white texture of the tightly closed petals in sharp contrast to the deep green stems and thorns below.

A slight chill made her tremble. Right now, her body could be deciding her future, and whether to bloom from a tight single bud into maternity fullness. A tiny speck of cells, moving slowly within her uterus, were determining whether to take the shape of another human being. Alissa's arms tightened against her. As another chill made her shiver, a short burst of laughter broke away from Allie. Or I could freeze to death, standing in front of an open window, from a draft forty degrees colder than the Los Angeles area heat I'm used to. Alissa closed the window part way and grabbed a sweater from one of the suitcases on the bed.

Alissa pulled on the oversized knit sweater as she headed through the kitchen and back to the car to finish unloading the groceries. She quickly filled the bottom two layers of the refrigerator with gold cans of Diet Coke. Granted, the teapot would stay filled and warm to chase the dampness away in the evenings, but nothing replaced the icy jolt of Diet Coke for her in the morning. It seemed odd not to unload a couple of bottles of local wine from the grocery sacks this year. Alissa had enjoyed most of the central California area's varieties and flavors in past visits. No alcohol for the expecting-to-be-expecting during this trip though.

A ringing phone broke the silence. Alissa quickly searched the rooms to remember where she put her cell phone. "Hello?"

"I just heard you were back," Carolyn squealed. News traveled fast around here. "You are coming to the playhouse tonight, aren't you? It's Friday, and a perfectly marvelous way to celebrate your return. Let me make reservations for you right now, please?" Her enthusiastic voice warmed Alissa through. "You have to come with us."

"All right, all right. I'm yours for the evening. But no fix-ups. I know you've had a year of working your matrimonial matching schemes on the local maleness, but spare me, I just got in." Alissa could hear her friend's pout coming through the phone lines.

"I'm crushed you would think that way."

"Carolyn, you do this every year. Leave you alone for a while and you're scavenging anything in jeans and sneakers from San Louis Obispo north to Big Sur. Not that you have bad taste, or anything. I'm not totally complaining."

"But tonight they're doing *Love Letters* at the playhouse. You don't want to see such a romantic story all alone?"

"I won't be alone, you silly goose." Alissa smiled, already knowing how this conversation would turn out. "I'll be with you and Bill."

"Al, I'm serious."

"And?..."

"And I already called him to see if he was available when I heard you'd come into the village today." Defeat sounded in her voice. "What are you doing here so early? It's not like you to arrive before Sunday."

"And I threw you off to have a second Friday night of setting up blind dates for me? What is he this time? A retired lawyer, a widowed rancher, or some ag student you found bussing tables at a restaurant?" Life was never dull around Carolyn. Alissa got comfortable in the kitchen chair and they caught up with the latest gossip. All but one important tidbit of gossip, Allie thought as she smiled to herself.

By the time she got off the phone, the sun had begun to set. Alissa grabbed her hat made of heavy-knitted yarn that matched her sweater and headed toward the cliffs. The first Cambrian vacation sunset...a magical painting of pigments in pastel pinks and blues, violet and peach, changing in hues as the sun dipped below the horizon of the ocean. Pelicans flew across the water in singular formation, skimming just above the tops of the waves. The rocks orchestrated a symphony as the thunderous waves beat into shore.

Alissa crossed her arms tight, deeply breathing the salty air off the ocean. Other people from the neighborhood came to share in the glory of the event, creating a small gathering on the bluff. Turning to walk back to the house after nature's dramatic ending, she noticed brush near the ranch land moving. Two young deer were grazing within sight of their mother. The doe stared at Alissa, waiting to see what she was going to do. The doe's coloring blended with the brush almost perfectly. As Allie watched, more deer became visible. She counted seven in the grassy field, a Cambrian first for Alissa. What a breathtaking display of grace and gentleness. The baby fawns suddenly noticed the strangers and brought their heads up quickly. Ears too large for their heads twitched like radar, waiting for their cue from the doe.

"No one's going to hurt them. Your babies are safe," Alissa softly spoke. Carefully, she turned around and headed back to her rental. The look from those dark brown eyes of the doe reflected in Alissa's heart. A mother's eyes, protecting, loving. Always on the alert for the safety of her charges—am I ready for that kind of do-or-die commitment? She placed her hand against her flat stomach.

Allie turned on the shower in the bathroom. It was time for her annual blind date à la Carolyn's continuous matchmaking dreams. She stepped into the warm spraying water, a smile playing at the corners of her mouth. Lathering soap over her arms, she knew she would spill the baby beans before the week was out, otherwise Carolyn would try to marry her off before next Friday. Since the first year they'd known each other, the woman had started making plans for an enormous gala wedding against an ocean backdrop for Allie.

Carolyn called Allie matrimonially challenged and, determined to find a cure, introduced her to anything in the central California area wearing men's clothing. Not quite true, Allie corrected herself. Carolyn's taste ran on the fussy side and her manly picks commonly had a few things going for them: money, looks, and/or personality. Nothing clicked for Allie in the heart department, though. She usually met them in the security of a double date with Carolyn and Bill. They dated, sometimes the guy slept over, and then Allie went back to Southern California. A few e-mails, a few phone calls, and poof! the men vanished. Allie ducked her head under the faucet and let the water drown out the thoughts. She felt like a sacrificial lamb going to slaughter.

Allie opened the glass door to the theater and scanned the lobby, looking for Carolyn and Bill. Elegant yet cozy, Allie loved the magic Cambrian porthole, where actors might be talented locals or a big name from Hollywood enjoying the chance of ocean-sprayed scenery during a gig.

Tugging the edge of a peach-colored shawl further over her shoulder, Allie spotted her friends near the refreshment bar. Allie's knees locked in place, though, when she noticed Carolyn smiling up at a chiseled piece of gorgeous granite. Allie started drooling in more than one body cavity as her eyes drank in the Brad Pitt nonchalance coating a Tom Selleck body. Omigod, a hunk. How was she going to keep her forced-into-celibacy hands off him? Gillian had warned her a half dozen or maybe a million times before she left the office to behave herself on this make-a-baby vacation.

"You've got sand, sea, and siestas scheduled, boss. No sex, no foul. Don't look at the studlies, and for goodness sake, if you do look, don't touch." Gillian had snapped his fingers. "Keep your arms and legs together at all times and have fun."

Allie forgot to remind Gillian of Carolyn's matrimonial habit of fixing her up with potential husband candidates. Visions of Gillian tagging after her in the Chinese restaurant pounded in her brain like a conscientious objector. No sex. No sex.

Check out the tight butt in those Dockers.

No sex…Gillian's ghost wagged his finger like a limp windshield wiper.

Look at the long legs, able to leap coffee tables in a single bound and wrap around you in ecstasy.

Play safe. No sex.

Carolyn looked over and, spotting Allie, gracefully waved her arm over her head, beckoning her toward the back of the room. Beckoning her to stand closer to the Herculean figure, closer to a nucleus of lust and sin. Tiny beads of sweat broke out under Allie's arms. So much for worrying about being cold from the coastal night air…Allie's face flushed with a scorching sizzle as the man turned slightly in her direction, looked where Carolyn was pointing, and flashed a megawatt smile that could light up Broadway all by itself in a black-out. Please don't let me hear "Strangers in the Night" while I make a fool of myself walking across the lobby.

Trying to remember how to breathe and walk at the same time, Allie excused her way through the groups of people standing between her and her night's destiny. Is that knight with a K, as in shining knight wearing casual street clothes? Two seconds later she stood next to the Chippendale dancer look-alike, the towering vision even more breathtaking close-up.

"Allie," Carolyn said as she leaned over and air-kissed the side of her cheek, "you made it."

Allie stared directly into Carolyn's twinkling eyes, noting that her friend's smug face reflected a cat that swallowed a pet shop of canaries. "And no jet lag, darling, since Cambria's in the same time zone as Rancho Cucamonga." Allie leaned into a quick hug from Carolyn's perfect spouse. "It's good to see you again, Bill."

No more stalling. Allie tilted her face upward and gazed into eyes colored an emerald green she'd only seen in travel posters of Ireland. Their depth, fringed in perfectly long lashes, pulled her into a breathless moment where her heart pounded loudly, drowning Carolyn's voice.

"…works as a reoccurring role in *Days of Our Lives*." Omigod, Soozi is going to die, Allie silently screamed. "You may know his character: Jim, Joe, Jeremy…," Carolyn's voice dropped, floundering in male names.

"Jason, a dark shadow from Salem's seedy side," purred a deep Barry White tone. "But that's only my alter-ego, here they call me Sam."

Subconsciously crossing her legs daintily at the ankles, Allie stood before him smiling. "I'm sorry I don't watch daytime television, I've obviously missed quite a bit." What am I doing flirting? Gillian is dropping his pink curlers right this minute as the GPS (Gillian protection system) sounded a siren in her brain.

Fortunately, the lobby lights flicked off and on, rescuing Allie from fantasies of throwing the man on the carpet and doing what any decent oversexed harlot would do. Sam gently took her arm in his and escorted her through a short passage into the theater. Their shoes echoed a few steps in unison on the wooden floorboards as a young woman took their tickets and handed them a program.

Fasten your seatbelts tonight, it's going to be a bumpy ride. Seatbelts, nothing—Allie heard a door slam with twenty deadbolts crashing into their holders and six chain locks forced into place when the heat from his hand, lightly touching her lower back as he guided her to their row, made her dizzy.

Allie stared at the ringing phone on the end table with blurry eyes. "'ello?" she croaked.

"So?" Carolyn asked.

"Do you know what time it is?"

"Two cups of coffee past breakfast, and I still don't know how your date ended."

"He's nice." Allie brushed a strand of stray hair from her face.

"Excuse me? You disappear on the arm of a gorgeous television star, and all I get is 'He's nice'?" Carolyn squeaked.

Allied stretched under her comforter and snuggled back into the warm spot. "Carolyn, he's nice and gay."

"Damn."

"You forgot the rule: If he's gorgeous and single, he's probably not straight. Jason knows half the entries in Gillian's little black book." Allie swore she could hear Carolyn banging her head against a wall.

"I…I just thought he—damn."

"Call me after you locate your pride."

Inside the mall of shops off Burton Road, Alissa stepped through a door to her right into a room filled with color and designs, a children's bookstore. Floor-to-ceiling oak cases showed books and stickers of the classics Alissa had loved as a child, as well as more modern fantasy characters she knew nothing about. Winnie the Pooh and all his friends, including Christopher Robin, were displayed in a variety of sizes along one wall with Bert and Ernie of Sesame Street fame dominating another corner.

Colorful stuffed animals interrupted the hundreds of books in lovable squished fashion on almost every shelf. A book and a cuddly, a perfect pair, what clever owners to mix and match the textures of childhood together, she thought. Good marketing. Her footsteps slowly creaked on the worn wooden flooring and brought a sense of wonder and delight.

Walking through the picture book section, Alissa ran her fingers lightly against the paper covers. How do parents choose a book these days. Allie scanned the assortment of animal stories, fantasy themes, and growing-up ideas that filled shelf after wooden shelf. What if she collected a few books each month? Alissa laughed under her breath. The baby would own a library before it was old enough to read.

Alissa touched a few books as she read the titles and authors, then stopped. She carefully slid a white and blue covered book titled *The Jolly Man* from its home on a top shelf. The two authors' names printed on the cover sent goose bumps down her arms. Savannah Jane and Jimmy Buffett, *the* Jimmy Buffett of Margaritaville fame and his daughter? She flipped to the back of the book and read the bio on the dust jacket flap. None other than the Key West man himself. This had to be a sign that she was doing the right thing, didn't it? If her musical idol for over twenty years could find happiness and contentment as a parent, so would Alissa. Not only did he enjoy the roller-coaster ride of parenting between albums and concert tours, but, together with his daughter, he had written a children's picture book from the lyrics of one of his songs.

Her baby-to-be's first book. Alissa held it lovingly to her chest and walked toward the cashier. Waiting in line, she opened the book and glanced at the painted illustrations and adventurous text below. She imagined sitting in a rocker with the baby on her lap as they read together through this story for the hundredth time. Alissa stood dazed, the edge of the book cutting into the inside of her fingers from squeezing it tight. Buffett's magic touched Alissa this time through a different link, far stronger than his music and lyrics, a parental bond. She lost moments daydreaming of her baby.

Jimmy Buffett's music created the background to most of Allie's adult life. After all these decades of singing along to the taleful ballads, Alissa realized she had never dragged Soozi to a Parrot Head celebration. A standing room only, singing nonstop, gyration-of-fun concert—how long had it been since she'd been to one? A wild, rebellious wave of energy flowed through her, time to kick off the old high heels and celebrate Buffett-style. Alissa thanked the quiet store clerk who handed back the book wrapped securely in brown paper. *The Jolly Man* tune played in her mind as she pulled away from the parking lot.

Excitement grew in the pit of her stomach at the thought of a Buffett concert. She'd been away too long because of too many deadlines bleeding over into weekend marathons of production and programming, with no time to be wild, wacky, and wicked.

Inside her closets back home hung colorful Hawaiian shirts of rayon and silk next to an assortment of T-shirts with Buffett logos painted in tropical settings. The wilder the better was the preferred dress code at concerts. Photos of Parrot Heads, fans of the Caribbean rock star, on various Web sites showed them enjoying the notoriety of dressing in colorful costumes of parrots, or in honor of two of his popular songs, shark fins and cheeseburgers.

Allie walked into the rental house as her cell phone jangled in her purse. She glanced at the number as she flipped it open. "This better be life or death, Gillian."

"A warm aloha greeting to you too, boss. I have some great news, but if you want to wait all these excruciating days until you return," he sighed, "I'll hang up now."

"Oh, brother. Go ahead—you've already interrupted my vacation mode. What's up?"

"This is fabulous."

"It better be."

"You're-going-to-die fabulous. I just sold your play."

"Say what?" Allie stared into space, her stomach beginning to tighten. "What did you say?"

"Your play, *The Crystal Prince*. I got producers to back the show and it goes into production next week. Isn't that utterly fabulous?"

Allie paced in the kitchen. "A—how did you find my play? B—I never authorized you to authorize for me on my private property."

"Piffle," Gillian sniffed. "Who's that little guy on *M.A.S.H.* with the glasses?"

"Radar."

"Oh, yes. I pulled a Radar on you. The papers were in a stack I gave you months ago. You've been so head-in-the-clouds with the baby process, you didn't even blink." Allie heard his office chair squeaking in the background. "As for finding the precious package, you didn't hide it or anything. Sitting in your bottom drawer makes it company property; I just exercised your options."

Allie increased the speed of her steps. Gillian sold my play? Impossible. Gillian found producers for my play? My play?

"Allie? Allie, I can hear you hyperventilating. Oh, and we've made it into

122

a musical. Most of your words are being used, but being put into song. You know how I adore Andrew Lloyd Webber. I feel such a connection to him right now, like we're twinsies."

"But…but how?"

"Darling, all the crew down at the Orange County Theater are buzzing about this. Oh, and Eric is in the chorus. Is that to die for?" The other line started ringing in the office. "Gotta run, Miss Playwright, business calls me. Congratulations, go celebrate."

Flicking the phone closed, Allie sank against the kitchen counter. The nerve of that man, rummaging through my desk drawers, reading my personal stuff—and selling it, of all things. And, and…oh, my heavens, he sold my play. She walked trance-like toward the bedroom and headed for the closet. She picked out a beige-toned tropical shirt. Twirling in front of the bedroom mirror with the shirt, Allie grabbed her long hair and pulled it on top of her head, locking it in with two sticks.

Allie patted her stomach. "Get used to it, kid. Your mother is a flaming Parrot Head and will be the talk of the playground for years." She was starving, and headed for the car and dinner with friends. Not too many Parrot Heads in this California coastal paradise, more like Yanni groupies or Mozart mavens up here. No matter, a few locals enjoyed her differences. I'm celebrating now, Cambria.

"You what?" Carolyn shrieked, then quickly looked around the restaurant at the morning customers. She fussed with the checkered cloth napkin in her lap. A soft redness flowed across her cheeks. "I can't believe it. I don't know what to say."

Allie hesitated. One part of her wanted to announce her possible pregnancy to Carolyn, to the world, that she could be pregnant right this very second, but sensible caution prevailed. And a touch of superstition, and a couple of invisible threats from Soozi. For years, Carolyn had schemed and plotted a wedding for Allie's future, pleading with her not to throw life away on just a career and to let her help find someone suitable.

"I'm going through artificial insemination," Allie repeated. "It sort of came up this summer like a Grand Canyon–sized sinkhole in my heart. Extreme cravings for holding a warm miniature body tsunamied me." Allie twisted the edge of her napkin. "Close your mouth, girl."

Carolyn leaned back into the chair and folded her arms. "Allie, you look confident. You've a fire in your eyes, a twinkle," she said. "So, you're joining the other side."

Carolyn and her husband, Bill, both agreed "no children" early in their relationship. Artistic jaunts across the country, mixed with long periods of low finances, left the decision about raising a family easy for them. Scratching out a living in clay for two adults was one thing, but children demanded hard work and expensive responsibilities, Carolyn had told Allie more than once over the years. The pair enjoyed their self-involvement and let the rest of the world be their family.

"I thought you were happy without a tiny terror?" Carolyn questioned, playing with her food. "We were going to travel as a foursome after you got married, remember? See the world and enjoy ourselves. Grow old and make memories in countries around the world."

"Don't pout, it makes wrinkles on that sweet face. I know all about your here-comes-the-bride fantasies for me." Allie settled back in her chair. "You wanted us to play *The Honeymooners*, Alice and Trixie, with our crazy, mere-male husbands. Despite all your hard efforts, Carolyn," Allie patted her friend's hand, "there just doesn't seem to be a guy out there for me."

"But a baby?" Carolyn scratched her face with the tip of her finger.

"Carolyn, it's exciting, trust me. Do you know what I found right here in Cambria? Jimmy Buffett published a children's picture book. Even my Caribbean wild man found parental happiness.

"I came here to keep my fingers and legs crossed, I guess, and give my egg and the sperm time to do their thing. Relax with the ocean and let nature take her course." Allie placed her hand on her stomach.

Carolyn shook her head back and forth. "You want a baby. What an idiot I must have seemed Friday night setting you up on a date. Why didn't you stop me?"

"How do you stop a moving train? Carolyn, I couldn't get a word in edgewise; you were talking a hundred miles an hour, as usual."

"I thought he'd be the one," Carolyn sighed.

"Yeah, he would, for Gillian. I appreciate your efforts making my first night back special. You always make my trips exciting—I'm like a pet project of the mad matrimony madam. Well, I'm going straight into Maternity 101, do not pass throwing the rice, and go directly to the nursery. Can you keep up with me?"

"Yes, of course. I think. Maybe. It's so weird. I can't imagine you pregnant."

"Me, neither." Allie stared at Carolyn with blank brown eyes. They burst into laughter.

"No making you a fellow member in the wives' club? How long before you find out if the process took or not?"

"I'm waiting till I get back," Allie said, crossing her legs under the table, "if I don't get my period by then. I don't know how women handle this emotional roller-coaster ride month after month."

Carolyn nodded at an older couple just leaving the restaurant, then looked back at Allie. "Sorry. Go on about the roller coaster."

"You should have seen me when it didn't take the first time. Pit-i-ful. I can't handle the rejection of my own body. You put your heart on the line and nature slaps back and says, 'No, not you.' You take it personally." Allie laid her head against the back of the booth. "I have such respect and compassion for anyone fighting to get pregnant and facing that red devil over and over for years. I'm not that strong."

"Bill and I never even had a dog. Too much responsibility—your freedom is imprisoned between guilt and exhaustion. Are you sure you've thought this through? You didn't get sucked in on some new Pampers commercial? No sniffing baby powder from a paper sack in the bathroom?"

"I know…different, huh? I have to go with this." Allie flagged the waitress for more tea.

Carolyn held up her cup, too. "Well, is the father cute?" Allie heard the resignation in her friend's voice.

"He's number forty-five on the charts. Tall, brilliant, athletic, and very young," Allie teased. The worst seemed to be over. Carolyn didn't have a heart attack nor end their adults-only friendship.

"Young? Oh, great. I suppose you'll be spending your vacations at Sea World now. I'll never see you again." Allie watched Carolyn's lip tremble as she bit down to still the quiver.

Allie came around the table in two steps and hugged her. "Carolyn, the baby has fifty weekends a year to visit Sea World or Disneyland. We live in Southern California, one big amusement park all by itself. We'll be coming up here for fresh air and hiking with a four-wheel-drive stroller. The little thing will learn to crawl among the tide pools, and cut its teeth on abalone shells."

"A baby. Wow."

Allie flipped her hair over her shoulder. "And Auntie Carolyn can teach her the difference between loganberries and ollieberries."

Chapter 11

Allie stood before the shelves of boxes at Kmart. Sealed cardboard boxes of various colors and sizes that could announce the biggest change in her life. Or cruelly register a negative, sending her back onto the table at Dr. Adams'.

"What do I want again? They all look alike."

"If you hadn't panicked and taken those other two back, we wouldn't have to be here. You want any pee-on-a-stick method, don't you remember?" Soozi impatiently tapped her painted fingernails against the handle of the shopping cart. "I waited forever for your stupid vacation to end, and this isn't how I thought we'd be spending our time."

"I thought they would expire or something, how am I supposed to know what kind of shelf life these things have? This is all new to me." Allie chewed on her fingernail. Did her jeans feel a little snug today or was she just imagining it? Too much rich food in Cambria, most likely, or could she really be pregnant? "Wasn't it easier for women long ago? Either you were or you weren't having a baby, and nature let you know about three months into it. Simple, straightforward, yes or no before ultrasounds and ovulation kits."

"You'd have been crucified back then, too, remember. Women barely had the right to vote, let alone have a child by themselves. You'd be run out of town with a scarlet A clashing with that gorgeous hair of yours. We had no choices as women, Allie. Simple is not always better, my friend." Soozi grabbed Allie's shoulders from behind. "Don't forget where we've come from. Women were oppressed, depressed, and regressed. You wash your mouth out when you get home for even thinking the past was better."

"Well, I'm tired of making decisions." Allie felt like stamping her foot.

Soozi shook her friend. "Take two of them and confirm whatever fate has in store for you. This isn't brain surgery." Soozi reached over Allie's shoulder and grabbed the brand she'd used with Zoe and one other different brand. "Okay, this and this one. Now, let's get out of here."

The cashier in front of them didn't look old enough to be in high school, let alone handle people's money. "So, like, do you want it to be positive?" she asked as she scanned the UPC codes across the register.

"Yes." Allie looked over at Soozi.

"Cool. Congratulations, like to both of you, you know. I'd freak if I was pregnant right now." The girl handed back Allie's change with fingernails painted in bizarre black and neon-colored designs, and then put the boxes in a plastic bag.

"Oh no, she's not, uh, she's not with me. I mean she's with me, but we're just friends."

"It's cool. No biggie."

Soozi squealed outside, bending over in half as they walked. "She thought I was your significant other! She thought the baby was ours."

"Well, don't have a cow. We do make a darling couple. I don't know how we'd break it to Randy, though." A nervous laugh broke out. "Can you imagine the look on his face if you told him you were leaving him for me?" Laughing harder, Allie crossed her legs while digging for her car keys inside her purse. "I'm going to pee my pants."

"If you are pregnant, you have to get used to running to the potty often, my dear. The fetus sits on your bladder all day and night, pushing for the heck of it. Don't ever be too far from a commode after the fourth month or so. The little darlings keep pushing and kicking from then on. Bruised ribs and battered bladder—oh the joys of being pregnant." Soozi got into the car and shut the door.

"Stop it. So, tomorrow morning it is. The first pee of the day, huh? What time do you want the news, Aunt Soozi?" Allie started the car and pulled out of the parking space.

"This is your call. The kids are usually up by seven and the NFL games start at ten or something. That's how my Sunday mornings usually go. Only the sports change, to let Randy know the year is passing by," Soozi snorted. "Men are such uncomplicated creatures. Snacks and sports fill up any weekend, rain or shine."

Inside, the car was toasty warm from the sunshine. The brisk breeze raised goose bumps on unprotected arms, but Allie turned on the vents and let the fresh air in. Some days a sweater was not enough outside the car and too much inside the car. Welcome to Southern California.

"What are you doing tonight? Have you planned anything special?" Soozi put her sunglasses on and looked over at her friend.

"Um, actually, yes."

"Well, that was evasive. Give it up—what?"

"Gillian scheduled his favorite masseuse for me at my house, a relaxation treatment." Allie quickly glanced at Soozi, then back at the traffic. "Don't start pouting over this. You came with me today, and you'll be the first one I call tomorrow with the results. Don't make this ugly," Allie warned.

"What are you talking about? I think it's a great idea. You'll get a heavenly chance to turn your mind off about everything for a while, and be all loose and snuggy when you go to bed."

"But?" Allie pulled into Soozi's driveway.

"But I wish I'd thought of it first," Soozi spit out. "Damn him—Mr. Orange County feel-good always butts in." She jumped out of the car and Lenny ran across the front lawn toward her.

Allie sighed. Thank goodness for Lenny, I owe him one. "I'll call you tomorrow. Lenny, take your mom in the house and tell Daddy to get her a cup of tea," she yelled from the car.

"Daddy's got football on. I'll do it." Lenny ran back to the front door as if he were allowed near the microwave, let alone could use it.

"Now look what you've done. I have to go rescue my kitchen. *Ciao*," Soozi blew a kiss back toward the car and headed into the house.

Driving home seemed mere minutes as Allie stopped the car in her garage and grabbed her plastic sack. Gillian told her they would come over with dinner and all the stuff for the massage around seven. Allie's chores were clearing a place in the bedroom for the table and taking a shower. She walked over and kicked on the thermostat. The house held a slight chill, not the best temperature when lying practically naked in front of a stranger.

She walked back out across the front yard and checked her mailbox. The afternoon sun felt good on her face. The day had warmed up to over seventy degrees, but couldn't combat the chill left from the night before in the shadows. Anything below sixty-eight degrees felt chilly to Allie. Her thin blood lived on desert Santa Ana winds and tropical sun rays most of the year. Standing in front of her freezer with the door open for too long was intolerable.

One minute after seven, Gillian came through the door with a small cardboard box smelling scrumptious in his arms. Behind him followed a tall young man in a black leather jacket, with matching leather pants. A brilliant white polo shirt underneath the jacket practically glowed against his skin. The man carried a folded table and had a navy blue gym bag slung over his shoulder. Allie couldn't take her eyes off the young Adonis. *I'm supposed to take my clothes off for him?*

"Darling, breathe. This is Eric. Eric, Allie, my boss and prospective mother-to-be. I want your talented hands to ease her wretched body of all concerns and tensions tonight, and hopefully we'll all live happily ever after tomorrow."

Gillian put the box down on the dining room table. He noticed the candles and placemats. "I didn't know you owned any. Nice touch. I'll unpack dinner in here. Allie, show Eric where to set up his table and oils." Gillian spoke over the sounds of unwrapping cartons from the box.

Eric had already skimmed out of the leather jacket and tossed it onto the back of the nearest chair. Allie stopped dead for a moment at the size of his biceps chiseled into his tanned arms. Anything large and beefy would do as a description. His white shirt, neatly tucked into a tiny waist, created a perfect upside-down triangle of maleness. With pants so tightly stretched over his body, Allie wondered why she didn't see the folds of the shirt where it was tucked. *How do men do that?*

"Uh, this way, Eric. I hope there's enough room for you and everything.

I've never had a massage at home before." Allie rambled on as she led him up the stairs to the master bedroom. Of course, there's enough room, you idiot. A queen-size bed and a few bookshelves only took up half the master bedroom floor area. A massage table would be no problem.

"This will be fine. I can use the dresser top for my equipment?" Eric's slight accent tickled Allie's ears.

"Sure, no problem. Is there anything I can get for you?" Allie asked. Coffee, tea or me, gorgeous. Where does Gillian find these guys?

"Maybe a couple of towels, please?" Eric unpacked a handful of lotions from the gym bag onto the dresser.

Magical potions for your instant enjoyment. Allie brought in some towels from the bathroom cupboard, and watched him set up the table.

"Downstairs, you two, before the food gets cold," Gillian called up the stairs. "Allie, do you have wineglasses? All I can find are these ancient cartoon jelly jars in the kitchen."

Allie rushed down the carpeted stairs and into the kitchen for the requested goblets. I don't think I'll be able to eat a thing in front of that hunk. And I surely do not want a full stomach when I'm lying there naked under a sheet for this guy. The smells from the dining room were exquisite, though. Allie's mouth actually watered every so slightly, draining her of any resistance.

"I found this darling Asian place in Anaheim, Allie. Not too rich, not too spicy. Enough protein to be satisfying, but mainly vegetables. The man is a genius with a wok. Eric, would you pour the wine, please? None for Allie, she's strictly nonalcoholic for the next nine months." Gillian glowed in the candlelight, serving as host. A dinner party, any excuse of one, animated him all the more. "How did your day go?"

"Soozi and I picked up the necessary supplies for, uh, tomorrow morning," Allie stuttered out. Rather a delicate subject to be discussing in front of Eric. She glanced across the table at the delightful view.

"Oh, don't fret about Eric, love. I've told him everything. He's quite easy with it all, eh, Eric?" Gillian patted the man's thigh to his immediate left.

"Right. I hope it all works out, Allie." Eric nodded his head slowly and picked up his glass of wine in a salute.

"Eric is from Australia, Al. Don't you just love his accent?" Gillian again reached over to pat his thigh and left his hand resting there under the table.

Allie covered a sigh by putting veggies into her mouth. Gillian would not be sleeping alone tonight. Allie looked down at her plate. Gillian's personal life had always been exotic and flavorful like the menu on her plate, especially next to her dull and mundane calendar. Eric was not the first of Gillian's friends Allie had met over the years, their phenomenal looks always breathtaking.

Gillian laid his chopsticks down. "Eric is playing the character Alexander in *The Crystal Prince.*"

Allie almost choked on a piece of celery. "Uh, wow, congratulations, Eric." She had never imagined Alexander as drop-dead gorgeous.

"Everyone is excited about the musical, Allie. You've done a great job on the story line."

Gillian purred, "See, I told you so." He clapped his hands together. "I will clear away the table, you two head upstairs. Allie, prepare yourself for the most luxurious hour of your life. Eric's hands should be insured by Lloyd's of London, they are that powerful. I will not see you again tonight, my dear. You will melt like butter into your bed when he is through with you. Eric will tuck you in. So give me a hug now and I will await the good news tomorrow morning." Gillian came around the table to Allie.

Eric pushed his chair aside, drained his glass of wine and went up the stairs.

"Gillian, thank you so much for everything. The food was excellent. I can't even begin to tell you how much I appreciate the massage. You've done a great job, as usual, in distancing me from my own worries. This is perfect." Allie put her arms around his neck, and felt the hesitant, brief tightening of his arms around her body. Allie leaned back and kissed Gillian briefly on his cheek.

"Go, boss lady. Your table of pleasure awaits you. I will clean up these few dishes, and then dive into this marvelous book I brought, Bette Midler's autobiography. I can't wait to begin. Hurry along, go indulge, go," Gillian teasingly pushed her toward the stairs.

Inside her bedroom door, Eric had set up a bowl of hot water and the bottles of lotion were now warming inside. A small CD player sat next to this with a Mozart concerto filling the room.

"Take this sheet with you into the bathroom and completely disrobe.

Wrap the sheet around you with the opening in front," Eric handed her an expensive flat sheet of soft blue.

Lying face down on the table with the sheet now covering the lower half of her, Eric slowly began working the first warm oil onto her back. A soft, indescribable fragrance touched her nose. Allie drifted away with the strong movements of his fingers. Once, Eric had her roll onto her back but Allie scarcely remembered the effort. He practically lifted her from the table in helping her roll over. Lloyd's of London should *definitely* know about these hands, Allie mused, no longer cognizant of her body except wherever Eric's hands or fingers were.

Eric eventually straightened to his full height and reached for one of her bath towels, briskly rubbing his hands of excess oil. He spoke not a word. Allie couldn't move a muscle of her relaxed body, nor did she care, watching Eric turn down the quilt and sheet on her bed. In two strides he was beside her again and easily slid his arms under her. Lifting Allie to his chest, he put her limp arm around his neck. He turned and headed back to the bed.

Allie wished she could savor this moment. She felt like a character on the cover of a romance novel. The sheets of her bed felt cool against her relaxed body, the massage had warmed her skin all over. Eric, indeed, had tucked her in and quietly began to pack his gym bag. Allie fell asleep before he finished and left the room, closing the door carefully behind him.

"Eric." Gillian closed the book on his lap, watching the gorgeous male walk down the stairs. "How is she?"

"She will sleep longer tomorrow, I'm sure." Eric put down the table and bag, reaching for his leather jacket.

"Excellent. Let the ol' witch of day care and bon-bons cool her heels waiting for Allie's call. This is one time Allie will not be up before dawn." Gillian smiled in delighted satisfaction. His plan had a dual edge—for Allie to ward off any pre-test stress, but also delay and spoil the she-wolf's anticipated morning wake-up call of test results. "Soozi won't dare ring first tomorrow and risk calling before the test is complete." Gillian finished his glass of wine, flashing a perfect smile at Eric.

In ten minutes the boys had the house locked up and the baggage stored in the trunk. Gillian drove off into the night with Eric at his side.

Allie awoke from the most glorious dream, though she couldn't remember a single detail of the adventure. A soft smile played on her lips as she rolled over in the bed and stretched her long legs under the cocoon of covers. Her body felt liquid and limber, deliciously calm. If only she could remember what day it was. Something nagged in the back of her mind, some insistent speck of nuisance trying to swim through the haze of waking up.

The sun peeked through the edges of the curtains, forcing its way into the bedroom in beams of flecked yellow. Looks like another sunny day in Rancho Cucamonga, what a surprise. Do I have to be somewhere today? What is it I'm supposed to remember? The pillow cushioned Allie's face as she moved, the new area cool to her cheek. She hugged her arms around its softness. Weekend mornings are luscious. Is it Saturday or Sunday? Can't be that important, if I don't remember.

Moving her legs under the sheets, Allie realized how smooth they seemed against the fabric. A slight fragrance brushed her nose as the sheets ruffled from the movement, a sweet fragrance of a gentle perfume. Slowly the activity of the night before slipped back into her conscience: a massage table, Eric's strong bronze hands kneading her naked body from one end to the other, being carried to bed, an exquisite night. Eric. Gillian's Eric.

"Gillian's Eric?" Allie's eyes widened. "Oh, my gawd. Last night, Gillian, Eric. It's morning. *The* morning." Fear gripped Allie across the middle and held her fast in the bed.

"I've gotta get up. The test. It's time," Allie whispered. She moved the covers with pitiful force, her arms refusing cooperation after the glow from last night. The bedroom air chilled her skin, raising goose bumps. Grabbing her dependable chenille robe, Allie walked to the windows, drawing the curtains wide after the first feeble attempt. Outside the sun gleamed brightly. Allie squinted from the glare of the late morning rays. She'd overslept pee-on-a-stick day.

She walked into the bathroom, ignoring her disheveled image, duplicated in all the mirrors. Morning hair, twisted and tangled down her shoulders in rust-colored chaos times six, followed her carnival-style across the floor.

"That poodle in leather! Wait till I get my hands on him, making me late." Allie reached for the opened cardboard box on the marbled counter. She had memorized the directions and information leaflet from inside it yesterday. Her hands shook slightly as she pulled the plastic container out of the box. Who created such a compact contraption? How can something so small make or break my day?

Allie's bladder gave an insistent pang, rousing her from reverie. No use standing here thinking about it, just pee and get it over with.

She felt as if she released two gallons of liquid from her body, yet the directions only asked for a few drips and drops. Had she diluted her urine? Would the test be inaccurate from too much water yesterday? Allie wrapped the worn robe back around her as she flushed the toilet and laid the instrument on top of the box.

She flicked the radio on and the room filled with something mellow. The words floated around her, something about "It'll be all right...on Monday." Jimmy! "Dang, I wish I knew how long this song was. I should have brought up the kitchen timer," Allie told her reflections in the room. "Give me strength, Jimmy."

Bending over the second sink, Allie began brushing her teeth. Her heart pounded in her chest and the foam from the toothpaste splattered on the mirror. She concentrated on the tube of toothpaste in front of her. Do not glance over, it's too early.

Jimmy's voice finished his soft rock hit, and another song followed without any commercial interruption. Allie kept her back to the box. Don't look, don't look. You'll jinx the test. Goose bumps traveled the length of her clenched arms.

Finally, she gave herself permission and turned around. She stepped closer to the plastic stick, still squeezing her arms. The tiny digital view screen sat in front of her, a definite pink mark in the center of it. Positive. The test is positive. I'm pregnant. I'm going to have a baby. Allie's hands shook as she picked up the test, afraid that jarring the instrument would make the mark go away.

If I keep this in a souvenir box for the baby, would it always show this wonderful pink mark? She could write today's date on the tester with a permanent marker anyway to remind her of this plastic-encased perfect moment.

Allie slid her feet into her worn, scruffy slippers. She had calls to make. She took the tester with her into the kitchen downstairs to make a cup of tea. *I'm pregnant.* She looked at her stomach, just below the tied knot of her robe, and whispered, "What would you like? Apple cinnamon or berry tea, since we're celebrating?" The metal teakettle banged against the side of the sink, echoing in the empty kitchen. Water from the tap splashed inside as it filled.

I'm going to be a mom. She looked out at the trees in the backyard through the large kitchen window. The branches danced in the motion of a late summer breeze, painting the area in various shades of green. Allie leaned against the sink, watching the modern dance routine of nature before her.

Wherever you are, Mom, you're going to be a grandmother. Tears escaped down Allie's cheeks, she ached deep inside at not sharing this moment with her mother. As limited as their relationship might have been while Allie grew up, this new life, this new generation might have filled in gaps and holes. What was her mother's pregnancy like? How long was she in labor? Family information was lost as she'd brushed off the pain and cobwebs of the past. *I've got to call Soozi before she drives over here and takes the test for me.*

"And you didn't tell them I was pregnant?" Allie quizzed Soozi for the three-millionth time as they drove to the restaurant together. "How? How could they not have worn you down with incessant questioning? Aren't they curious?" Allie had made Soozi wait to meet with the group until the next normal lunch, without calling a special date to arouse suspicion.

"I told you, I didn't say anything, they have lives of their own, you know. They aren't sitting in the kitchen watching the calendar religiously about you." Soozi turned her head, watching traffic around them. "You're driving me insane. You know that, don't you? We get there, you blurt it out at the table—bingo, everyone will know." Soozi smacked the steering wheel with the heel of her hand. "Like I'm going to leak it to Janelle or Cindy and have the rest pout for not being the first to find out? I don't think so. I'd be shredded to pieces at our next potluck dinner, for sure." Soozi tapped her brakes and slowed for the red light ahead of them. She turned and looked at Allie, placing a quick hand on her knee.

"This is your news. I've been there, done that a couple times already, especially with this Midol group."

While walking to the glass front door of the restaurant from the parking lot, the sun warmed their backs and a cool breeze from the west brushed strands of their hair forward. Soozi hesitated then turned and quickly gave Allie a hug for support. The women inside were like family, only better, and this was Allie's moment to break the wonderful news to her sisters. Allie squeezed her friend in return, and they locked eyes in prenatal conspiracy.

"It's about time you two finally showed up. We were ready to spread romantic rumors about the both of you to the tabloids," blurted Cindy, working on her second glass of wine.

"Sit down, sit down. Allie, how was your trip to Cambria?" was the first question shot from the noisy table.

"She goes there every year. Same ocean, same pine trees, yadda, yadda. More importantly, how are you feeling? Are you pregnant yet?" Janelle leaned forward, staring hard at Allie's face.

"Ex-cuse me, Janelle. I was being polite." The friend shoved Janelle in the shoulder. "Miss Manners would slap your face. You don't jump on Allie about the baby situation." Tempers caught up quickly; all seated guests started talking at once. The animated women chose sides of manners versus curiosity, and protocol was thrown around like darts.

A sharp whistle pierced the air and caught the pack's attention. Soozi stood by her vacant dining chair with her hands on her hips, glaring at them all. "Behave."

"God, I've never been able to whistle like that," Allie said, laughing at the frozen faces around her as she pulled out her own chair from the table. "Look, I'm sorry we're late for lunch; it's my fault, and I know how anxious you all are. Second, I'm not sorry to say," she paused, "that I *am* officially late." Allie waited, watching the shared quizzical looks as she eased herself into the padded seat.

"You're late? Of course you are, we agreed on twelve-thirty," one snippet declared.

"You're late? You're late!" Like a cartoon lightbulb over their heads, the group squealed in delight.

"Soozi, sit down for heaven's sake. Omigod, this is fabulous. Girl, tell us everything," Cindy said grabbing Allie's hand from across the table.

"What's to tell? I peed, the stick turned pink, and then pink again. I'm pregnant."

"We got two tests, just to be sure," Soozi added. "Looks like we're adding another charter member to the Mommy and Me class next year." Soozi waved over their heads to the hostess at the front of the restaurant. The woman nodded and headed to the restaurant's kitchen door.

"Did you take the tests to Cambria? Such a perfect place," one of them asked loudly over the others discussing the good news among themselves.

"No, I waited until I got back. Gillian sent over his masseuse, Eric, to my house for a private session the night before to ease the stress of waiting. What an intoxicating feeling, lying on his table. The man is drop-dead gorgeous and can do the most fascinating things with his large, strong hands." Allie teased the group with testosterone details.

"I'll bet. That's what I want in my bedroom, one of Gillian's young friends with his hands all over me. I wonder—if I tell Santa Claus I've been very good this year, will I get my wish?" Janelle snickered with a slap at her neighbor's arm.

The sexual twittering among the women stopped as two waitresses pushed a cart toward their table decorated with pink and blue helium balloons. A beautifully decorated cake and a chilled bottle of champagne in an ice bucket perched on top of the cart.

"Sooz, you sly devil, you! This has your signature written all over it. Okay, I admit you actually kept the secret from them, obviously you were too busy planning your own surprise." Allie leaned over and hugged her dear friend in the next chair. The cart came to a stop before Allie, and she read the top of the cake: "'Congratulations, Allie and #45.' Cute, real cute, girl."

A round of applause broke out among the women. "Viva number forty-five and his future offspring!" The other patrons of the restaurant joined in the applause. Allie glowed in their support. One waitress popped the bottle's cork, the other brought out glasses.

"Just iced tea for the mother-to-be," Soozi reminded them.

The women raised their filled glasses high. "To Allie, our newest rank in motherhood. May the baby be healthy and happy."

The clinking of glasses and congratulations filled the area.

Allie quickly changed the subject, embarrassed from all the maternal attention. She needed normal ground and focus on something other than herself. "How many babies have been born on TV's sitcoms?"

A groan came from the group.

"Well, the first was little Ricky Ricardo, wasn't it? Lucy broke the censor ceiling going into labor on the tube for that one," Cindy said, starting the trivia game. They should have known Allie couldn't keep from playing, pregnant or not.

"Okay, too easy, we all knew that one. What about Samantha Stevens? She had two babies over the length of her television show, Tabitha and Adam. I get two points for two babies."

"Hey, what about Mr. Kotter's wife, she had twin girls. I should get two points, too."

"Were they the first twins on a series? Vinnie Barbarino showed up in more than one dream for me."

Heads bobbed around the table as the clink of forks to plates played in the background.

"Dr. Quinn had her baby in the wilds of Colorado under some tree with that hunk, Sully. Remember, they were looking for Cloud Dancing, and she went into labor in the woods. God, Sully was gorgeous."

"What about movie babies? I have the DVD of *Yours, Mine and Ours.* Lucille Ball had a baby on that one, too. That should count."

"The game is television sitcoms, not movies. No cheating."

"Murphy Brown had a baby boy. I win the game, as she was also a single mother."

"Not so fast, Rachel was single on *Friends.* I win," said Allie.

"Not much birthing on sitcoms. Most women don't find being left behind by the hysterical husband funny. Nor can we chuckle as she practically bends over in half during the middle of a contraction. Birth is a prime-time drama thing."

"No contraction stories," Allie interrupted Cindy. "I warned you before I started all this baby stuff. No war stories—I want happy stories from here on out."

"*That Girl* never had a baby, nor did Mary Richards. Well, they weren't getting anything between the sheets. No scx, no babies."

"A-hem." Soozi roughly cleared her throat. "Excuse me? Present pregnant company hasn't been laid for quite a while. Nature has her own practical helpers nowadays."

"Oops. Sorry, Al. Who *has* had sex in a while? I'm more frustrated than ever, and I'm married. Maybe I'll attack Chuck when I get home; somebody remind me. The man can't keep his hands off the computer long enough to make love. I swear he's fooling around on me in cyberspace."

"Ah, it's a good thing God made them cute so we can tolerate the rest of their stuff."

"They are cute. Remember Keith Partridge? I wouldn't have minded having his baby."

"Can you name all the Partridges?" Allie threw out. She took another bite of cake.

"I got this one." Janelle jumped at the question and sat up straight. "Danny, Laurie, Chris, Tracy, and Keith. Though for a while I had a crush on Mr. Kincaid."

"Eww. Mr. Kincaid?"

"That was absolutely correct. Okay, what about the Brady Bunch?" Allie asked.

"With my eyes closed, if I don't fall out of my chair: Marsha, Jan, Cindy, Bobby, Peter, and...and," Cindy put her hand up to her forehead, wrinkling her face in concentration. "Shit. I'm too buzzed. Sugar and alcohol have erased a few memory chips, I swear. I can see the checkerboard squares in the opening, with Alice and Mike Brady, does that count?"

The other women started teasing her unmercifully. "How can you forget the one we all wanted to sleep with?"

"Speak for yourself. He wasn't my type. Too dark for my taste."

"I really can't remember."

"Girls?" Allie held up her hands. "Gre-eg!" they chorused.

Other diners looked over at the women. "No, we will not break into the theme song," Soozi assured the strangers. "You can go back to your normal lives unharmed."

"How can you compare Greg Brady with Keith Partridge? No way. Geez, we had a great line-up of male flesh on TV for a while."

Allie pushed open the glass door to Novel Software humming the theme song from *The Partridge Family*. She grinned at Gillian as he turned around in his chair.

"How are your wild, wicked women doing? Is it safe for a mere male to cross the street this evening?"

"Happy for me, and not at all concerned about you. We celebrated with chilled champagne, and I endured a quart of iced tea. It's going to be a long winter without Diet Coke, I'm afraid." Allie sighed dramatically for sympathy she probably wouldn't get. "I won't miss the alcohol, though the champagne today looked inviting. What am I supposed to do without Diet Coke?" Pouting had no effect in this office.

"You will live by the gold can, O wise one, until the end of gestation." Gillian closed his eyes and put his hands together in front of him. A serene calmness on his face enhanced his good looks.

"You were supposed to say 'little grasshopper.'"

"Excuse me?" Gillian wrinkled his nose with disgust.

"Never mind, it's a David Carradine joke. Sheesh. You're too young for *Kung Fu?* Sometimes I'm amazed at how far apart we are in childhood memories."

"Allie. It's not truly an age thing; we're only about twelve years' apart. I lounged outside on the beach, listening to music during my daylight hours of growing up. And in the evening, the television was rarely turned on in our household—such a vulgar distraction. Our family attended productions in Orange County or downtown Los Angeles. My father found much more entertainment value for us than *All in the Family*."

"Don't go down that road. Parent issues are not my favorite subject."

"Sorry, boss. I forgot." Gillian handed her the day's mail.

Allie walked into her office reading the stack of papers. She dropped the majority on her desk, but focused on one envelope. A regular business-size one, thick with papers, but she didn't recognize the name and address in the corner. She picked up her letter opener and sat back in her chair. Out came a sizeable check and a signed copy of a Novel Software agreement.

"Oh, Luuu-cy," Allie called out. "You have some 'splaining to do."

"Yes?" Gillian stepped into her office and casually propped himself against the chair in front of her. Every hair in place, striking a model's pose. Allie wondered how he did it so naturally.

"Who is the Educational Committee of Lake County, and what is this check for?"

"It's a baby present from me to you. While you were out getting pregnant, I sold a copy of the Hear Ye software to a fabulous company back east. I thought you could start the baby's college fund."

"Well, I don't know whether I should be pleased or frightened. Are you planning on taking over the company next time I go to lunch?"

"Can't a slice of male mortal-ness help out around here once in a while without you freaking out?" Gillian turned an injured face to her, a perfect pout.

"You're right. A big thank you is in order. That was sweet of you to think of its dowry already."

"Every child of royalty should have its own kingdom in savings in case of hostile takeover."

"Cute. Back to work, slave, before I think of a way to replace you."

"Never. You get lost on the freeway, let alone the superhighway." He pushed himself away from the chair like a sleek, confident tiger, and headed down the hall.

"I do not."

"Do, too."

"Do not. And *I'm* the boss."

Gillian sighed. "Sure, throw rank in there. It's the only way you win."

Chapter 12

"Okay, here's some practice at being a mommy."

Allie watched her best friend unload armfuls of supplies.

"Zoe's probably due for her afternoon nap in about an hour. In the meantime, do not let your eyes off her at any time. She can clear out a kitchen or bathroom cupboard in nanoseconds." Soozi came in and out of the front door.

"I shouldn't be too long, though this is not Lenny's idea of a great time," Soozi threw out over her shoulder, dropping off a diaper bag, a car seat, and various toys, before setting the toddler and her blanket on the couch. One corner of Allie's living room looked like a colorful tiny tot disaster.

"Who enjoys the torture of trying on clothes for school, even if it's only preschool? How many dressing rooms did we whine and mope through at Sears in our younger days?" Allie reached over and kissed Zoe's curls on the top of her head. A couple hours of babysitting the toddler should be fun.

"Yeah, right. I'll take him to McDonald's for lunch if we survive the clothes-buying thing. She's good for a hot dog or PB and J sandwich, whatever you've got in the kitchen. Nothing too rich like fettuccini or pâté, Auntie Allie. Call my cell if she gets too much for you. Just remember, when yours is this age, you won't be able to give it back to anyone after a couple of exhausting hours." Soozi flashed a wicked grin as she walked toward the front door and her own challenging afternoon.

Allie waved at Lenny, waiting in the minivan outside. He looked pitifully small behind the window glass, his turn at the generational persecution, trying on clothes. Soozi would have her hands full getting more than one pair of pants on him for size today, without also having to chase Zoe, running in the opposite direction. Allie was ready for babysitting.

Right on cue, about an hour into playing with a sack of plastic blocks, the toddler sat there glassy-eyed in the middle of the blocks, but nothing registering.

"Looks like nap time for short people," Allie whispered. She set up a couple of pillows on the couch in the family room with a sheet under them and laid the tiny munchkin down. The dependable security blanket magically appeared from the diaper bag and was immediately clutched by tiny hands. In a few minutes, Zoe zonked out.

Allie popped in a favorite video. A bowl of microwave buttered popcorn, a box of Kleenex, and *Wuthering Heights* made a perfect diversion during Zoe's nap.

As Allie blew her nose for the third time with Heathcliff and Cathy's ghosts walking hand in hand up Pennington Crag, Zoe squirmed and moaned on the end of the couch. Moaned? Allie stared at the curly-topped peanut across from her. Do toddlers moan? The baby's face sported two bright red roses for cheeks. The air-conditioned living room curbed the California heat; why is the baby's face red? Are they supposed to get red when they're sleeping?

Allie moved quickly to the couch. Smoothing a stray curl from Zoe's forehead, Allie's hand touched a small nuclear heating unit. She's burning up! Carefully picking her up, Allie felt Zoe's head roll against one shoulder. Allie's neck stiffened from the heat radiating from the baby's skin.

Allie took the stairs quickly with Zoe in her arms. She threw open the medicine cabinet and rummaged for a thermometer. Nothing. The catch-all drawer below the sink proved empty as well. "Dang." She moved Zoe to one arm, balancing the limp fireball against her hip, and ran back down the stairs. Think, think. Grabbing the diaper bag and her purse, Allie rushed outside to the car. No car seat. Great, what kind of aunt doesn't remember the car seat.

Allie bundled the sick child into the back seat with the diaper bag, and then rushed back into the house. Allie dropped her keys as she searched for the door key. Slamming the door out of the way, Allie grabbed the seat and got to the car before the front door slammed shut. She strapped a seat belt through the chair, and tucked the still-sleeping Zoe inside the buckles.

Turning the car sharply on Baseline Road, Allie imitated an Indy 500 driver and screeched to a halt in front of a small emergency clinic in ten minutes flat. The parking lot looked fairly empty for a Saturday afternoon, a grateful Allie noticed. She grabbed the precious child and diaper bag in her arms and entered the single-story building.

"Hi, I'm Zoe. No, wrong. This is Zoe and she's running a fever. I'm babysitting, but I have an emergency piece of paper thingie from her mom somewhere in my purse."

A young woman handed her a clipboard with blank forms to fill out. "I'll need to make a copy of that for our records. Do you know if the child is insured?" she asked crisply.

Allie piled the bags on one of the waiting room chairs, and propped Zoe up in another. "I'm sure she is, but I haven't a clue about group numbers or anything. I'll pay cash for now. Will that work?" Allie dug out a worn folded piece of paper from her wallet. She hadn't used the emergency form before, nor the older one for Lenny that was probably in shreds from age and non-use. The nurse took a copy and handed the creased paper back to Allie.

Zoe leaked a soft whimper from the chair behind her. Allie turned and pulled a bottle of Kool-Aid from the diaper bag. "Here, sweetie. Drown that ol' fever for me, while I fill out these papers." Zoe's sleepy face leaned toward her.

"This is Auntie's favorite flavor of Kool-Aid, grape and lemonade, I guess they call it Purple Rex something now, since it comes in its own packet," Allie babbled. "I used to mix the two separate flavor powders together when I was a little girl. Guess I wasn't the only one enjoying the combo." Allie propped Zoe and the bottle up with a soft pink blankie, then went back to the forms on the clipboard.

"You've probably heard the Kool-Aid story from me before," she continued. "It's like my Aunt Kitty telling me all the time about having to walk three miles in the snow every day to school. I have Kool-Aid stories; it's a parent thing, Zoe." Allie finished filling out the papers and quickly handed them back to the woman behind the glass.

"If you'll come through the door on your left, the nurse will take you back," the receptionist said, giving Allie a knowing smile.

Scrambling to pick up the lethargic baby, diaper bag, the bottle of Kool-Aid, and her purse without dropping anything, Allie wondered why there wasn't a summer Olympic event on how much a woman could gather up in her arms in thirty seconds. Hips were an important part of the process. She was ushered into a cubicle-size medical room in the back of the building. "Let's take the patient's temperature. The doctor will be with you soon, only one patient ahead of you," the nurse said, picking up the hand-held device. "Just hold her on your lap." The nurse carefully poked the plastic-covered tip in Zoe's ear. One click and it was over. "One oh two point eight. It's good you brought her in." The nurse threw away the temperature cover. "How long has she had the fever?"

"Sometime before Cathy died in Heathcliff's arms."

"Excuse me?"

"Oh, sorry—maybe an hour. She was fine when her mom dropped her off."

"Doctor will be in soon." The nurse closed the door quietly behind her.

Allie shuffled through her purse and flipped open her cell phone. She dialed Soozi's number, but the battery failed before she finished the speed dial. "Damn. Zoe, remind Auntie Allie to plug in her phone when she gets home."

Allie cradled Zoe in her arms and paced the floor. Zoe snuggled on her shoulder and fell back to sleep with the rhythmic walking. Allie hummed a nursery tune and caressed the soft curls on the fiery head.

The door opened after a brief knock and in walked a Gillian clone. A healthy bronze glaze glowed from his face and exposed lower arms. When did men get so young and tanned?

"Hi, I'm Dr. Richmond, and this must be Zoe. Why don't you lay her on the table for me. Has she had all her immunizations?"

"I think so. I'm not her mom, I'm a family friend. Soozi is really Super Mom about their physicals and all, so I'm sure Zoe is up-to-date, if not ahead of schedule in any medical mandates." Allie let go of the warm bundle and laid her on the cushioned examination table. The thin paper cover crinkled from Zoe's weight.

"Is she going to be okay? She was taking a nap on the couch, and the next time I looked she had these bright red cheeks. I don't have any Tylenol for kids or anything, so I didn't know what else to do but bring her here." Allie tried to breathe. She slid her hands under her arms. The room felt chilly after letting go of Zoe.

"I'm sure she's going to be fine. Some children spike a fever. Let's have a look at her ears. That's the usual culprit for children at this age." He reached up to a black scope attached to the wall and bent over the tiny lump.

Allie watched this perfect head of great-looking blond hair and tropical-hued skin bend down over Zoe. Southern California must grow these guys in the foothills somewhere by the dozens. He doesn't look old enough to be wearing a white coat and to know what to do with a stethoscope. This man should still be playing doctor in some dormitory room with a coed, or me, if I remember how to play. The gorgeous doctor straightened up, and Allie snapped back to her responsibilities.

"Hmm, just as I suspected. Both ears are infected. I'm surprised she's not a lot fussier about it. Usually kids take it out on the world when they have ear infections." Dr. Richmond put the examining equipment back on the wall. He kept a hand on Zoe's chest. "Let's have her sit up, and pull her shirt up, please." He placed the end of the stethoscope on the child.

"All clear in there." Dr. Richmond ran a few more tests, checking to be sure he wasn't missing something else, and took out a prescription pad.

Allie stared at his groomed fingernails. Down, girl, he's probably gay or married. Gillian, where are you when I need you to check your Rolodex for the scoop on this guy.

"Let's get her going on amoxicillin and Tylenol liquid. She should be kept quiet for today to give the medicines a chance to work." He handed the piece of paper with scribbling on it to Allie.

"Are you babysitting for the weekend?" His dark eyes locked gazes with Allie. "I could call you later to see how she's doing." He leaned against the table, with a hand in the deep pocket of his white coat.

"Uh, no, her mother is clothes shopping with Zoe's older brother. I'm just minding her till they get back. You're sure she's going to be fine?" The obvious pass from the doctor flew two feet over Allie's head; he looked like a model from a magazine cover, something L.A.-ish. She brushed her hand over the back of Zoe's curls and got a valiant attempt of a smile for her efforts.

"She'll do fine. If the fever isn't broken in two days, she'll need to see her regular doctor. Otherwise, just have the mother make an appointment for a recheck with her pediatrician in about ten days. Are *you* going to be okay? You look a little peaked yourself." Dr. Richmond stepped closer to Allie, staring at her face more closely with a professional concern.

"I guess I panicked. I'm okay. I'm not very experienced with babies, though I'm hoping to be soon. I've just found out I'm pregnant," Allie said, and then found herself spilling her guts to this stunning medical creature. Why was the handsome doctor volunteering to call her later to check on Zoe? Do they always do that?

"I've heard of Dr. Adams' work—she has had significant success with AI. I'm assuming that's the method you're using? I'd love to talk to you about your reactions to the doctor and procedure. Would you like to have dinner some night this week? I hope I'm not being too forward." Dr. Richmond finished washing up and leaned against the porcelain sink, crossing his legs at the ankles while he dried his hands.

Allie stuttered slightly. "Uh, well, I don't know." Allie picked Zoe up in her arms. "Could I call you later? I'm not quite myself yet with this fever thing about Zoe. Are you here at the clinic often?" Since when did cute doctors ever talk to me? Oh, sure, give me a couple of shots of some other guy's sperm and suddenly I'm tantalizing? Give me a break.

"We rotate shifts here at the clinic. My practice is over in Upland, not too far from here. Why don't you give me a call this evening, and let me know how curly-top is doing? I'll be here until nine or ten o'clock and we'll see how you're feeling by then, too." Dr. Richmond stuck out his right hand.

"Sure. I'll call you later. At the clinic." Allie twisted to the left to extend her hand to the doctor. She couldn't move too far from Zoe on the table, as the toddler leaned her limp body against her.

"Great, look forward to hearing from you. Take care, Zoe. You're going to be back to your old self before these adults around you catch their breath." And he walked out of the room, leaving the door open.

Filling the prescription went smoothly, as the baby zoned in a fevered world while they waited on a vinyl-covered bench seat. Flashes of the good-looking doctor came and went for Allie. *Soozi will be hysterical. I know I'm dead for not calling her.* People came and went constantly as Allie rocked Zoe gently in her arms and played back the short conversation with Dr. Richmond. "I'm sure it's a professional curiosity thing," Allie whispered to the sleeping bundle in her arms. "He's asking me out to learn more about Dr. Adams, don't you think, Zoe?"

The pharmacist explained the dosage and process to Allie before sending them on their way back home. The amoxicillin looked liked melted strawberry ice cream, and the pharmacist dropped a syringe into the paper sack for injecting the thick liquid into the baby's mouth. *Modern medicine strikes again; something simple in concept, yet effective. I'll bet a mother/doctor dreamed this one up.*

Zoe didn't contest the pink stuff, nor the purple Tylenol squirted into her mouth. Allie followed up the medicines with a fresh, cool bottle of juice and sat with her on her lap. Rocking against the back of the couch, Allie starting softly singing a Buffett song to Zoe. Allie loved to sing, and had entertained foolish thoughts long ago of being a lounge singer in her other spare time.

Most of the songs Allie sang when alone came out like blues. It didn't matter what the song intended to be originally, fast tempo rock or an old Dixieland melody played in ragtime, when Allie sang it, the words lingered slow and haunting in the air.

Even now Jimmy Buffett's words trickled out slowly, each syllable caressing the toddler with emotion. Allie half-listened, smiling at the old childhood fantasies of dimly-lit bars, leaning against a baby grand piano, dressed in a sequined dress split up the side, and blinded by a single spotlight. The Saturday afternoon movies on television glamorized the job in black and white for Allie. Chorus teachers in elementary school had praised Allie's voice and talent, lending some credence to her fantasy.

Today the words of the song sounded different. Allie bent her head slightly trying to catch the nuance. Same slow-paced melody but almost crooning, like an antique lullaby. Goose bumps painted Allie's arms as a strange sensation passed over her. All these years of pretending to be a crooner, wanting to sing the blues at a coffeehouse or nightclub, and she was actually singing lullabies? The warm, deadweight of sleeping Zoe gave strength to this new maternal concept. Allie continued rocking and singing various songs of Jimmy's, dragging out lyrics on a single note forever to her sleeping charge.

"Did you miss us?" Soozi barged in the front door with Lenny almost glued to her side. "Someone didn't want to wait in the car. Hope you don't mind." Soozi, surprised, spotted the sleeping bundle on the couch.

"Lenny, why don't I get you a granola bar, and you run out back to my hammock. I'll bet you could use a swing after all that hard work trying on clothes," Allie said, heading for the kitchen.

"I got new school jeans," Lenny said, following her like an eager puppy from a pet store.

"You'll look so sharp, Len. Here, take this outside while Zoe's napping." Unwrapping the snack, Allie pointed him toward the back door.

Soozi quickly grabbed some glasses from the overhead cupboard and a bottle of wine from the refrigerator.

"Make mine virgin, please," Allie chided her friend.

"Shoot, I forgot. I'm not used to this baby thing at all. Lenny wore me to a frazzle out there in mall land. He's telling me he can't wear black pants to school. Since when? He's in preschool, for crying out loud." Soozi poured a glassful of zinfandel for herself and took a large swallow.

Allie filled the second glass with club soda. "Gang attire worries in a preschool?" Allie took a small sip. "You can't be too careful anymore. I, uh, had a teensy kind of crisis of my own while you were gone," she said, and she filled Soozi in on the doctor visit.

Soozi fell against the edge of the counter. "I'm sorry, girl. I thought she might be teething, but I didn't expect ear infections or I never would have left her with you like that."

"Don't beat yourself up. She's got drugs, she'll be fine. Besides," she paused for special effect, "I think I got a date out of it." Allie deliberately spun away from Soozi, tossing her hair to the side, and walked to the kitchen window to watch Lenny outside.

"Did I hear the word date come out of your mouth? How do you get a date from a sick child?"

"The cute doctor that examined her at the emergency clinic on Baseline." Allie rolled her eyes. "You'll never believe this. He got excited when I blurted out about being pregnant through Doc Adams. Wants to have dinner soon and talk about the artificial insemination."

"You told him you were pregnant? Are you nuts? The first cute guy you see, and you tell him you're having a baby on purpose?" Soozi practically shouted at her.

"Don't wake up Zoe, she's had a rough afternoon."

"You tell him you're pregnant and he asks you out? Is that like weird, or what?" Soozi poured more wine into her glass. "Are you going out with him?"

"Hey, you snap my head off 'cause I'm home every Friday night and now you're questioning if I should go out or not? He's a doctor, not a serial killer. Doesn't that count for something in the integrity clause?" Allie laughed at her. "He's Gillian cute, Orlando Bloom cute. He works weekends for sick children. Do you want a note from his mother?" Allie waved her hand toward the living room. "Besides, Zoe likes him—isn't that a good recommendation?"

"Yeah, right. She's a flirt, Allie. Anything with facial hair comes by and she's all smiles and batting eyelashes." Pitiful whining came from the living room. "Speak of the siren, herself."

Both women walked back to the couch in the living room. Sitting up, Zoe rubbed her left ear. Her curls were tousled, with a couple sticking straight up in the air. When she saw her mom, the volume of whimpering increased twofold.

"Hey, it's okay. Do you have an owie?" Soozi sat down and gathered up the child and her blanket onto her lap. "Did you have an adventure with Auntie Allie?" The miniature head barely bobbed up and down in acknowledgment. Soozi rocked her sweetly, her cheek lying against soft strawberry curls.

The kitchen door in the back slammed, and a burst of colorful energy ran for the couch. Lenny leaped over the arm and landed just inches from his mom.

"Is Zoe sad?" Lenny stuck his face close to his sister's flushed face. Zoe reached out and shoved him away, growling against her mother's chest. "Zoe, don't," Lenny argued, trying to climb onto his mother's lap.

"I see where this is going. Allie, get the bubble gum syrup stuff out of the refrigerator, please. Len, you get the diaper bag for me. You're the big brother, you can help. We're out of here, group." Soozi snuggled Zoe tighter to her chest and grabbed her car keys. "Let's give Auntie Allie some rest."

Allie helped Lenny gather the baby's stuff back into the Sesame Street diaper bag. The group walked out the front door toward the van in the driveway.

"Call me and let me know what the doctor says," Soozi yelled from inside the car.

Allie waved her off and went back into the suddenly too-quiet house.

"You're seeing a medicine man for short people? How chic, darling." Gillian held his coffee cup up to his lips with both hands. "A local shaman, I assume?"

"Yes. Zoe stayed with me Saturday afternoon, and she woke up from her nap with ear infections. This guy works at a clinic down a ways from my house. I took her to the nearest emergency spot, and there he was." Allie picked up her pink phone message slips and headed to her office door.

"Does he know you're in the, uh, family way?"

"It's just dinner, Gillian. But, yes, he does know I'm expecting. That was sort of his pick-up line, I think. He seemed interested in hearing about Dr. Adams and her program." Allie slumped against the doorjamb. "Maybe it isn't me at all—he probably has the hots for Adams and he's going to pump my brain for details."

"Don't go hormonal over this. I just wondered if you were passing out the maternal information to available men and the general public." Gillian cleared his throat and turned his desk chair around. "Of course he asked you out. You're gorgeous, you're fun. Why wouldn't he take advantage of a hot combination? You'll see." Damn, she's moody lately. He had to watch everything he said or risk setting off a maternity emotion explosion.

When Allie answered the doorbell, the doctor stood before her in freshly pressed blue jeans and sports jacket, black loafers and socks. Nice touch, Allie thought, she was tired of the bare ankle look. The view was just as pleasant as that day with the white coat and stethoscope. Maybe even better. Allie's blood pressure was definitely lower tonight, and the man had a delightful grin as she invited him into the house.

"Would you care for a beer or something before we go, Doctor?" Allie asked as a good hostess. She wasn't truly interested in staying around the house; her stomach growled rather loudly. But she didn't want to seem too eager to eat, either.

"Call me Keith. No, I don't want to drink alcohol in front of you. How are you feeling? Any residual effects yet from the pregnancy or the insemination procedure?" He came in and leaned against the end of the couch.

"No, knock on wood. The second procedure went quite smooth, and I haven't noticed any nausea or anything." Allie felt embarrassed going right into medical talk about her condition. "Uh, do you always ask such blunt questions on a first date?"

"Sorry, am I being rude? I just hadn't talked with anyone that had worked with Dr. Adams before. Being a baby doctor, I guess it intrigues me, the type of woman who would want a baby so much as to go the extra effort. I don't mean to be a klutz out of the gate with you." He crossed his arms over his chest. "I'm used to working with kids, and you need to say what you mean around most of them. They don't let you get away with anything middle of the road. If it's time for a shot, they want to know up-front."

Allie laughed. "Not my idea of a good time. I think I'd rather have the needle sneak up on me. The anticipation seems worse than the injection."

"Kids today play a different game," he agreed. "Should we get going? I made reservations for us. I hope you don't mind if I chose the restaurant?"

"No. There's not much that comes by waiter that I don't adore." This time they both laughed. Allie grabbed her purse and set the lock on the front door.

"Did they forget your driveway in this tract?" Dr. Richmond leaned over and unlocked her car door.

Allie admired the profile she remembered from his office. "The realtor didn't call these 'doll houses' for nothing. You get a tiny driveway for a tiny car and a tiny front yard. That was supposed to be a selling point for professionals who were first-time buyers."

"Well, I guess they succeeded. Looks like a packed street."

"When my friend, the mother of the toddler I brought to see you, comes over with her minivan, she hangs over the sidewalk quite a bit. I guess they want to force you to park your car in the garage for aesthetics. It's the only place a real car fits." Allie climbed inside the dark blue Lexus. The doctor closed the door after her.

"How is Zoe?" he said when he entered on the driver's side.

Allie raised her eyebrows. "You remember her name?"

"Hey, how do you forget the angel that brought you into my office?" The words flowed like velvet out of his mouth.

Allie tipped her head slightly to the side. She'd been out of the normal dating loop for so long, she pricked her ears to his melodious line. Is he a good witch or a bad witch? Her warning flashers came on low beam. "Zoe is doing fine. She finished her meds and seems back into terrorizing her older brother."

"Good to hear. Her mom took her in for a recheck? Sometimes one dose isn't enough."

"Yeah, I guess she knew that." Allie felt like her tongue tripped over every syllable. "I have a lot to learn about raising children." Allie played with the edge of the seat belt; she was out of practice with this male-female conversation thing.

They rode in silence the rest of the short way to the restaurant. After pulling into the parking lot the doctor came around and opened her car door for her, extending a hand to help her out of the car. Allie smiled and reached out as his hand enveloped hers tightly. As she stood up he brushed his body against hers, closing the car door. Allie tensed a brief moment, staring at the front of the restaurant. Dr. Richmond put his arm around her and started to lead them forward.

"I hope you're hungry," he crooned into her ear. "They have excellent entrees here, healthy choices for a new expecting mother." His words blew warm against her hair as he practically nuzzled the side of her head, and his arm held her in a tight embrace.

Oh, my gawd. Allie's eyes opened wider. Surely, this couldn't be right. Granted she had first date jitters being too long out of the saddle, but the warning flashes were getting stronger. Maybe he's just friendly and I'm overreacting.

Keith stepped forward and opened the door for her. The loud activities and energy of the place washed over her and dispelled any negative thoughts. Get a grip on yourself, she thought. Don't freak out with the first nice guy that invites you to dinner.

The young hostess greeted them and acknowledged the reservation for Dr. Richmond, flirting with the young doctor while ignoring Allie. Her actions were exaggerated for Keith's benefit as she hailed the waitress to escort them to the table. Allie rolled her eyes, and followed the appointed woman. She wouldn't look back to see if the hostess detained Keith a moment extra. The guy is definitely good looking. The female population around here confirmed that well enough. Allie needed to relax and enjoy the evening.

Keith moved into the booth beside her, sliding his arm up onto Allie's shoulders, not an inch of empty space between them as the waitress handed each of them a menu. Keith accepted with his free hand, and laid it on the table. His motions were fluid in turning the pages of items, and placidly caressing Allie's shoulder with his other hand as if they'd known each other a long time. His touch was more familiar than Allie appreciated.

"I would recommend something with a lot of protein while in the first trimester. You can maintain your weight with vegetable plates and salads later. Give the embryo a good strong beginning." Keith turned his head slightly toward her and caught Allie's gaze.

How can something so young and gorgeous be so weird? Allie laid her arm across her stomach protectively; the man was acting as if this were his baby. "Sounds good. Would you care to order for me?"

"My pleasure," he said, and he went back to studying the printed items in front of him.

Watching his attractive profile, a part of her reacted to his physical sexuality. The soap opera looks sent electric shockwaves to the pit of her stomach, assuring her that she may be pregnant but she wasn't dead, not by a long shot. Her traitorous body was interested in fooling around with this young medical stud, but her mind was on red alert.

The waitress came and took the order, bringing back two glasses of herbal iced tea. Keith picked up his glass and twisted slightly toward Allie, never letting his left arm move from around her shoulders.

"A toast to the wee one and its beautiful mother, may you both be healthy and happy all the days ahead."

Allie's glass stood frozen in front of her, and her eyes stared registering the look on Keith's face, one of flushed excitement, intensity. Keith clicked his glass against hers, breaking the reverie, and Allie tried to smile, forcing a sip of tea down her dry throat. Holding the glass, she struggled with a second sip, confusion running rampant in her thoughts.

"You have a great body for a baby." The doctor's voice was deep and breathy. "Dr. Adams couldn't have hand-picked a better woman—you are remarkable."

A wave of nausea began inside of Allie. She rubbed her hand across her forehead as he crooned words as if in some bizarre foreplay. She couldn't believe what she was hearing.

"How did you feel when Dr. Adams inserted the sperm? Did you enjoy it?" Keith's face looked flushed, moving in closer to Allie, saying the last words into her hair, practically caressing it with his lips.

Stiffening with disgust, Allie placed a strong hand against his chest and gave a slight push. "I'm sorry, Keith, but I'm feeling a little sick to my stomach. I need to go home. I can't stay." She forced herself not to grab the front of his shirt with her fist to accentuate her demand. "Please, would you mind canceling the order and taking me home? First trimester, you know. I'm really sorry."

Keith's face kaleidoscoped through various expressions in a matter of seconds—disappointment, resignation, and concern—before he said, "Certainly. Maybe this was too soon. I'll find our waitress. Sit quietly until I get back. Try a few sips of tea, and take some deep breaths. I'll get you home." He slid out of the booth and headed toward the front of the restaurant.

Leaning against the back of the booth, Allie closed her eyes and agreed a few deep breaths would help. The noise of the restaurant began to filter through, as the past few nightmarish minutes faded with Keith's absence.

People were enjoying the food, and conversations were animated and fun, the weekend promising more of the same for most of them.

When Keith returned he didn't bother to sit down, but he extended his hand and helped Allie from the table. He had found her with eyes closed and head resting on the back of the booth. "All taken care of, let's get you home. Come on, you need to get to bed and some rest."

A moment of panic raced through Allie's heart. Had she made it worse by canceling dinner? Did Keith fantasize that he would personally undress her and tuck her into bed next to himself? Surely not. This is a physician, sworn by oath to take care of sick people, not have a fetish for pregnant women and rape them.

She reached for his offered hand and stood up, careful not to get too close. She looked up into the face that had earlier given Allie her own fleeting fantasy, and found compassion and innocence. Dr. Richmond had returned, the alter ego gone. She forced a pitiful smile. "I'm sorry to end the evening so suddenly, I just don't feel well."

"Not at all. Please don't give it another thought. Listen to your body, and let's get you home." He pulled her in close as he led her outside.

She found herself melting. His young firm body felt good against her as they walked slowly through the parking lot. Disappointment for what could have been a nice time sat heavy. Now seemingly removed from the darker Mr. Hyde inside the restaurant, Allie enjoyed the feel of a man's arm around her and the warmth two bodies generated. She missed this kind of contact.

Keith opened the door and stood close, ready to help her into the car. Allie smiled. He acts like I'm seven months along. His concern would be touching if not for the perversion lurking somewhere inside the Adonis frame. Allie did not want to tempt fate between here and home. She focused straight ahead and tried not to look as he entered his side of the car and started the engine.

"Are you joking? He hit on you in the restaurant?" Soozi held the phone in one hand and a glass of wine in the other.

"He leaned into me, talking about the act of insemination like in a porno movie. He got hotter the more he talked about it, and I'm trapped beside him in the booth. Any second and his other hand was going to scout the territory under my skirt."

"Yeee-ew. The man's a pediatrician, for God's sake."

"I didn't look, but I'll bet his crotch was busting stitches. He's whispering in my ear questions about the procedure, like if it felt good." The violation of the night before still felt fresh.

"Who'da thunk it? A cute creep plays doctor with children by day and lusts after pregnant women by night. Your luck in dating is catastrophic. You haven't been out in eons and the first credible invitation is Jack the Ripper of the maternity ward." Soozi drained what was in the glass, and poured herself another.

"Too weird, I'm telling you. Like a bad B movie, and I kept listening for sinister music, or some director yelling cut and saving me from this guy." Allie moved the phone under her ear. "What are you guys doing today?"

"The kids are in the family room, digesting a box of sugared cereal, and then I'll take them to the park to run it off. It's cool out there, but they'll keep themselves warm with hyper-ness from the cereal explosion. What are you up to?"

"After last night? I don't think I'll go out of the house for the next few months except for work. Some part of this week I have to hit the grocery store. The proverbial cupboards are bare, and I don't want the baby to starve."

"Cute. You haven't gained an ounce yet."

"I probably lost a few. I couldn't eat anything last night after we skipped dinner at the restaurant and he dropped me off. Breakfast doesn't sound too swift, either. How could a guy be like that?"

"It takes all kinds, sweetie. Some are uglier than others." Soozi put the rest of the wine bottle in the refrigerator. "Okay, I gotta chase these kids outside for a while, before they kill me. You rest up, don't concern yourself about groceries until later in the week. Check out those frozen packages in your freezer. You probably have enough in there to feed a small village. I'll talk to you later."

Allie convinced herself she liked grocery shopping late at night. Her excuses sounded reasonable—less crowded, more time for reading the fat content or carb level of product labels without being in someone's way, not having to reach across someone else's cart. The real reason? Not leaving the office until long after a typical workday, usually late evening.

Having inherited a sluggish metabolism, Allie tried to carefully select the food she put in her cart. Temptation lurked on every aisle. A pattern of gold Diet Coke cartons lined the bottom of the cart, with a few packs of Fruitopia thrown in for dessert. Fresh produce bins, a major attraction, kept her busy for a while, adding clear plastic bags of one or two bell peppers, a single cucumber, and a stalk of celery to her load.

Allie's unconventional taste buds meant she didn't need meat and potatoes often. She'd make an entire meal of four or five ears of corn during the summer with a little "I Can't Believe You Put Butter in a Spray Bottle" for a low-fat dinner, washed down with a glass or two of icy skim milk. And cereal wasn't just for breakfast anymore. A bowl of Sugar Smacks hit the spot after a rough day of clients and Gillian.

Allie dawdled in an aisle reading bottled dressing labels for an autumn salad she was going to build of spaghetti squash and a one-pound package of prepared greens. When another cart rammed into the side of her cart, jarring it out of her hands.

"What the—!" Startled, Allie jumped quickly to the side, stepping squarely on the foot of the guilty shopper.

"I'm sorry—ow, shit, that hurt." The man tripped over his apology as he grabbed his foot in a single hop motion. "You've got spikes on your feet. I think you broke the skin."

"I didn't mean to step on your foot, I was just trying to get out of the way. Is it bleeding?" Allie regained her composure. "What's the hurry? This is a grocery store, not a freeway."

The man's dark hair hung down in front of his face while he bent over rubbing his foot. He straightened up and swept his hand through his hair, revealing a pleasant looking face a foot above Allie's. "Oh, it's you," he mumbled. His blue eyes searched Allie's face for assurance she was all right or she wouldn't hit him with her purse next.

Allie stared back. "Whoa, the married guy," she whispered. Straightening her shoulders, she said, "At least you're not on the phone this time."

159

"Huh? Yeah, I, uh, just got off work, and I've got two hungry cats at the house. Trying to grab something for all of us. I wasn't expecting anyone in the aisle at this time of night, and I guess I took the corner wide."

Allie couldn't take her eyes off his face.

The man rubbed his hands on the front of his pant legs. "Hi, I'm Jack." He stuck his right hand out tentatively. "Local fool and pathetic cat owner."

Allie giggled despite herself. "Allie," she said, taking his extended hand in hers. "We've got to stop meeting like this. Someone's going to get hurt, more hurt than your foot, I mean." Smooth, Allie. "I understand your urgency. Cats can be quite demanding this time of night. I hope you'll be forgiven when you get home." Allie turned and started to push her cart down the aisle. "Take it easy on the straightaways, Jack, there's a speed limit in this store, you know." Does his wife know the man is dangerous with a shopping cart?

Jack mumbled some words and watched her walk away.

Allie found her breathing a little erratic as she stopped at the end of the aisle, and the coolness of the dairy case in front of her felt good blowing across her flushed cheeks. Nothing like running into Mr. Married Guy at the supermarket again in the middle of the night. What's with all the cute ineligible guys running right into her. She put a half-gallon of generic skim milk in the cart. I hope his wife knows she has a good one. Randy would never shop at night for Soozi.

She placed a few more items in the cart and headed for the only open checkout stand. Allie found herself behind Jack. On the moving counter, Jack unloaded five or six large cans of cat food and a twenty-pound bag of dry food.

Allie raised her eyebrows. "Are these tigers?" she inquired, nodding toward the items.

"It's, uh, cheaper to buy the larger sizes, you know. They get half a can in the morning and the rest at night." Jack started to blush at the explanation. He turned to finish unloading his groceries.

Allie stared at his back. Cute, married, and thrifty. She struggled to think of something to end the awkwardness. "Good idea. Our cats wouldn't touch anything more than an hour old. I think my mom spoiled them rotten."

"Your mom must love cats a lot." Jack edged closer to the cashier as the line moved.

"Oh, she did. But she and my father were killed ten years ago." Why did she blurt that out?

"I'm terribly sorry. I guess I just thought she was, um..." He closed his eyes for a moment and said, "This isn't working out, maybe we should start over." He stuck his right hand out toward her again. "Hi, my name is Jack Strong. Do you come here often?"

Allie started to bristle. I hate married guys who flirt, especially with that little boy innocence in their faces. She took his hand again, squeezing hard. "As a matter of fact, I do. Every few days or so. Eating has become a habit."

The man rubbed his hand, staring back at Allie, and reached for his wallet.

"I'm sure your wife has the same kind of habit." That will show him.

"Huh?" Jack froze. "Wife?" he stuttered.

"Aren't you married?"

Jack turned and looked behind him, then back at Allie. "You talking to me? No, no wife, just cats."

Allie blushed. "But on the phone—before. You said..."

Jack looked confused, then smiled. "Oh, Sherry? She's my sister. She asked about what happened that night."

Allie finished unloading her cart and Jack paid the cashier for his groceries. He hesitated by his cart while he put his change and wallet back into his pants' pocket.

"Um, I really have to rush home right now and I, uh..." He took a deep breath. "Would you like to have a cup of coffee sometime or something?" The girl stopped moving the food across the bar coder for a split second, watching the exchange between the two late shoppers.

"Well, I'm usually pretty tied up during the week."

"Sure, no problem. I understand." Jack ducked his head down.

"But maybe Sunday afternoon would be okay." Allie moved a step closer. "We could meet at the art fair by the Plaza. Do you know the one? Maybe on the bridge, I think there's a coffee place close by, if you want."

Jack stared. "This weekend?" The corners of his mouth tipped up. "That would be great, sure. At the art fair, yeah. Uh, around two o'clock?"

Allie smiled. "It'll be fun. I haven't been there in ages. Around two-ish, if the cats are still speaking to you."

"Oh, gosh, gotta go. 'Bye, uh, see you Sunday, Allie." Jack hurried toward the glass sliding doors and out into the night.

Allie caught the eyes of the young cashier. "Well, isn't that always the way? As soon as you're pregnant, some Prince Charming runs you down with a shopping cart." The girl's eyes got huge. Allie was sure this was the most excitement she'd had all evening.

Allie took inventory of the information she knew: a good-looking, tall guy named Jack works late, has two cats, not married, and a sister named Sherry he adores. Soozi will shred this late night story to pieces. Allie sighed, and heard herself tomorrow convincing Soozi she hadn't done anything wrong, no personal details, the man doesn't know where she lives or works for stalking purposes.

Soozi should be proud Allie hadn't let the Dr. Keith nightmare scare her from speaking to the male species. She'd made a harmless date for Sunday, in broad daylight at a crowded setting. At least Allie hoped it was still a local gathering place. The summer tourists would be winding down, but surely someone would be there, wouldn't they? If less than fifty people aren't on the premises, Soozi will have Allie dead and buried near Mount Baldy before sunset. Shoot, Allie couldn't win a conversation even when Soozi wasn't there in person.

"You did what? You actually made a coffee date this weekend with a strange man who owns two cats?" Soozi shouted, with what sounded like happy tones into the phone over the din of the kids playing behind her.

Allie's confusion showed. "You're not giving me grief? Where's my lecture on stupidity and vulnerable risks, etcetera. Remember Dr. Octopus? He was a chance meeting, and a professional to boot."

"Girl, that man was a pervert. You haven't been out on anything remotely romantic, like a Sunday afternoon at the park kind of thing. This will do you good, maybe make up for Doctor Deviate. The hormone deposit is working better than you think, Al. This number forty-five seems to be pretty potent."

"Soozi, I don't want to sleep with the man—I'm pregnant. We're just having coffee and conversation. He is kinda cute, though, in an innocent, manly sort of way. Nothing like the drool factor the doctor had."

"Let me exchange phones, the kids are drowning you out. I want details and this isn't going to work. Randy! Take over in here with these monsters. Allie has a date, again. Yeah, really." Soozi picked up the portable phone and clicked off the other one to a noticeable drop in noise level. "Now, tell me everything."

"Okay, that's the second time today I've caught you in a dreamy smile," Gillian remarked. "You look more like the Cheshire cat, not the glow of pregnancy. Lunch was semi-delicious, but no big deal. I give up, what could your virtually perfect brain be hatching that's creating this cloying grin on your face?" Gil stood before her with one hand on his hip, the other tapping on his cheek.

"What are you talking about? Can't I be grateful it's Friday?"

"Grateful? You? Oh, my…you have a date!" Gillian said. "An honest-to-goodness date, twice in one month? Not with the masher, I hope? Look at your face, you're blushing." Gil fired off questions like an Uzi, as he grabbed a side chair and plopped his tight jeans down for the latest dirt. "This looks serious; your face is practically mauve. What's his name, what does he do, where did you meet him?"

"It's a coffee date at the art fair. Nothing serious. I sort of bumped into him at the grocery store earlier this week."

"Rather trendy, I must say. One of the top ten places to meet your fellow singles is at the market. Was it near the pasta packages at least?"

"Close, he ran me down in the salad dressing aisle."

"A brute, eh?"

"More klutz than brutish. Oh, and he has cats."

"Oh, well, there's a definite reason to hang on to him." Gillian rolled his eyes.

"Anyway, we saw each other again at the cash register, he popped the question about coffee, and I said sure." Allie twisted in her chair. "So, yes, I have a date on Sunday with a man I met at a grocery store. Do I have your approval?" Allie asked in a nasal, whiny tone.

"I don't know, boss. On the one hand, it will be good for you getting back in the saddle after all this Sandra Dee celibacy. But aren't you in the middle of a certain maternal project right now?"

"It's a lousy cup of coffee in public. Sheesh, you're as bad as Soozi. I'm not going to attack this guy. Coffee, small talk, broad daylight, many people around." Allie's voice bounced off the walls. "It has nothing to do with me being pregnant."

"Down, girl," Gillian sniffed.

The reference of equating him with Soozi stung, and Allie stared at her pained cohort. "I'm sorry. I know you are concerned about my social welfare. I didn't mean to snap at you. I guess I'm a tad nervous about this."

Gillian swiped a dismissing hand in the air. "Let's get to the important details. What are you going to wear? You want casual but not sloppy, smart but somewhat revealing; hmm, sexy with sandals. How about a hat? Or more of a Lana Turner approach?"

Allie smiled at her assistant and patted her flat stomach. Uncle Gillian had found a topic he loved best and would be on a roll for a while.

Sunday turned into a typical Southern California September day. Warm breezes kept you in summer clothes when all the women's magazines showed fashions of wool sweater sets and dark colors. Allie leaned against the old wooden bridge, staring into a man-made creek below. The water made soft splashing noises against preformed rocks.

"Hi, you made it." His voice spoke behind her left side as he stepped onto the bridge.

Allie turned and smiled. Jack seemed taller than she remembered at the store, and great-looking legs with powerful thighs were exposed under a pair of pressed khaki shorts. "Did the cats give you hell when you got home that night?"

"Oh, yeah." Jack leaned against the rail. "Fickle felines, though. As soon as they ate, I was their best friend."

Allie began the game of small talk. "What are their names?"

"Hoo, uh," Jack spoke quickly and dropped his gaze down at the trickle of running water below them.

Allie couldn't understand a word. "It can't be that bad. Spit it out." Allie couldn't believe her eyes. His cheeks were crimson splashes.

"Look, I inherited the cats from my sister. She moved into an apartment about six months ago and couldn't keep them. I let them stay with me so she didn't have to send them to the pound. She named them...," he paused and took a deep breath, "Pixie and Dixie." Jack looked her square in the eyes with reserved defiance from his ill fortune and his sister's childishness.

Allie burst out laughing, touching his arm in sympathy. "'I hate you mieces to pieces'? Boy, that's an old cartoon. My animated childhood favorite will always be *Beanie and Cecil.*"

Her touch was not lost on Jack as he tried to stay nonchalant. "'Hey, Beanie boy; I'm coming, Beanie.' Good choice. Do you know the name of Captain Huffenpuff's boat?" Jack smiled at the beautiful woman next to him.

"The *Leakin' Lena*! Be careful, I'm a champion at television trivia. You don't know who you're up against. I drive my friends nuts with trivia." Allie's face glowed. Great legs, cute face, and a brain? Not a bad combination for someone found in the grocery store.

"Okay, name your favorite Western," Jack said.

"All of them."

Jack laughed. "Didn't girls have a crush on Michael Landon, or any cute guys in leather?"

"A lot you know. The horses had a big part of our hearts," she said. "But unlike most girls on my street I enjoyed the Wild West stories for more esoteric reasons." Allie twisted a strand of hair, looking out from the bridge. "The creak of leather saddles and the chinkling of reigns gave me goose bumps, like I'd lived there before, you know? Like reincarnation with theme songs." Allie pushed away from the wooden railing. She put her arm through his and led them toward the outdoor umbrella tables.

"Gee, and I just lay on the floor and enjoyed the gunslinging and the fighting."

"Now you're making fun of me, dude. And we don't take kindly to teasing our womenfolk around these parts."

Jack laughed at the horrible impersonation. "Sorry, ma'am." He tipped an invisible hat. "It's not every day a woman uses a word like *chinkling* in this here town."

Allie let go of his arm and sat down at a patio table near the creek.

Jack tilted his head to one side. "What can I get for you?"

Allie grinned at his masculine shyness. "They have a wonderful apricot tea here—I'd love a cup. With a packet of honey, please."

Allie watched Jack walk toward the service window. The view didn't bother her eyes at all. She hadn't realized how long-legged this colt was, nor how comfortable he seemed to be with himself. She couldn't believe how brazen she'd been in taking his arm on the bridge.

Jack turned back while in line and caught her stare. They both blushed at the awareness of their attention. Neither broke off the eye contact, though Jack had to finally pivot when it was his turn to place their drink order at the window. Allie leaned forward and put her elbows on the table. She traced a small design absentmindedly with her fingertip.

Her cell phone buzzed in her purse. Flipping it open the alert flashed two text messages. One from Gillian: "Soooooo?" Allie clicked back, "Fine, go away." The other from Soozi: "Details. Take notes." Allie clicked a short: "No problem." The two busybodies were more alike than they'd ever admit.

The afternoon felt comfortable. A warm flush rose on her cheeks as she watched Jack place a steaming cup and saucer in front of her.

"I don't think I've seen such a lovely shade of natural blush before. I hope those are good thoughts."

"I'm sorry. It's such a beautiful afternoon, my mind drifted for a moment. How, uh, are the cats?"

"Impatient to meet the gorgeous vision who attacked me in the number three aisle and made me late for their dinner."

"You lied," Allie shrieked, giggling. "You lied to two felines, telling them it was my fault, and then tried to sugar-coat it by calling me gorgeous?"

"Yeah, did it work?" He stared into her face.

The banter continued through a second cup and the sun began to dip toward the west. The palm trees covered the patio area in shade and a slight chill followed. The two pushed back their chairs in grudging mutual agreement and started to walk toward their cars in the parking lot.

"I had a nice time, Jack. Too long since I've slowed down enough to enjoy a Sunday afternoon with someone. I guess I forgive you for the collision at the supermarket. How is your foot by the way?"

"Fine, no scars or lingering disabilities. I had a great time, too, Allie. Would you like to do lunch sometime, or take this a drastic step further and try dinner somewhere? I could ask permission of Pixie and Dixie for a night off, if you're game." Jack took her hand to help her over the landscape and conveniently kept it in his.

"Make sure you feed them first, and I'll consider it." Allie liked the strong feel of his hand against hers. They had a natural pace together.

"What about steaks at Charley's, Friday night? We could meet there, if you'd rather, after work. I'll have my neighbor's daughter feed the two bruisers so they don't wreck the furniture and you won't fret about their welfare." They had reached Allie's car. Jack took her keys and opened the door for her.

"Sounds like fun. About seven-thirty?"

"That's a date. Umm, how can I get a hold of you should something come up; uh, I don't mean it will, but if one of them tries faking a hairball or something, where could I call?" Jack stuttered through his request.

"I'm at Novel Software on Haven Avenue above Sixth Street. We're in the phone book."

"Great. I'm looking forward to Friday night then." Jack hesitated a moment by the car door, his face creased as he squinted in the late sun. Then he handed her keys back and took a step backward.

Allie noticed his hesitation. She didn't know whether to be flattered or frustrated he didn't try to kiss her. This guy definitely isn't a stalker or a professional heartbreak machine. Allie liked his little-boy shyness. "Bye, Jack. See you next Friday," she said, and closed the car door herself.

She left him standing in the parking lot, watching her car pull away. She glanced in the rear view mirror and waved her arm through the open car window. She lost him when turning onto Foothill Boulevard with the evening traffic. The late afternoon air felt cool against the side of her face as inside the car felt warm and secure. She pushed the button to bring up the window while replaying the afternoon delight in her mind.

Chapter 13

"So, what happened at the art fair with you and the grocery guy? Please tell me this went better than the doctor fiasco," Soozi said. She'd returned Allie's call after the miniature tornadoes were safely tucked into bed. Sunday night mayhem had been deafening earlier when Allie first called.

"We had fun, perfect weather, not too crowded. An-nd," dragging out the word, she continued, "he knows a lot about television trivia. We played a few rounds together."

"You started on this poor guy right off the bat? Girl, that's a kooky habit of yours. You could have sent him running off into the mountains, never to be seen again." Soozi's voice went into a whine. "Allie, you drive me nuts with that stuff. Honest to God, you do."

"Sooz. He started it."

"The man's a saint, Al. Marry him now or I will find one of our group who will." Soozi poured herself another glass of white wine, with the phone cradled on her shoulder. Was this her second or third glass tonight? Soozi listened to Allie droning on about Mr. Dullness. What were the odds of Allie finding a guy to play TV trivia with? Oh, brother, now we'll hear about this forever. Didn't this guy play sports as a kid?

"Are you seeing him again? Or did he give you the classic he'd call you and the phone will never ring." Soozi dripped in sarcasm before she could stop herself. Maybe it was three glasses already.

"Ouch, Friday night for dinner," Allie continued. "Why are you being catty about this? I thought you'd be happy for me, you know how much Dr. Dickhead freaked me out. I needed a nice guy—if nothing else, to do a get-back-on-the-bicycle sort of thing."

"Sor-ry. I didn't know you were sensitive about him already. You bumped into him at a grocery store, for Christ's sake, in the middle of the night." Soozi stared at the empty glass in her hand. Where did the wine go?

"Are you all right? Did I forget your birthday or something?" Allie asked.

"No. Forget it. I don't know what got into me." Other than a whole bottle of wine, as less than half a glass poured out when she tipped it over. Soozi dropped the empty into the kitchen trashcan, then flinched at the loud clatter. "Sounds like a sweet afternoon. I think I need a couple of Tylenol and a soft pillow, I'm tired."

"Call me tomorrow at work. I worry about you, girl. You sure you're okay?"

"Sure. I'll call. G'night." Soozi hung the phone back into the cradle. She rubbed her hand against her forehead. Behind, she could hear a faint laugh track from the television. Randy would be nearly through his *Los Angeles Times* crossword puzzle and wanting conversation. I can't face going in there tonight.

"Honey, I'm going up and taking a shower," Soozi called toward her husband.

"'Kay," came the dependable answer from her college sweetheart, husband, father of her two children, defender of the faith and the mighty.

The carpeted stairs moved slightly under Soozi's bare feet. She grabbed the polished oak railing for balance and began a slow trek upward. What is going on with me? Soozi asked herself. This is nuts. Drowning my brain in alcohol again; what am I doing? Shower. I need a hot shower.

Soozi stripped off her clothes in the middle of the bathroom, bumping against the sink. Her clothes lay in a colorful heap on the floor. She pulled back the plastic curtain and carefully stepped into the tub, keeping a hand on the wall for balance. The tub's porcelain felt cold on the bottom of her feet.

As she snapped the curtain back into place, Soozi bent and twisted the water handle. A freezing spray of water splashed against her white skin. The shock made her quickly inhale, and she bit down on her bottom lip to keep from screaming. Her body ached with tense muscles against the frigid shower. Slowly the temperature began to change, and Soozi couldn't stop the flood of tears.

She stuffed a washcloth into her mouth, as the water splashed across her face, muffling her racking sobs. She crossed her arms around her chest and fell against the wall. One hand pushed against the washcloth as the sobs turned into screams of frustration. The shower water insulated the rest of the family from the desperate noise.

"It's only me. Traffic this morning was a nightmare, I swear." Gillian flounced into the office over a half hour late. He dropped his briefcase on the desk and headed for the coffeemaker in the kitchenette.

"I need caffeine. Pull-eeze tell me you put real coffee in here and not some mother-to-be watered down trash," he whined pitifully out into the office.

"Relax. I made myself cocoa this morning. That pot's for you." Allie walked into the kitchen area, smiling, in too good a mood to play with Gillian's stressed-out head. "You owe me, you know."

"Anything, my queen, anything. But make it a few minutes from now; my nerves are frazzled. What is wrong with people? The gas pedal is the one on the right and the brake pedal is on the left. Elementary physics, you cannot go faster than the car in front of you. Accidents everywhere." Gillian swung his arm high into the air for dramatic emphasis.

Allie ducked at his swing. "Move out here to the Inland Empire and you won't have to commute every morning."

Gillian made a disgusted look as he walked back to his desk. "Be serious. Now tell me all about the strange man with a cat fetish you had coffee with yesterday."

"Gillian, we had a lovely time and talked for hours." Allie leaned against the side of Gillian's desk, sipping at her cup of cocoa.

"Talked. You do lead such a charmed love life. And what, pray tell, did you two kids talk about all afternoon?"

"Television." Allie turned her back and hid her smile.

"You've got to be kidding? You grilled him with those asinine questions you grill me on? Is he old enough to answer them or do you explain the story lines?"

"He's my age, and plays well with others. The hours flew by. We laughed, we shared, we challenged." She turned back toward him, smacking her hip against his desk. "Ow, that's going to linger."

"Well, well. The boss has found someone to play with. I'm happy for you, Al. Seriously. What more could you ask for than a trivia playmate for a fulfilling love life. Did he kiss you?" Gillian leaned back in his office chair.

"Not exactly."

Gillian sighed into his cup. "Either his lips found themselves planted against yours in some sort of passion or they didn't; you'd remember."

"I think he thought about it, but nothing happened."

"Wonder boy didn't try anything? We're glad he's not a tramp like the kid doctor, but come on. He's not one of my rejects, is he?"

"Not all cute guys are your throwaways. At least Jack knows Angela Cartwright is not related to the Cartwright boys from *Bonanza,*" she snapped at Gillian. Could it be Allie wasn't Jack's type? Surely not. He'd suggested dinner, a second date.

"Darling, the man gets brownie points for even knowing who Angela Cartwright is. But did Mr. Trivia know who the all-important god, Jimmy Buffett, is?" Gillian accepted her rebuff and raised her a comeback. He was learning to hold his own against the pregnant hormone queen.

"I didn't probe into his blood type or druthers of music. He's got great legs, though," Allie taunted her coworker.

"Now we're getting to the juicy stuff. You've been holding out on me. So, there is some potential to this Jack fellow. The scenery is nice close-up, hmm?"

"Gillian, he's sweet—a rare gentleman found in a valley of braggarts and maulers. He escorted me to the car, and we made a dinner date for Friday." Allie flipped her hair off her shoulder. "No heavy breathing, no slobbering or drooling on either of our parts. He's nice."

"Nice? Oh, please. That's what you say about your Aunt Kitty, not a man. Let's hope on Friday his real personality shows up and not some lactose replica of male testosterone." Gillian stretched and lifted himself out of the chair. "'He's nice,'" he said, imitating Allie with an uncanny likeness. "Really." He walked back to the kitchen for a refill.

Allie appreciated the view of Gillian's exit. The man dresses for success, that's for sure. The cut of those tight pants comes from a personal tailor. Why does Gillian work when he doesn't need my money? Must be nice. Allie giggled to herself. Gil would bite her head off, using him and the word nice in the same sentence.

Jack *is* nice. That's nothing to be ashamed of, she thought, going into her office to try and get work done. She sat and turned her chair toward the window. Okay, she had cheeseburger and Diet Coke tastes instead of caviar and champagne. Gillian would have to live with it.

The unfamiliar creak of the outer office doors an hour later got her attention away from the computer screen. Unless Gillian scheduled a meeting with clients, those doors rarely opened during the workday.

"Does Allie Thompson work here?" a strange voice asked from the reception area.

Allie came around her office door in time to see Gillian accept a cut-glass vase of flowers from some young man in tailored shorts.

"I'm Allie," she said, facing the kid before Gillian practiced his charm on him.

"Sign here, please." He handed her a clipboard and pen with a quick professional flip of the wrist.

"Go, girl. Looks like Mr. Nice With Cats scored points on the Gillian scale of romance. And an extra point for requesting specific flowers, not the dreary standard issue of a basket of pitiful posies." Gillian delicately touched the petals of the peach-colored gladiolus. The tall stalks were nestled in a forest of greenery. "Definite possibilities, Allie."

The delivery person nodded his head. "Enjoy," he said, and let himself out the door.

Allie looked at Gillian with twinkling eyes, then back to the flowers. "Look at this." Instead of the typical florist card, a Hallmark envelope was tucked on the plastic cardholder wand. Allie reached for the card, noticing a sticker in the corner printed with Suzanne's Flowers.

"I like men going the extra energy. A special card, too—good touch, Mr. Nice," Gillian agreed.

The envelope held a Shoebox greeting card that made her laugh.

"Take this Kleenex moment into your office, please. I have work to do out here. Somebody has to run this company before you go on maternity leave."

"Hey, don't get your hopes up. I may bring a midwife into the office and drop the baby in my office during lunch."

"You would, too, spoiling my fun."

"Get over it."

"Yes, boss. Whatever you say, boss."

Allie set the vase on her desk, and pumped her fist in excitement. Flowers and Hallmark. Allie punched a button on her phone. Soozi was number one on her speed dial.

"Hello?"

"I just got flowers, and they had a Hallmark card tucked inside."

"Oh, yippee for you."

"Hey, what's bugging you? Last night you almost took my head off over this Jack thing, and now you're peeing on my flowers."

Sooz choked on her laughter. "Sorry. Your call got me off the kitchen floor scrubbing up Zoe's oatmeal. A food critic at two feet tall, and she flung handfuls of mush everywhere. This stuff is like glue."

"Remind me not to ask you for the recipe. Okay, can we start this conversation over? I got flowers from Jack. Gorgeous peach glads."

"Young love. I am so jealous. Did you say he put a real card with them? I never heard of such a thing. The grocery guy with the cats? You have to let Randy meet him, maybe something will rub off."

"That sounds like my ol' Soozi. Double-dating would be fun. Let me see how the dinner date goes and make sure this guy doesn't have a Mr. Hyde complex, too."

"Still traumatized by that man?"

"Yeah, I guess, let's not go there. We're going to Charley's for steaks and I think he deserves a decent thank you for the flowers, if he's a good boy."

"Behave yourself, you're a mother-to-be." They laughed together.

"Mrs. Peel, of course," Jack stated before plunging the forkful of food into his mouth.

"For her body or her talent?" Allie shot back, carving into her steak.

Jack had lost some of his shyness after two bottles of Miller Genuine Draft. Allie nursed a virgin strawberry daiquiri and watched his sweet face.

Jack nearly choked in swallowing his mouthful too soon. "That's the whole point of the fantasy. Mrs. Peel's talents with judo and stealthing helped sculpt her body. A woman who could take care of herself, and do it all while poured into a one-piece bodysuit."

"What about *Charlie's Angels?*" Allie stabbed at her vegetables, not sure she liked playing the game of gorgeous celebrities of the past.

Jack held up his hands. "I'm totally guilty of watching them bounce across the screen, praying for a cold day scene to enhance their, uh, shirts." Jack reached for his water glass. "Don't get me in trouble. I know about your daydreams of Burt Ward, remember? Someone wrote 'Mrs. Robin' all over her school notebook."

Allie blushed and lowered her eyes. "God, he was adorable. What a discovery, going from *Lassie,* rated G, to Robin in spandex, an easy PG-13 for my young, lustful soul. Puberty messes with your television viewing."

"What about other heartthrobs," Jack continued, teasing her. He found himself encouraging the blush. "You're going to tell me you didn't have the hots for Vinnie Barbarino?"

"Too street tough." It felt delicious to be out on a Friday night. The dim lights gave a soft glow to the other tables and patrons. The familiar background noise of conversations and orders filled her ears, this time like music, not possible rescuers from danger. Allie tucked a loose strand of hair behind her ear.

"Okay, back to *Batman.* What say we try and find some of the old episodes on cable, and you can get your fix of Robin and I'll force myself to watch Julie Newmar as Catwoman."

"Wasn't she a knockout?" Allie reached over and touched Jack's arm. "See? I noticed the rest of the characters besides the caped crusader's sidekick. In fact, I met Frank Gorshwin years ago when he was in a play out here in the valley. He still had a glint in his eyes, just like his character, The Riddler."

Jack looked down at Allie's hand lingering on his arm. Allie noticed his glance and retracted her hand slowly.

"Now, what did you do that for? I kind of liked it there." Jack spoke hardly above a whisper.

"I, uh, need my hand back to cut my steak. It takes two hands to eat food politely in public, you know. I have all the Miss Manners' books at home." She lightly passed the moment off.

"How is your steak by the way? Do you know in some states, you'd be arrested for eating meat like that? Meat is supposed to stop moving before you eat it." Jack pointed at her plate.

"I love my steaks rare."

"There's rare and then there's what's on your plate. Animal lovers are going to picket your dinner choices. I like mine cooked. What else do we not have in common? Let's get the annoying nuisances out of the way and concentrate on the good stuff." Jack raised his eyebrows in surprise. "Did I say that?"

Allie stared at her new friend. "Why, Mr. Jack, I think you're flirting with me. Or is the beer bringing out another side of you? Should I order you another Miller?"

"You bring out another side of me, Allie." Jack lowered his head and played with his napkin in his lap during his confession. "You've got my attention, Allie, and I hope, would you mind, maybe we can do something next weekend? I mean, if you're not already booked or something."

Allie touched her fingers to her lips to still the smile, and turned her head to the side. "My social calendar is pretty dusty, Jack. The last couple of years have been full of working overtime, getting my company up and running successfully. Dating took a back seat to Novel Software."

They both smiled, and this time Jack reached across the table toward Allie. She met him halfway, and their hands came together by the basket of rolls. Allie could feel deep strength in his large hand, but his touch was gentle.

"I'd love to do something next weekend. Did you have anything special in mind?"

"Maybe a ride up to Oak Glen for apples? We could take a picnic basket."

"That's perfect. I used to go there with the neighbor's family, across the street as a little girl. My parents never seemed able to pull away from their work long enough to smell the apple cider. How fun, I'd love that."

Jack reached for his glass of beer and appraised the woman across from him. Her face glowed in the candlelight at their table. Her dark eyes twinkled with the dancing flame and gripped his heart. "Oak Glen, it is. I will take charge of the pick-a-nick basket for us."

"Yes, Yogi." Allie laughed, jumping into the cartoon character.

"Your job, Boo Boo, will be to keep an eye out for Mr. Ranger." Jack squeezed her hand.

"I'll have to call you back, Sooz. I don't feel good," Allie said as she slammed the phone down and rushed to the downstairs bathroom near the kitchen. She held the toilet rim as her breakfast cereal came back up. She dropped to one knee on the cool tile, heaving again and again.

When the attack subsided, Allie wiped her mouth with a washcloth from the towel bar above. Her hair dangled damply at the sides of her face. Allie waited on the floor, catching her breath, before trying to stand up. The phone began ringing. Allie listened for the answering machine to pick up.

"Allie? Allie, are you okay? Call me. What's going on?" Soozi sounded worried on the tape. The click of her hanging up stopped the machine.

Allie got to her feet. Her legs were rubbery and unstable as she headed out of the bathroom. Her mouth tasted like battery acid. She went upstairs and brushed her teeth, swiping the brush on her tongue. As she rinsed her mouth, she caught her pale reflection in the mirror. *I must really be pregnant. This is the second morning in a row I've knelt before the toilet god. Yesterday I thought maybe an early flu bug, but this is nuts.*

Allie went over to lie down on her bed and picked up the phone from her nightstand. "Sooz? How long does this morning sickness stuff last? I'm sick of it already and it's only been two days."

"Hopefully only a month or so, though I've heard some women stay sick through the whole nine months. You better toughen up, old girl. Morning sickness is just a wake-up call. You have so much to look forward to: swollen ankles, stretch marks, your hair breaking off because the baby is stealing all your nutrients."

"Tell me again, whose maternity idea this was?" Allie mumbled against the receiver. She laid her other arm over her eyes.

"All yours. Come on, nature is just getting started. We won't go into the nightmares of labor, where you think it's the end of the world. And labor ain't nothing close to what that kid is going to do to your heart and soul once it gets here. It will shred you apart."

"Lenny giving you a tough time this morning, Miss Good News?" Allie would smile if she didn't feel so lousy.

"He let his sister put her Pop-Tart in the VCR to see if it would play a Pop-Tart commercial. Honestly. Then Zoe is screaming because she thinks the machine ate her breakfast. There are crumbs everywhere inside the machine. The guys at the shop are going to love this one."

"Whatever happened the time Lenny put the toaster waffle in the machine, complete with syrup?"

"We got a new unit—this one. The syrup had dripped and hardened over everything by the time we found out. Shoulda bought a locking kit for the new machine."

Soozi changed the subject abruptly. "Have you told Aunt Kitty you're pregnant yet?"

"No. I'm not sure how she's going to take the news her niece is having a baby without benefit of a father. And doesn't have a clue who the father is." Allie's stomach rolled again ominously. She took shallow breaths hoping the bed would keep still.

"Sperm all looks alike going in, what can I say?" Soozi burst out laughing at her own joke.

"Cute. She practically raised me, and yet I haven't talked much with her lately. Life gets complicated and time slips past before I know it. I did send her a birthday card last spring, almost on time, too."

"Allie, invite her over for dinner or take her to lunch, we won't discuss breakfast in your delicate condition, and break the news to her. Who knows, she might surprise you. She's a feisty thing."

"You're right, you're right. Okay, I'll call her today and set something up for next week. Most of her evenings are packed with bridge and social hours at the senior center. For someone who never married, she's sure making up for lost time with the octogenarian set. She's the Barbie Doll of the bingo parlor."

"Well, rest up. Keep some soda crackers or Cheez-Its near your bed, and suck on one or two before you get up in the morning. It helps take some of the acidity out of your system. Call me later. It's been too quiet in the other room. I don't know if Randy has tied them up or vice versa. *Ciao*."

Allie pushed the button on the phone and listened to the dial tone. She punched in her aunt's phone number and waited for her to answer. Her mouth still tasted awful under the thin layer of toothpaste.

"Aunt Kitty? It's Allie. How about penciling me into that overbooked calendar of yours for dinner some night this week? It's been ages since we've seen each other."

"Sugar, how nice. I'm sure I can cancel something. You let me make some phone calls and I'll get right back to you. You doing all right?" she asked suddenly.

"Yes, pretty fair, why?"

"You sound a might peaked. You're putting in too many hours at that business of yours, just like your mother. You better slow down, it ain't good for you, staring at that computer all day long."

"Aunt Kitty, you'll never guess what I'm doing next weekend." Allie adored her family matron. It had been too long since they'd talked.

"Taking over the world, I suspect?" she teased with a wheezing cough.

"No, I have a date with a man I met a couple weeks ago. We're having a picnic at Oak Glen. See, I will be out in the fresh air and nature. Do you want me to bring you back some apples?"

"Absolutely, child. I love making applesauce."

"I didn't know you were still doing much cooking."

"Oh, lands, it's easy anymore. You put them in one of those Crock-Pots in layers, sprinkling cinnamon on each layer." Aunt Kitty covered the phone with her hand while coughing. "Sorry. Fill it to the top as far as you can with the lid on, and let the apples cook overnight on low. I wake up to a house smelling like apple pie and have hot applesauce for breakfast." Allie heard her take a sip of something.

"You sly girl, holding out secret recipes from your own flesh and blood—a great breakfast and room deodorizer in one. Check and see what you have available this week, and let me know. 'Bye, Auntie." Allie put the phone back in its cradle and rolled over on her side. The bed still was unmade from getting up early this morning, and Allie reached down to pull the sheet and blanket back over her. Me and the baby are taking a nap.

"Are you sure you're feeling okay?" Jack asked Allie for the second time. She'd been rather quiet during the first part of the trip.

"Maybe a little rundown from work," and tired of throwing up in the mornings, Allie thought to herself. "It's been a hectic week. This is exactly what I needed, to get away and relax in the country." She reached over and patted his thigh, and left her hand there.

Allie was still pale from the morning's knee services at the toilet, despite her extra care with makeup, and Jack looked concerned over her appearance. As the car headed for the apple orchards, Allie picked up the conversation and tried assuring Jack everything was fine.

"I love this time of year. I was the only kid on my street excited for school to start. I'd have brand new pencils and a new notebook. What could be more fun than breaking in a new pencil box?"

"You are an odd one, Allie." Jack reached down and laid his hand over hers on his leg.

"I loved writing, on anything, about anything. I wrote scads of plays, you know, where the neighborhood kids played all the parts." She looked over at Jack. "I actually reworked one story line from back then. It's been buried in a drawer forever, and my assistant found it."

"Is that a good thing or a bad thing?"

"With Gillian, you can never be sure. Anyway, somehow with his gazillion contacts I guess he found a couple of producers, and my play is going to be performed in Orange County." Saying it out loud was such a delicious feeling. Allie fluffed up the back of her hair to cover her enthusiasm.

"Wow. I'd love to see it."

Allie looked out the window, blushing, erasing the last of the morning paleness. "Yeah, me, too."

Oak Glen cast a magical spell on the two of them. The picnic feast Jack brought consisted of sandwiches, cold salads, and two delicate wineglasses for the fresh cider they bought. Under a shaded canopy of California oaks and other trees, they sat on a king-size quilt and gossiped about life in general.

The autumn sun warmed in marbled patches through the overhead branches. Earth tones of dark greens, mixed with the beiges and yellows of the dried field grass and dead leaves, painted a familiar childhood landscape for Allie.

After lunch, the two packed away the basket and quilt in the car, and walked, holding hands, along a dirt path. Their steps and the swishing of their windbreakers when they brushed against each other broke the silence. They didn't walk far, nor at any brisk pace, enjoying the fresh air together. Jack rubbed his thumb gently against hers in their clasped hands. Eventually they turned around and headed back to the car. Their steps slowed, not wanting to leave the glen.

Allie broke the spell. "It's been decades since I've been up here, yet most of it hasn't changed at all. Just me."

"Changed for the better, I must say," Jack added.

"Well, older anyway."

"Hey, I'd be arrested for what I'm thinking if you were underage, Allie." Jack's words were as soft as the afternoon breeze.

"You, with impure thoughts? About me?" Allie teased her friend, but her heart pounded in her chest.

Their steps slowed until they stopped under a tree. Allie leaned against the trunk. Jack stepped close and put his hand up against the bark of the tree, above her shoulder. His face came in close and they both stared into the eyes of the other. "Allie, I'm not a Boy Scout anymore. I confess, I've thought about you more than I probably have a right to. You are so damn beautiful, it makes me want to do this," and he leaned over the rest of the way and gave her lips a gentle kiss.

When he moved back, Allie broke into a crooked grin. "Why, Mr. Strong,

180

I do believe I've wanted you to for an awful long time." She reached up for his shirt and pulled him in for their second kiss.

A slight groan escaped from Jack, as the second kiss blended into the third and the counting stopped for both of them. All that mattered was the delicious taste of each other, standing together in the woods. Jack pulled her body into his, wrapping his arms under her jacket, rarely letting his lips move off hers. Allie combed her fingers through his soft dark hair.

The sun began to dip below the hills, and a chill came up from the shadows. Despite the heat the two of them generated, Allie shivered. "I guess I'd better get you home." Jack pulled his face away and brushed her hair with his words.

"I guess we should." Allie closed her eyes and etched this moment into her heart. The perfect fit of his body entwined with hers, and she tasted his mouth as she carefully licked her tender lips.

"You know, this was destiny." Jack stepped back and held her at arm's length.

"Oh, really. How so?" she asked.

"Look," Jack said as he pointed over their heads.

Allie looked up into the branches and saw a huge clump of mistletoe. "Jack, I forgot that stuff grows wild out here. How perfect." She leaned over and planted a quick kiss on his surprised face. "Come on, this body doesn't handle anything below seventy degrees."

They moved in close, side by side with their arms wrapped around each other's waist, and headed for the car. Jack kept her close as he unlocked her door. Allie slid into the warmth of the car and waited for Jack. He put the car keys into the ignition, but before he could start the car, Allie reached over and kissed his lips. The car kept out the chill of the air, and they stayed a while longer enjoying each other.

Gillian came into the office Monday morning and set his briefcase on his desk. The lights were on, but where was Allie? He walked into the kitchen area and saw the preparations of coffee out on the counter, but no coffee. Then he heard the flush of the toilet in the back of the office. He finished making the coffee and went back to his desk to grab his cup. A bedraggled Allie came through the bathroom door and shuffled toward him.

"My gawd, are you contagious? You look horrible. Shouldn't you be home in bed or something?"

"Thank you, Mr. Blackwell. No, it's not contagious unless you're pregnant. That would be fun, then we could both share the joys of morning sickness together." Allie tucked her hair behind her ears and walked toward the kitchen. Smells of the fresh-brewed coffee forced her back into the bathroom. She slammed the door.

"And women want to do this on purpose?" Gillian shook his head as he poured himself a cup of coffee. Looked like he'd be in charge of the office today.

"Do you want me to call Dr. Adams?" Gillian called out loudly as he set out his work for the day.

"No…" Water ran in the sink, drowning out the rest of her answer. The door opened slowly. "I'll be okay; this has to pass." She straightened her sweater and brushed the knees of her nylons. "Maybe for the next week or so, could you pick up your coffee at Starbucks or something before you come in? Just until this phase of baby-making is over?"

"Sure, boss. No problem. Can I do anything for you?" Gillian worried over the pale form in front of him. A few weeks ago this woman had been glowing, now she looked like something dredged up from the Los Angeles River.

"I've got crackers at my desk." She started walking across the office as the phone rang.

"Novel Software, may I help you?" Gillian answered, keeping an eye on Allie.

"Oh, Jack. Yeah, she's, uh, busy right now. Let me check and see if she's available." He put the call on hold. "Are you up to talking? I take it everything in the woods went well with Prince Charming. He sounds annoyingly chipper for a Monday morning."

Allie stopped in her tracks and smiled at the thought of Jack.

Gillian lightly slapped his cheek with his hand. "What did you two naughty kids do that makes your sickly cheeks red?"

Allie didn't waste time answering him, but moved as quickly as she could into her office and closed the door. Gillian stared at the painted door; he didn't remember her ever closing the door for a phone call. The blinking light on his phone went solid.

"Well. This is a man I definitely must meet." Gillian swiveled in his chair and turned on his computer. "We need mood music for the occasion. Hmm, maybe a little Andrew Lloyd Webber will spice it up around here."

Almost an hour later a sheepish Allie opened her office door and leaned against the jamb.

"Well, boss, have you decided to work today?" Gillian flipped the question over his shoulder, not bothering to turn around.

"He's taking me out to lunch this afternoon."

"Good, it's time I met Romeo."

"You behave yourself, or I'll—" She ran to the bathroom before she could finish her threat.

"You can't fire me, boss. You can't even keep your breakfast down." Gillian leaned over and turned up the volume of his CD player, drowning out the noises from the bathroom. "Don't forget to brush your teeth before you come out," he shouted over the music.

Twenty minutes before Jack's proposed arrival time, Gillian took a small, soft-sided bag from a cupboard behind his desk. He walked with purpose into Allie's office. "You have a date coming and look like death warmed over. Turn your chair around and let me fix your pitiful face." The emergency stash of cosmetics in the office was Gillian's idea because he refused to attend business meetings unless she looked decently professional. His talent with a blush brush far exceeded anything she could do. "There, the cat man will fall in love with you all over again."

"Don't start, Gillian." Allie saved her file on the screen and exited the program. She knew his talent with Revlon could make all traces of morning sickness disappear. "Do not shred him with those pointed claws of yours. Be nice. I haven't begun to explain you to him."

"You don't trust me with Jack?" Gillian feigned shock and hurt. "Obviously, you must be lightheaded from this morning's workout over the porcelain throne. I'm happy for you. It's about time you had a man for yourself."

"We haven't done anything." Allie squirmed in her chair with the turn of the conversation. "We're just friends."

Gillian laughed and picked up the tubes and brushes, putting them back in the bag. "You keep telling yourself this isn't serious."

The outside glass door creaked. Gillian stopped what he was doing and stared at Allie. "It's him," she whispered. Gillian dropped the bag into her top drawer and walked out before Allie could stop him.

"May I help you?" Gillian advanced toward the tall male.

"Hi, I'm Jack Strong, here to see Allie," he put his right hand out toward Gillian.

"Charmed, I'm sure. Gillian Nation, Allie's assistant. She'll be right out, if you'd like to take a seat." Gillian walked around his desk after shaking Jack's hand. He quietly pulled out a tissue and wiped his hands. The poor man had wet palms. Disgusting, reacting like that over a woman. He wanted to shake the man. Get a grip on yourself.

Allie came out a moment later, her eyes twinkling and all traces of the morning gone. Gillian noticed it wasn't his talented efforts that made her face seem flushed and vibrant. She went up to Jack and they hugged each other. They both started talking, and then laughed. Jack leaned in and planted a quick kiss on her lips.

"Uh, Jack, did you meet Gillian?" She pulled herself reluctantly out of his embrace.

"Before you came out." Gillian grimaced. How can something that cute be so gaga over Allie? "Why don't you two kids go off and have lunch. I'll manage the company until you get back."

"You're welcome to come with us, Gillian," Jack piped in.

"Thank you for the gracious invitation, but no, I have other plans this afternoon." Gillian winked at his boss as Jack turned and opened the office door. He gave a thumb's up behind Jack's back. Allie mouthed a thank you and they were gone.

"Hello?"

"Soozi, did you get your invitation?" Allie sat up straight on the exercise bike, keeping a steady rhythm as she adjusted the phone mike in front of her mouth.

"How fun is that? Our own little reality show. Carrie's going for a younger man, and we get free eats; works for me."

Allie wrinkled her nose; food still wasn't on her top ten list. Carrie, a friend from the gym, won the leading lady role in *The Crystal Prince* and had fallen in love with her leading man, Adam Sanders. She blamed and worshipped Allie in a roller-coaster of emotions over the past month, and Allie twisted the blame onto Gillian for selling the play in the first place.

"I gotta ask a question, Sooz."

"Shoot."

"Is it too early in the relationship to ask Jack to a wedding?" Allie couldn't hold her breath on the bike, but felt like it.

The pause on the other end lasted longer than Allie expected. "Well, hard to say, Allie. In my case any excuse to get out of the house is great; I'd drag Randy anywhere. With Jack, I think you play it by ear. This isn't some long drawn out religious occasion, this is Party Carrie. The whole thing should be a lot of fun. Yeah, bring him, and we'll see what happens between him and Randy."

"True. It's a good chance for them to swap stories. I don't think Randy's ever met one of my dates."

"Allie, none of us have met your dates, because you don't have any. Randy is a little curious about what number forty-five looks like though."

Allie mopped her forehead with a towel. "Yeah, that would be interesting. Okay, I'll call Jack and see what he says. Who knows, maybe he'll be booked that night." Allie heard a call-waiting beep in her ear. "That may be him now, gotta go, sweetie. Kiss the kids for me."

"You bet, talk to you later."

Allie slowed to a stop on the bike and punched the flash button on her phone. "Hello?"

"Maniacs, they are nine-maniacs, I swear."

"Hey, Gillian. Who are you sniping about now?" Allie climbed off the bike and reached for a bottle of water.

"Carrie and Adam want everything in nines. The wedding is on the ninth, they're having nine attendants, and everyone must be seated by 7:00 because the ceremony is to start at exactly 7:02 P.M. It's insane. You can't order people around like this."

Allie laughed. "It's their party—yes they can. Hey, I've decided to invite Jack, do you think that's an Emily Post no-no?"

"He needs to know what he's getting into. Might as well meet the whole gang in one room."

"Gillian, we're just dating."

"Gotta run. Eric is in the wedding party, and I have a million things to do. *Ciao.*" Gillian hung up.

Allie pulled the headset off, and after a few stretches headed for the shower. She'd call Jack tonight.

At the stroke of 7:00, the conductor raised his baton and the musicians stopped. The nine-piece orchestra had played softly as people filed into the room and sat in rows of folding chairs, which were set up on either side of two aisles leading up to the stage. A backdrop from *The Crystal Prince* decorated the hotel's raised stage with silk trees adding a nice touch of greenery. The center section of chairs was packed, and the overflow of wedding guests filled in most of the side sections. When the conductor tapped the music stand in front of him, the audience quieted to silence.

The baton went up, and at 7:02 the strings started a haunting melody. Allie looked to her left at Jack, and then Gillian. Butterflies were dog-fighting in her stomach. Soozi sat on her right, leaning against Randy. When Allie caught Gillian's eye his slight nod barely broke a degree.

The back doors opened, and a young woman dressed in layers of thin seafoam green chiffon, with a tight bodice and a handkerchief skirt, walked down the left aisle. She reached for a single white rose from a basket in the back and began singing "Forever," stretching the word into long notes.

From the other aisle a striking young man answered with a deep, clear voice singing "On this day." They stepped in time to the music, turning their heads toward each other as if nothing separated them. Another woman stepped out and picked up a rose, harmonizing with the first woman as they echoed "On this day." As the last note faded, a second young man came into view and with the first, sang "Forever."

From behind the backdrop a group of players came out dressed in shades of blues and greens, the women with flowers and ribbons in their hair. The nine voices blended beautifully into the love song from *The Crystal Prince*. "On this day…one love beats from two hearts…forever."

An oboe soloed a few notes and the groom stepped out. Adam looked breathtakingly handsome as he raised his head, taking a deep breath. "Once I felt hopeless and lonely," his voice sang out through the room. "One heart I never would find."

Allie gasped at the sound of her words in song. Adam walked across the front of the stage and stopped at the edge. The other attendants moved together toward the back and Allie recognized Eric in the line-up.

The music softened to just the violins. "I wondered where I would find you," Carrie sang as she stepped out from the back door, her voice sending shivers up Allie's back. Soozi grabbed her arm as they watched their friend enter the room in shades and layers of white, an incredible vision of lace and pearls, with glints of twinkling lights as the Austrian crystals sewn in the gown caught the lights as she moved. Her veil draped softly over her curls.

The music enveloped everyone as Adam answered back, staring at his bride, "I wondered where I would find you."

Carried lifted her left hand toward the stage as she picked up a small bouquet of white roses and ivy, trailing ribbons and crystals with her right. "How would I know you?"

Adam hesitated a heartbeat, his eyes filling at the sight of her. "How would you know me?"

Allie found her own tears trickling down her cheek. Jack glanced over and reached into his jacket pocket for a handkerchief. A quiet sniffle next to Allie meant Soozi too felt the power of love in the room.

The attendants harmonized in chorus as the bride came closer to the stage. The minister stood in the middle.

"The purest heart…" Adam crooned.

"An open heart," Carrie answered.

Adam reached out and took Carrie's hand, leading her onto the stage. Their voices blended in perfect timing; the director watched the couple. A few inches separated their faces as they sang only to each other yet projected the words to every corner of the room. They held a single note as the attendants moved closer, singing in chorus.

The couple took a deep breath and held the last word, "Forever," as the orchestra finished the piece in majestic glory.

The deafening silence echoed against the walls. There was not a dry eye anywhere; women dabbed their eyes and sniffled in the quiet.

Adam and Carrie turned and faced the minister.

Allie wondered how Jack felt as the couple exchanged their vows. Her cheeks blushed as she felt his fingers caress hers. Soozi leaned against her side. When the minister said, "You may kiss each other," the audience erupted into applause. A perfect kiss, and then the happy twosome turned to face the cheering mob.

"May I introduce you to the new Sanders family."

Another wave of applause, and the orchestra began the same melody, now in brisk, delightful chords. The attendants started singing in unison: "On this day…they found one heart. On this day…the purest heart." Adam and Carrie walked up the far aisle. The orchestra played, and the attendants followed the happy couple. The director watched as the last went through the door, then he brought the orchestra to a crescendo and finished the piece. The audience sighed.

Allie moved to stand up and Jack leaned over and kissed her lips. Allie's face flushed and she heard Soozi gasp ever so slightly behind her. Gillian's eyes, outlined in wet eyelashes, glittered back at Allie.

"If the rest of *The Crystal Prince* is anything like that number, you have a hit on your hands."

"I don't know what to say," Allie stuttered. "I recognized the words, but, wow." Soozi squeezed the back of her arm, and Allie continued, "Gillian, I never imagined it could be like this."

Gillian leaned past Jack and brushed his hand across her cheek. "No problem, boss."

The room empty, the group realized everyone was gone. They moved to the aisle and started toward the back door.

Gillian stepped through first and then moved to the side. As Allie walked into the foyer, applause broke out from the attendants. Allie stopped suddenly as Soozi bumped her from the back. "Author, author," they called out. The instant accolades caught Allie by surprise.

"This is not my time—you have all given life to the pages of text. And wonderful memories to Carrie and Adam."

Gillian started working the crowd. The reception was in the ballroom across the hall. The hotel staff opened the double doors and beckoned the crowd to enter. White netting hung in soft waves across the ceiling with white lights twinkling through the gauze. Each table, covered in white, glowed in candlelight with white centerpieces reflected in the mirrors underneath them. Murmurs of delight came from the guests because at each place setting rested a small crystal heart.

Soozi placed her clutch bag on a table and turned to Randy. "Get me a flavored vodka, would you, please?"

Gillian watched Randy head for one of the open bars in the corner and stepped closer. "How does it feel to see your best friend as a playwright?"

A red flush crawled up Soozi's neck. "You know I wish her the best of everything," she spit out.

Gillian purred, "Career, baby, cute guy, a musical." He let out a short sigh. "Isn't she wonderful?"

Soozi looked impatiently around for Randy, trying to ignore him.

"Look at how success seems to follow her everywhere. People adore a winner." Both Gillian and Soozi watched Allie in an animated conversation with a group, her hand nestled inside Jack's.

Randy stepped up, and Soozi grabbed the chilled glass from his hand. She took a large swallow, and Gillian smiled over at Randy.

"How's it going, Gillian?" Randy asked.

"Never better, my dear fellow."

Soozi started to drain her glass and caught Gillian's perfectly trimmed eyebrow raise. Lowering the glass, Soozi patted Randy on the arm. "I see a friend across the room, I'll be right back." As soon as her back blocked Randy's view she finished the drink and headed for the bar.

"That pampered poodle better stay out of my way," she mumbled. "Tell me to celebrate Allie's success. Insinuate I'm a loser next to Allie, while he wipes his nose on the hem of her skirt."

Though busy listening to whoever's turn in the conversation, Allie followed Soozi's mad dash across the room for the bar. Tilting her head she saw

Gillian standing by Randy, grinning in prideful malice. Looks like the score is Gillian one, Soozi nothing. But the night was young. With a heavy sigh, Allie leaned against Jack.

"Will you excuse Soozi and me for a few minutes?" Allie said as she pulled Jack toward their table. "Would you save our seats by Randy over there, I need to talk to Soozi."

"Didn't you just see her?" Jack teased. "Go, I'll miss you, but I understand. A woman's gotta do what a woman's gotta do."

Allie gave him a quick peck on the cheek and headed off into the crowd.

Allie found her friend at the gift table with a fresh drink, looking at a book. She slipped her arm through the one holding the drink. "Give me a sip."

"Uh-uh. Alcohol." Soozi didn't look up and turned a page of the book.

"What are those?" Allie let go and gazed at the display of books, all with photos of the happy couple on the cover. A small sign reading FOR OUR GUESTS rested above. Picking up one of the soft-covered books, she flipped through and saw baby photos and school portraits of Carrie and Adam.

"It's a journal of how they grew up and when they met. Is this fun or what?"

The last pages thanked everyone for attending and sharing in their new adventure of matrimony.

"I love it. Look how adorable Carrie looks. I didn't know she was a cheerleader."

"Who?" Two men arm in arm came up behind them. "What are these?"

As Soozi passed them each a copy, the four read bits and pieces out loud. "These are priceless. How clever." One said, "I'll bet Gillian thought this up." Allie watched Soozi's jaw clench and her eyes narrow. Not what Soozi needed to hear. Allie sighed.

The group at the book table grew in size until the disc jockey tapped on his microphone. "Ladies and gentlemen, please welcome Carrie and Adam Sanders."

Allie grabbed Soozi's arm and urged her, "Come on, we'll be missed by the guys." Soozi tucked her copy of the book under her arm and finished her drink. "Ready." Allie hoped Gillian had moved far away from their table.

Chapter 14

"I've thought of new names for the baby. Check this out, Jackson if it's a boy or Cheyenne if it's a girl." Allie squeezed the lemon slice in her iced tea. She hadn't lunched with Soozi in a while. Almost every day since the wedding had included Jack, and Allie felt guilty.

"What did you two do, go to Knott's Berry Farm this weekend?" Soozi picked up half her tuna sandwich from the plate. The tables around them were starting to empty as the lunch hour crowd disappeared. Her wineglass was almost empty, and Soozi looked around. "What do you have to do to get service around here?"

"No, Jack and I went to a late movie." Allie was confused at Soozi's testy remark. I thought she'd be happy in sharing ideas of naming the baby.

"Then where'd the Wild West names come from? Some John Wayne retro festival in Los Angeles? Is this my second glass of wine or first? Obviously, not near enough."

"I just liked the names—different but kind of solid, you know?"

"This isn't part of that childhood crap where your parents wouldn't let you be a cowboy, no matter how many *Bonanza* episodes you memorized, is it? We could never get you outside to play hide and seek at night when that show was on. And I swear, every channel had a giddy-up program back then." Soozi grabbed the saltshaker away from Allie for the second time this afternoon. "No more, you've had enough already."

Allie frowned.

"How serious are you getting with this guy? Doesn't it sound a little kinky thinking of Jackson as a name for the baby?" Soozi glanced around the room again for their server.

"What are you talking about?" Allie choked on the french fry in her mouth. "What do you mean 'kinky'? How is the name kinky?"

"Jack's son? Jackson. Hello? Wouldn't Freud have a field day." Soozi moved back in her cushioned chair and straightened her back.

"Get over it. Are you going to eat your pickle?" Allie reached across the restaurant table toward her friend's plate. "Names are a heavy responsibility. It's weird naming a new human being you haven't even met first. How did you know Lenny was a Lenny before he was born?"

"We agreed to use our grandparents' names for the first one. For a boy it was Leonard or Elmer. Thank God for Loony Toons, Randy couldn't get past other kids making Elmer Fudd jokes about the baby so Leonard won." She shrugged her shoulders. "The kid's a Lenny now."

"How did Adam handle naming all the animals in the Garden of Eden? Can you imagine if he'd had a bad day and named the lion a beagle?"

"I don't think they had beagles back then," Soozi said curtly and signaled the waiter for refills.

"You know what I mean."

"Maybe dingos or terriers, but no beagles, I'm sure. I can't imagine Snoopy in the Old Testament."

"Okay, okay—I got your point. Sheesh. So, you don't like the name Jackson?" Allie wiped her mouth with her napkin.

"I didn't say that, I just think it's like one of those *Modern Romance* stories to pick a name close to a guy you're dating that's *not* the father of the baby." Soozi said. The waiter came and set a fresh glass in front of Soozi. She downed half the white zinfandel.

Allie put her hand out toward the waiter to stop him. "Could we have a slice of carrot cake, slightly warmed, with vanilla ice cream, please?"

"Right away, ma'am."

"You don't have to eat for two, you know. The baby's no bigger than a peanut. Don't go gaining thirty pounds and come whining later about feeling like a beached whale." Soozi applied fresh lipstick. "One of us has to be strong."

"Yes, Mother," Allie said, grinning. She wouldn't be the only one sticking a fork into the cake when it arrived.

"Have you told Jack you're pregnant?"

"Not exactly."

"How not exactly? Either you have or you haven't."

"Well, the subject hasn't come up yet."

Soozi leaned forward on the table. "Excuse me? Do you expect him to ask? 'Are you allergic to cats? Oh, by the way, are you pregnant?'"

"Sooz. He's a gentleman. He hasn't tried anything carnal yet. His kisses are sweet, like that first love where you can't catch your breath. Just a regular good guy."

"His kisses are sweet? Whoa. There's a romantic image I won't get rid of soon. Allie, you have to tell him you're expecting. This relationship has gone way beyond a couple dates, shake hands, and have a nice life."

"Look what happened when I told Michael, and I've known him for years. The man disappeared before I finished my glass of Perrier," Allie pouted. She'd been avoiding this subject.

"Sleaze is as sleaze does." Soozi took a long drink of her wine, leaving a perfect lip imprint on the glass.

"Making love to Michael was The Colossus of roller-coaster rides." Allie sighed with the passionate memories that seemed like another century ago. Michael hadn't called her at all since she told him.

"You don't build a lifelong relationship on physical acts that make you think of a roller coaster continuously. You don't eat New York cheesecake every night for dinner." Soozi continued her motherly sermon. The wine had loosened her tongue. "You need substance to survive, and so does a relationship. You can get wild and crazy once in a while, but it's the day-to-day stuff that makes a couple last, gets you through the cold winters and stock market crashes or whatever."

"Sheesh, I thought for a minute it was snowing outside, with all the violins playing around us. I'll tell Jack, in my own way, soon. I'll tell him," she assured her best friend. "It's not like I'm showing yet, or anything. What if I'm overreacting and he doesn't feel serious about me? Then I've cut off a great friend for nothing. Why should I tell him before I know he's going to be around for a while."

"The man is nuts about you. He calls, sends flowers, books your weekends in advance. Even the wedding went great, meeting everyone. Gee, what makes me think that he should know a little more about you than he does?" Soozi held her wineglass in front of her face, turning it slowly so the sunlight bounced off the coloring. "He needs to know, Allie. He deserves to know you're carrying someone else's child." Her voice came out strong and demanding.

"Could you, like, say it any louder? I don't think the people in the next building heard you. I know I'm pregnant. I don't want to rush in where I might be wrong." Allie picked up a fork. "Are you going to help me enjoy this delicous carrot cake or what?"

Allie came back from lunch and pranced into the office, the carrot cake having satisfied a sweet-tooth craving she'd had all morning. Gillian's face was in his computer screen with something dramatic playing on the stereo. Allie stared at his back, his tight blue shirt accentuating the muscles, the dark blonde hair pulled into a neat ponytail, talent and good looks all in one terrific package. Allie knew her company would be in great hands when she took maternity leave.

"Hey, how are the changes coming I gave you this morning?" Allie asked him, leaning over his desk.

Startled, Gillian swung his chair around, clutching his chest. "Don't sneak up on a person like that, you almost gave me a heart attack."

"Turn down the orchestra, and you would have heard the door. You're not conducting the symphony, you know. You're supposed to appreciate music, not be dissolved into the score."

"How's the wicked matron of western civilization?" Gillian reached over and turned the volume down to conversational level.

"Seemed more up today. There's something going on with her. I don't have a clue what it is, and she's not spilling any hints. I'm sure when the time is right, she'll break this vow of silence. But I'm worried. She's been moody and almost vicious at times on the phone the last month or so."

Gillian sniffed, straightening a stack of papers on his desk that didn't need additional help. "The woman has always been a panther lying around, waiting to rip off an arm or a leg. She's obviously jealous about your relationship with Jack. It's a nasty Chicago kitchen knife in her side that you're happy with a man, means less of your time and attention for her. How is her Roy or Richard doing?"

"It's Randy. He's concerned too. I could tell at the wedding, he kept watching her." Allie moved a strand of hair from her forehead. "They've had their share of rocky times; shoot, they've been together since college. They've taken their wedding vows to extremes over the years: for richer or poorer, in sickness and in health. They've pushed all the bases of commitment, and things always work out somehow." Allie went into her office and put her purse away. Slipping out of her light jacket, she hung it up on the coatrack behind her door.

"Clicking the remote, what about the baby thing?" Gillian followed her into the room and dropped into a chair, dangling a long leg over the padded arm.

"The baby?" Allie tucked one leg under her as she sat at her desk across from him. "My baby? Why would the baby be a problem for Soozi?"

"Being Queen of Motherhood was something she had successfully done that you didn't. You have your own company, you're important, you've used your education and made a name for yourself out in the business world. Soozi has her name on a parent roster at preschool. Now, you have a new baby coming. Where does that leave the carpool madam of la-la land?"

"Gillian, do you really think she's upset about me having a baby?" Allie chewed on her bottom lip, tasting the last bit of frosting from the carrot cake. "She's volunteered through the whole process. The timing seems about right, though. She's been out of it off and on with me even before Jack, and it's been getting worse instead of better."

"Your new diaper dolly could be the answer. Give her some time alone to sort out her feelings. Why not give the phone company a break, and give

Soozi time with your new pediatric situation?"

"Hey, careful, you almost sound concerned about her. I suppose I'm impressed. I didn't think you cared, except winning at all costs against her anytime, anywhere."

"I'm not an ice cube, dahling. It's no fun to win in a contest of wits when the other player is having suicidal tendencies." Gillian played with the cuff of his shirtsleeve, his eyes averted from hers.

"I wouldn't go that far with the mental diagnosis, Dr. Brothers. I don't think she's hell-bent on destruction, but something is definitely bothering her she's not admitting to. How do I leave her alone without telling her why I'm leaving her alone?" Allie twisted in her chair, moving it back and forth with her hand on the edge of the desk.

"What was her problem today?"

"She wants me to tell Jack I'm pregnant."

Gillian perched on the edge of his chair and stared blankly at Allie. "You haven't told him yet?"

"No." Allie dropped her leg to the floor and sat up straight, ready for round one from the next challenger on this issue. "Look, this is the first guy I've really liked in a long time. I am not going to blurt out I'm expecting a baby and scare the hell out of him."

"Don't you think he's going to notice the change in your figure soon?" Gillian composed himself and leaned back into the chair. His boss was on guard toward any hysterics. This had to be handled delicately.

"I don't know, I'm not experienced in this maternity stuff. How long do I have before I start showing? With the morning sickness stuff I actually lost weight. That should buy some time on this adventure ride before I have to tell him anything."

"Allie, honesty has to be a part of this relationship. He seems like a nice guy, a tad dull around the Midwest edges, but he has some delightfully sexy areas about him."

"Stop checking his butt out every time he comes in here. This one's mine," Allie teased him. Jack does have a good look to him from behind, she'd admit. She loved the view of Jack from any angle.

"And if you want to keep him, you have to tell him."

196

"Gillian, you saw what happened with Michael. He dumped me on my butt."

"Excuse me? That statue of testosterone from Seattle was good for only one thing. Agreed, one great thing in a variety of venues, but really, sex isn't everything." Gillian shivered. "Can't believe I said that." He took a deep breath. "You are a quality woman, Allie. If this Jack person is someone you truly value, then you have to break the news to him about the fermenting bambino."

"I know." Allie chewed on her fingernail. "I should call and say, 'Hi, Jack. Oh, by the way, one thing I forgot to mention: I'm pregnant.'"

"Do you want me to come to dinner with you and Jack? I have quite the flair at bringing up sensitive subjects at your dinner parties," Gillian offered.

"Jack will think you're pulling his leg. He loves your sense of humor—he's one of your biggest fans. No, I'll decide something. I don't have to do it right this minute. Now, get out of my way, lunch isn't going to stay down." Allie ran for the bathroom with her hand over her mouth.

"Rather gauche, dear. Don't they have a pill to stop this sort of thing?" Gillian went into the kitchen area to wash his hands. *She has got to get over this heaving thing. It just isn't pleasant.*

The thought of telling Jack about the pregnancy made Allie cringe. Who would have thought at the beginning of all this that she would have to explain her actions to a gorgeous man? Allie felt as if life's deck of cards was shuffled all over the floor. Once the baby came, a man asking her out would know up-front he's involved with a single mother, recognizing the signs like a diaper bag for a purse, food stains on everything she owned, and sleep deprivation around the eyes.

How do you tell a guy you've met you're expecting a baby and it's not his? Why can't I just wait until my clothes don't fit anymore and he figures it out? Allie stood in front of her bedroom mirror and turned sideways. If she flattened her T-shirt against her stomach, the slightest outward curve could be seen.

What do I say? Do I write a monologue like Jay Leno or David Letterman and make a few cute pregnancy remarks? I know he likes kids, but this is rather a blunt test of that. Oh, Jack, you might want to mark your calendar,

I'll be somewhat busy around next May, so don't make any plans for the two of us.

It's not like we're engaged or anything. What if I'm jumping the gun? What if he likes me, but I've got the signals all wrong? I'll look like an idiot. Then, if I don't say anything and he makes a romantic move for the bedroom, do I blurt out the condom is for safety features only, I'm already pregnant?

The phone ringing by her bed interrupted the frustrating argument inside of her. She grabbed it with a sigh.

"Hello?"

"Hi, beautiful. It's been days since I've seen you. Any chance of getting together this weekend?" Jack kicked the conversation into first gear.

"I was just thinking about you."

"Uh-oh. Am I supposed to be worried or flattered?" Jack laughed.

"We-e-ll." Allie chewed on her bottom lip.

"Okay, I'm not sure I like the tone of that 'well.' Sounds like Mary Richards when she's about to spring some notion on Mr. Grant he's not going to like. Do you want to tell me? Or are you going to leave me in suspense?" The voice joked over the phone.

"Oh, Jack. I always think good thoughts about you." Allie curled up on her bed, leaning against her pillows. His familiar voice made her feel comfortable, appreciated. "You make me smile, and the past couple of weeks have been magical." Allie felt herself babbling. Stop, take a deep breath.

"So why does it sound like a big 'but' is coming and my palms are sweating? You're going to tell me a long, lost husband has returned to claim his blushing bride after all these years?"

"Jack, I told you I've never been married in this lifetime. Honest. And, uh, honesty is kind of what I need to talk to you about, though." Allie slowly let out the breath she'd been holding.

"Your real name is Alexander, and you attended an all boys' high school," Jack guessed.

"Oh, yeah, there's a *National Enquirer* headline for you. Please, would you wait and we'll discuss this face to face?" Allie twisted the phone cord in her fingers. Her heart was beating hard against her chest. I'm going to die.

"Sure, I guess, if you'd feel more comfortable. I'll wait until you're ready.

So, about this weekend, then, where would you like to spring this on me?"

Allie paused. "Could I give you a call tomorrow from work and let you know? I'd like to, uh, make it something special."

"Time is always special with you," Jack said, his voice low.

Allie could feel the blush of his cheeks through the phone. "I'll talk to you tomorrow from the office. Good night, Jack. I, uh, need to get to sleep. I have an important meeting in the morning," she lied. "Gillian will have my head if I'm not on my toes for it."

"Uh, sure, Allie. Good night."

Chapter 15

"Gillian, could you come in here, please?" Allie called out plaintively through her office door.

"Yes, Your Highness. Are you ready to get back to work? I have the Johnson contract ready for your lovely signature." Gillian sauntered into her office with a file in his hands and plopped down in the chair.

"What do you mean get back to work?" Allie quizzed in answer to his sarcastic question. "I've been here all morning. I haven't left the office."

"Excuse me? Since when have you made money staring out the window instead of at the computer screen? I swear this pregnancy has affected your short-term memory. Try a ginkgo fizz, please. Has the heaving stopped?" Gillian perched on the edge of the chair across from her desk, playing with the legal papers in the file.

"I think I'm done," Allie started, and then changed course. "Are you telling me I'm not pulling my fair share around here?" She squared her shoulders, eyes flashing at the hunk of gorgeous male genes in front of her. Gorgeous, hell, the man was still on her payroll, not the other way around.

"Hello, welcome back." Gillian set the file down and applauded. "Allie, you've been in Wonderland outside this office. There may be a warm body in your chair, but your mind is on hiatus.

"Not like you don't deserve a break, after the crunch of great stuff you gave the producers for the Christmas line this year." Gillian leaned back in the chair, crossed his legs, and checked his nails. "With my assistance, of course. But usually by now you are ankle deep in sketches for next spring, or beating yourself over revisions you wished you'd made. Instead, I find you daydreaming for hours."

Allie sniffed loudly and swiveled her chair back toward the window outside, giving Gil her profile. She stuck her chin out.

"This can't be all pre-baby blues, Allie, can it? I'm worried about your mental state. All this pouting is ruining my aura."

Allie didn't move.

"Is it a Jack thing? Of course it is, silly me." Gil dropped his voice with concern, and laid his hand against his face. "What did hetero-boy say when you told him about the baby?"

A tear traced down Allie's cheek as her bottom lip trembled. The light from the outside the window highlighted its liquid trail, catching Gillian's eye.

"Ah, sweetie, what is he doing to you?" Gillian leaned forward, grabbing the edge of the desk. "Tell Uncle Gillian all about it."

"He hasn't done anything—yet. He's wonderful. It's me. I haven't told him I'm pregnant." Allie's lip trembled more as other tears started to follow. "I think I've fallen for this guy. Why in heaven's name now? Whose crazy idea was this to get pregnant? Why couldn't I meet a guy *after* the baby's born?" Allie turned her chair back around with vengeance, facing Gillian. "What kind of sick joke is this, that I get them both at the same time? Now what am I supposed to do?" She slammed her hand on the top of her desk, then twisted to grab a handful of Kleenex off her table behind her. The box fell off the edge.

Gillian sat back. The rage of hormones in front of him made him blink from the attack. How does she do that? "Hey, I'm not the enemy. Just a pitiful player in the game of life, trying to earn a measly dollar." Gil was afraid to smile for fear of a fresh attack from the queen.

"I'm sorry. I don't know what I'm saying. Jack wants to get together this weekend, and I sort of told him I had something important to discuss. The guy doesn't have a clue as to what's coming in the conversation. I don't know, either." Allie suddenly leaned across her desk in desperation, forcing Gillian further back in his chair. "You have to help me. Think of something clever— do we go to Disneyland, and I whisper it in his ear in the darkness of the Haunted Mansion so it seems like a bad dream?" She got up from her desk and started pacing along the edge of the office.

"Or do we go to a fancy restaurant, and if he leaves me stranded I can at least get a taxi home? Eeew, no, too much like the Michael deal." She shook her hands up by her face and down at her sides. "I know you volunteered to chaperone the confession again, but that seems kind of cowardly, doesn't it? What should I do? Damn it, think of something."

Gillian tapped his manicured finger in earnest against his lips. This needed profound concentration. Men can be such brutes, Gil thought, but Jack was Allie's brute. "Jack is entitled to the truth, Al. If he's sincere about you, he'll need time to adjust to this. No matter how you say it, package it, frost it over, you have to give him space to digest the info. This is going to be quite a shock for the cat man. No two ways about it. Reality sucks, dear."

Allie stopped and turned to look back at him sitting in the chair where he always curled up in her office. Gillian glanced up just then and caught her stare. They both broke into peals of laughter, breaking the tension.

"Stop, I'm going to pee my pants," Allie hurried back to her chair, collapsing against the cushion.

Gillian grabbed the top of his nose in a slight pinch and laughed all the harder. "Is this the most asinine conversation we've ever had? Four months ago you and I are cranking out probably the top-selling software packages for milk-money-toting short people, and now this? Lord, give me strength."

Allie blew her nose.

"This oversized cubicle you call an office is giving me claustrophobia. Let's go do lunch somewhere and get inspired by the muses in the real world, if you can call the Inland Empire the real world."

"Excellent idea. I knew you'd help me on this. Soozi had nothing for me, zip, nada." Allie reached down for her purse in the bottom desk drawer.

Gillian sniffed loudly. "Please, do not strain this moment of frivolity by bringing up that woman." He went out the office door in front of her, pulling the rubber band from his hair, letting it cascade in soft waves down his back.

"And you say my hormones are out of whack. Not too long ago, you almost felt sorry for her. You have got to settle this war between you. I am not choosing sides when the baby is born." Allie turned off some of the overhead lights, ignoring Gillian's primping at a mirror on the wall. "Let's go. Lock the door behind you."

The lunch crowd at the Italian corner café had thinned somewhat by the time they were seated. Those customers still at their tables turned their heads to watch them pass through as they were taken to their seats. Normally, Allie enjoyed the obvious stares. She knew Gillian's tall, dashing looks were striking to both women and men. Not today; more important issues clouded her vision.

"I'm serious, Gillian. How am I going to broach the subject of the baby with Jack?" Allie handed her menu back to the waiter after placing her order for a chicken salad. She wasn't hungry, yet she couldn't listen to Gillian's retort if she went without eating this afternoon. Yesterday he'd told stories of starving babies in Africa because she skipped lunch.

"The confession has to be handled tastefully, dear. This is a most delicate subject toward a man's ego, emotional laws about a man's deflation factor when they find out they are not the daddy, yadda, yadda."

"Gillian, we haven't done anything horizontal yet," Allie quietly spit across the table. Blabbing sexual innuendoes was not helping. "He knows he wouldn't be the father. Biology 101 would tell him that much. My gosh, we've barely fogged up the windows of his car."

"He's a virgin?" Gillian pressed both hands to his face. "He has to be if nothing physical has happened between you two yet." Gillian stared incredulously at Allie across the table.

"He's kind of shy, maybe, I don't know. I'm not in position for a bedsheet playmate, as you've so rudely reminded me. I haven't questioned the chastity issue." Allie gratefully accepted the salad and interruption from the waiter. "How am I supposed to tell him about the baby?"

Gillian moved his salad plate closer to him. "This is more difficult than I thought. If you two haven't been lovers, where do you introduce a topic of the utmost maternal nature?"

"That's what I'm asking you, office boy," Allie stabbed at the lettuce with her fork with unnecessary pressure. "Get that creative pumpkin you call a brain in gear and help me."

"Insults are not necessary," Gillian reminded her. He flipped his hair over his shoulder and took a mouthful of salad.

Sighing with regret, Allie knew she had gone too far. "I'm sorry. You are brilliant, and I've taken advantage of your generosity by demanding a solution to this ridiculous mess I've gotten myself into." Allie laid her fork on the table and grabbed her napkin. "But I don't know what else to do." She bent her head as a new wave of tears flowed. Not a shred of eye makeup remained on her face as she sobbed into the napkin.

"You are a watery one, aren't you?" Gillian fidgeted in his chair from her lost composure. People were looking at them, and not with admiring stares. "Are you going to be like this through the whole pregnancy?"

Allie glared up at him from above the folds of the napkin.

"Just kidding." he took another bite of salad. Nibbling on a piece of carrot at the end of his fork, his eyes gazed out over the tables around them, trying to ignore the curiosity of the other customers.

Allie wiped her eyes and blew her nose on a tissue she found her in purse. Jack would never understand, no matter how she tried to tell him. She might as well face it, she'd lost him, and deal with it. Dragging the whole issue out wasn't going to solve anything.

Gillian set his fork on his plate with a clink, and stretched his arm across the table, a wicked gleam in his eye. "Okay, this is what you do, girlfriend. Trust me, this is phenomenal, even for me. You're going to love it."

"Jack Strong, please."

"One moment," the receptionist said and put her on hold.

At Jack's baritone voice, "Jack, here," Allie's face broke into a smile at the now familiar introduction.

"Hi, it's me," she said, twisting in her office chair, pushing the toe of her shoe into the carpet.

"So, are you ready to tell me what's up? I'm not getting work done worrying about your surprise."

His deep voice wrapped her in longing and tingles. She inhaled and said, "Oh, sure, put the pressure on, big guy."

"You started this. Seriously, Allie, I don't think you should be hesitant about sharing. I keep hearing a catch in your voice. I may be out of line, but I'd hope I'm worth trusting."

"You're probably right, but I need to tell you in my own way. Let's meet Friday night about eight o'clock. We'll make it, uh, a party. Should be our anniversary of some sort, shouldn't it?" She forced a small laugh. Oh, Jack, if you'll only listen to what I have to say. Hear me before you judge me.

"Oh, you ruined *my* surprise," he said, laughing back at her.

"What surprise?"

"I petitioned Hallmark online for a selection of 'sorta' anniversary cards, and now you've spoiled it."

"You are a sweetheart. Is it a date?" Allie chewed on the end of her pen. Her foot tapped a concerto underneath her desk. Would Gillian's idea really work? It had to, she had no other option at this point. Her creative well had run dry.

"Tell me when and where."

Allie smoothed the front of her skirt with her hands after she set her purse in front of her. Gillian had gone beyond himself. She had given him carte blanche to pick out an outfit, and he had dressed her in a business suit of pale peach, the jacket cut in a low classic style, showing the barest edge of white lace from a new teddy underneath. With three-inch open-cut heels to polish off the look, some of the male patrons in the store were getting whiplash with their second looks at Allie as they passed by with their carts.

She had taken the afternoon off and had tried to relax with a pampering facial and makeover at the Total Look Salon. Gillian had called ahead and arranged a barrage of treatments, finished off with a simple cut and hairstyle to accent the suit tonight.

"Classic lines for a classy lady," Gillian had said, helping her dress in her office after coming back from the salon. "You look scrumptious." He gave her a brief hug and stepped forward to open the door for her and examine the finished results with one last critical glance. "Good luck. He's worth it."

She leaned her hip against the plastic handlebar of the grocery cart. She'd been standing at the end of an aisle in the middle of the grocery store, staring off into space, when a pair of arms wrapped around her from behind. Allie could smell Jack's animal scent mixed with a fresh soap smell she knew and loved already. The hands came around her waist and pulled her back into his chest. She leaned into his body, and they both struggled a moment to get their breathing under control.

"I hope that's you, Jack," Allie giggled, tilting her head back onto his shoulder, "or I'm in big trouble."

"Do you come here often, Miss?" Jack loosened his hold enough to turn her around, facing him. "You look marvelous, Allie." He reached down and, closing his eyes, kissed her lips.

The moment lasted forever. People maneuvered their carts around the young couple blocking the intersection between aisles 4B and 4C. The other customers smiled and envied their romantic passion. Allie opened her eyes first and reluctantly pulled away from his embrace.

"Well. This grocery store will never be the same." Allie tried to smile bravely. Her lips still tingled from his kiss.

"I thought it was pretty special already, running into the prettiest girl in the world. Literally." Jack kissed her again, lingering his lips against hers.

Allie grabbed the handle of the shopping cart, fearing she would faint. A bead of sweat trickled down the back of her neck. Jack put one hand on the cart handle and one around her waist as Allie moved the cart ahead of her.

"I need to tell you something, Jack. I want our friendship, our relationship, to be honest and…"

Jack squeezed her close and kissed her hair from the side.

Her voice dropped to a whisper. "You're not making this easy. Most of my adult life I've been in control. I started a company on my own, I bought a house, and called it living."

Jack stopped the cart. "And survived quite well alone. I can't deny you are a very successful, complete woman, Allie. Is there room in that practically perfect life for a guy and a couple of cats?" He smiled down at her and touched the end of her nose with his finger. "Hmm, so serious—there's more?"

"Yes, actually. More has a lot to do with it. I wanted more in my life. I made some decisions earlier this year about something I didn't know I even wanted until recently. Meeting you in this store has made those decisions more…complicated for me."

"Allie." He pulled her close with both hands around her waist. "I didn't mean to make your life difficult. Just different."

"Jack…" Allie felt the edges of his jacket against her chest and for a moment wanted to forget telling him anything. Screw honesty. She just wanted to be in his arms forever. She took a deep breath. "The night we met, Jack, should have been in *this* aisle of the store."

Jack stepped back from her a few inches with a quizzical look on his face. "What difference does an aisle make?" He looked around briefly, but then shook his head.

"If you'll stop for a minute and look around instead of at me, an aisle makes quite a big difference." Allie pulled away from him and dropped her eyes to the parquet floor. She tried to exhale, but her chest felt constricted with tight leather bands.

The shelves around the two of them were filled with brightly colored plastic bags of diapers and bottles of baby lotions, leading into stacks of steel bins of baby food jars.

"I don't understand, Allie." Jack frowned and touched her face with his fingers to make her look up at him. "This is the baby products aisle."

She tried to nod her head but couldn't find the strength. "I'm pregnant, Jack. I'm going to have a baby next year."

Jack blinked.

"As I told you, I've been in control of everything for myself, and I decided I wanted a baby. Well, I never thought I wanted a baby, but then I did, and it was all I could think about. I have been going through artificial insemination, and just before I met you," Allie took a deep breath, "it seems to have taken." Allie didn't know what else to say.

Jack's face was frozen in time. His jaw clenched, and Allie could see a tsunami of emotions going through his eyes: shock, anger, disbelief, trying to make sense out of her recent admission.

"Had you run into me that night in this aisle with baby powder and diapers in my cart and a jar of juice in my hand, would you still have asked me out?" Allie tried to control the panic in her voice.

"I, uh, I don't know. I don't know what to say. I don't know if it would have made a difference that night." He stared at the floor.

"I see," Allie choked out stiffly. "Maybe I should give you some time to think about it. Maybe you can let me know when you figure it out."

Jack winced at the words. She spoke softly though no one else was in the aisle. The store seemed deserted.

Allie turned and started pushing the cart out of the aisle. She couldn't remember to breathe, but she couldn't stand there looking at the confusion in his face anymore. The wheels of the cart squeaked and whined as she walked toward the back of the store.

Jack watched her walked away. He should say something, he should call her name, but nothing happened. He rubbed his hand across his forehead and stared at the printed labels with smiling infants staring back at him. Cans of formula stood like sentries on the shelf. She's pregnant? His mind blanked. Allie was farther down the aisle, and he couldn't move. What was he supposed to do? A woman with a half-filled cart came around the corner, and hesitated before asking him to move.

"I'm sorry," he mumbled, and shifted to the other side of the aisle to let her pick up the items she needed. The woman looked at him. "I'm sorry," he whispered again out loud. "I'm really sorry."

At the back of the grocery store, Allie felt the cold chill of the dairy section she had passed the second time she saw Jack. She remembered the warm flush of her face, the giddiness of their chance meeting, and picking up an icy carton of milk. The refrigeration had been a pleasure. Now she stopped and crossed her arms in front of her, trying to ward off the chill, a cold penetrating deep into her soul. She twisted her body and looked over her shoulder. The aisle behind her was empty; Jack was gone.

Chapter 16

Allie chewed on the end of a pen, rocking slowly in her chair. Her hair draped thinly over her shoulder. She didn't bother to fix it.

"Hello? Anyone home?" Gillian softly called out, knocking on the office door before walking in.

"What?"

"Look at you. You're adding ten years with all those wrinkles and creases. What could be that bad you'd sacrifice your face?" He knew, but the subject was taboo.

Allie tried to rouse enough from her depression to carry on a conversation. "I took your advice and haven't called Soozi for days."

"And for that you have to look like Albert Einstein?" Gillian wanted to hold her, she seemed fragile, breakable. *Mr. Jack hasn't called you either,* he thought.

"She hasn't called me to find out why I'm not calling her. Is she sitting home drinking herself into a slow grave? Or has she found a new best friend to replace me?"

"Get serious. You two grew up together in this godforsaken area of California; you can't duplicate that on a whim of bad emotions. I'm telling you, she'll come around in her own time." Gillian leaned against the doorjamb, crossing his legs at the ankle. He ached for his boss. *This should be the* happiest time of her life, and look at her. Pathetic.

"Everyone's gone." Allie chewed on her fingernail and rocked her office chair with renewed energy.

"You're going through vampire woman withdrawals." He winced. "Stop chewing on things, get back to work."

Gillian sighed and quickly moved back to his own desk. The subject of Jack's absence since Allie broke the pregnancy news was crowning right over the top of Soozi's silence. If Jack doesn't make a move here shortly, I'll take the bull by the horns myself. Gillian smiled wickedly, then shook his head. No, he'd promised he'd leave Jack alone. But a tasteful conversation over cognac some evening might just be the herbal remedy to turn the foolish man's head back in the right direction. Baby or no, Gillian was sure Jack was deeply in love with his boss.

Allie sat in her office and pondered Soozi's attitude and absence. Allie had the sense of Soozi's marriage grinding on essentially out of habit, a house, and a couple of children, with pension funds and retirement ahead. She was concerned there wasn't much more between the two.

She turned back to her desk, working on reading the contract file Gillian had brought in. The phone rang. A moment later, the intercom button buzzed from Gillian. The blinking light was for her. She dared not hope.

Soozi's voiced tweaked half an octave higher than normal over the phone. "Allie? Any chance we can have lunch today? I know this is rather last minute—if you're busy, I'll understand."

"Sure." Allie pretended ignorance, but her heart was racing. "What's up, sweetie?"

"I've got to get out of this house. Can you meet me at the Buffalo Inn? Maybe around one-ish. I should be able to have someone watch Zoe for a couple of hours."

Allie pumped her fist in the air—yes! "A juicy hamburger and their buffalo chips sound perfect to me. Holding out till one o'clock may be a problem. I'll have Gillian run out and get me a bagel until then."

"I've warned you before about believing in tooth fairies, ogres, and eating for two. Lay off the snacks."

Allie smiled. "Yes, Nurse Ratchet. Lunch sounds great, I'll see you there."

Allie hung up the phone and stared out the window. Her mental antenna was in full force; something was wrong at the Jones' house.

"See? I told you there was nothing to get your hair extensions in a braid about. PMS has once again passed and she's ready to be half-human again." Gillian kept working at the computer as Allie stood behind him. He didn't want to look up and blow his cover over how worried he'd been about Allie.

"Remind me to slip a Prozac into your coffee every morning. Or should I get you a bowl of milk? Meow." Allie turned on her heel and went back into the office to finish up whatever was on her desk. Her concentration, she agreed, had been mush all morning. She'd show Gillian a management thing or two.

Before she got through the door, Gillian turned slightly in his chair. "Take your umbrella with you, boss. You haven't noticed in your spaced-out condition, but it's pouring rain out."

"I would have figured it out," Allie said, "when I got wet." She smiled. Nothing was going to dampen the fact Soozi was talking to her again.

"Cute. But you wouldn't have come all the way back up here for it, you'd catch your death of cold, and you're not allowed to take Nyquil for the next five months. I'm not listening to pitiful sniffles if you get sick."

When Allie finally bustled out of the office for her lunch date, with umbrella firmly in hand, Gillian stared at the phone on his desk. This Jack thing needed a teensy nudge from someone who knew the main characters involved. A lunch meeting between the two men sounded perfect; Allie would be gone for at least two hours, making up over gawd knows what with Soozi. Jack would probably listen best over food and a bottle of beer about his boss and her pediatric dreams.

Gillian pulled out a business card and started pressing the numbers into the phone. Your precious cavalry to the rescue, my dear. Mr. Jack needs to know the whole score of this production.

The hostess led the two women to a table up on the second floor, nestled away in a corner of the darkened restaurant. They quickly placed identical lunch orders and chased the waitress away.

"Okay, spill it. I've had really weird vibes from you lately. Not to mention I haven't heard from you forever. What's going on?"

Her friend took a deep breath. "I've met another man," Soozi whispered with her head down.

"Excuse me? What other man, when did you meet another man? What are you talking about?" Allie hissed. She rubbed her hand roughly through her hair. Her stomach twisted with tension. How did this happen? Allie tried not to panic.

"I met him at the mall," Soozi forced out. "Zoe and I were window shopping and this guy comes up behind me with Zoe's bottle in his hands. He tells me she dropped it, and when I went to take it away from him, he didn't let go right away."

"Soozi, this is ridiculous. You're married. To Randy. Remember him? Husband, wedding vows out in the backyard, lots of people and family standing around, not too many happy, but hey. I can't believe this; I *don't* believe it."

"Look. He stood there beside me with Zoe's bottle and this great smile on his face. Zoe's asleep, so when he asked if I wanted to get a cup of coffee, I couldn't resist. A strange, good-looking man asked me to get a cup of coffee in the middle of the day. I melted. Hundreds of people were around us—it's not like he was dragging me off or something to rape me."

"Did anyone see you go off with this guy? Do you know how dangerous that was in itself? What if Randy's mother had been there? She's not real fond of you; she would have used this against you for years. Does she have a case? What did you do with this guy?" Allie tried to breathe.

"We had coffee. You did it a few months ago with a strange guy, too, if you remember. I was happy for you."

"I'm not married. In case you've forgotten, I can do that sort of thing."

"Details. We just talked, for almost an hour. Then Zoe woke up and I had to go. He asked if we could meet there again the next day."

The waitress came back with their drinks, and Allie almost screamed out loud. She had been concentrating so strongly on Soozi's bizarre story, she hadn't noticed the waitress come up with a tray in her hands.

"Tell me you didn't go back?"

"I can't."

"You didn't."

"More than once." Soozi sipped slowly at her drink. Her hands were shaking as she returned the glass to the table.

"I don't know what to say." Allie held her glass but couldn't trust lifting it to her mouth without spilling. "What was so fascinating about this guy you would jeopardize your marriage to Randy?"

"I don't know. He's cute. He thought I had something worthwhile to say. Someone paid attention to my thoughts, my dreams. You can't imagine what that feels like after years of Randy sitting there with a crossword puzzle in front of him night after night, and the television blaring over the kids."

Allie reached over and playfully tapped Soozi on the back of her hand. "Excuse me? I have a date once a year, maybe, and you have the unmitigated nerve to tell me I don't know what it's like not to have someone of the opposite sex listen to you? You've had Randy for all these years, I've had no one, and you're whining about being lonely?"

"I knew you wouldn't understand."

"Understand what?" Allie smacked her hand on the table, ignoring the stares of the other customers. "You're right, I don't understand. Am I supposed to believe this is midlife crisis number nine hundred and two or what?"

"T—"

"Don't you dare give this man a name." Allie childishly threw her hands over her ears. "Don't you civilize this thing by making him human. No."

"Civilize what thing? We just talked, we didn't screw around. He's supportive, he likes me. Why are you defending Randy? What about my needs? You are so caught up in this baby thing, you never think about me at all. I talked about me during our times, not children, not utility bills. Me, doing something for me, like going back to school for my master's."

"Back to school? You only wanted to get an M.R.S. degree from college. You got Randy and a diploma, mission accomplished."

"This is different, Al, you've got to listen. I'm lost—I don't know what I want to be when I grow up. I always wanted to be like you, and now you're having a baby and being more like me. It's all crazy."

"Is that a bad thing? Did I miss something during the station break? All my life, people have been telling me to be more like Soozi, shoving it down my throat. Why can't you be like Soozi, quiet like Soozi, a good girl like Soozi. Saint Soozi of the sandbox. Now you're complaining because I'm too much like you, whatever that is. I'm so confused." Allie laid her head in her hands.

"Who told you to be like me?" The news surprised Soozi.

"Everybody. Aunt Kitty mostly, but I think there were even a few teachers in elementary school that slapped me with your name a couple times. Settle down, be like your friend Soozi."

"I was just a kid. How did I know you were taking a lot of heat about me? It would have occurred to a seven-year-old? You never said anything. I idolized you, Al. You and those silly plays you were forever putting on in the backyard." Soozi looked away from Allie. "I knew someday you were going to be rich and famous, and I would be stuck here in this valley, in a dumb old tract house with a bunch of smelly kids." Soozi carefully wiped a tear from her eye, trying not to smear her makeup.

"Hey, your kids smell wonderful. You never let them get dirty." Allie tried to make her smile.

"I wanted to be somebody, too, back then. I wanted to find a cure for cancer. Life is what happens when you're looking the other way, though. Then Lenny came along as my thesis and Zoe became my doctorate. Now I make sure their shoes match and hope they grow up to find the cure for AIDS."

"What is this all about, really? If you're unhappy with your life, change it. If you want to go back to school, go. You're a big girl. But is that all that happened? Soozi, you're making me nuts. You've been in a blue funk for months. You practically chew my head off when we talk. Now you've met a man, and you're telling me he wants you to go back to college to get your master's. And then what? Support this masher in his old age? Desert your kids?"

"Al, settle down. It's okay. I know it wasn't the kosher thing to do, but whatever it was, I loved every minute of it. I felt alive for the first time in a long time." Soozi searched Allie's face. "I've been so pissed about everything lately. We met over coffee, Allie, not over bedsheets. We sat at the mall in the food court in plain sight, for God's sake. We shared life stories, sitting together at a small Formica table, sometimes holding hands. He made me laugh, and it felt like a shot of adrenaline.

"I've been floundering, lost in a sea of perfect suburban boredom. You don't understand. Even now you're off on a new adventure yourself, having a baby. He helped me see I want more out of life, to go back to school and be something more than a wife and a mother. I want to do something with my life, for me."

Allie leaned back as the food baskets were put in front of them. Allie's appetite had diminished in the wake of Soozi's outburst. Allie shuddered. How could Soozi have been so unhappy all this time without saying something? Hadn't they always shared everything together? This baby has caused more ripples in the pond than Allie ever could have imagined, and it was not even born yet.

"I don't know how to tell Randy about going back to school. He'll freak. He'll have to help out with the kids a helluva lot more than he does. No more two-hour crossword puzzles and sitting in the john three times a day."

"If he doesn't hurt himself jumping off the couch to help sharpen your pencils. The man is crazy about you, he's just forgotten to tell you. Could be a pretty big turn-on to the guy, though, sleeping with a college coed again." Allie finally took a drink of her iced tea, her hands steady again. She winked at her best friend across the table.

Soozi laughed in spite of herself. "What about the kids? What do I do with them? Stuff 'em in my locker during the day?"

"Have you thought of putting Zoe into the same day care school with Lenny? They probably have a discount for multiple kids, like car insurance. You know Zoe would love it. Girl, there could be some terrific bennies from this. Maybe they'll potty train her for you." Allie watched Soozi take a healthy bite from her burger. Hers lay cold in front of her; how can lives get so complicated?

"What about the guy?" Allie demanded softly of her best friend, who had danced foolishly close to cheating on her husband.

"He's gone. It's over. Fini."

The waitress stopped and asked how everything was going. Allie sighed with frustration and waved her off. Who are these people who keep interrupting? This is worse than commercials on late night television.

"What do you mean he's gone? He vanished, just like that? He comes into your life, and then disappears?"

"He was only here on a business trip from Cincinnati. His company flew him home yesterday once his project was finished, and I think I miss him." Soozi's face dropped into her hands. Allie passed her napkin over to her friend. Tears stained the paper, as Soozi's shoulders shook from crying.

"You didn't call me about this until after he'd left?" Allie threw one of her chips across the table at Soozi's bent head.

Soozi nodded with the tears still flowing into the napkin against her face.

"I don't understand you, Soozi. You hold my hand through the artificial insemination during the day, but when I'd call at night, you'd growl at me. Don't you know how concerned I've been about you? I was afraid you were becoming an alcoholic. I haven't been worth shit at the office stressing about you, and trust me, Gillian has let me know it."

"You've been busy with work and getting pregnant. Then Jack came along and I thought I'd die from jealousy. You had it all." Soozi blew her nose, and looked around for another napkin. "When I met Thomas I didn't want to share him with you."

Allie stared at her with an open mouth.

"Not like you were the enemy, but you belonged in the same world with Randy and the kids. I used the alcohol to numb the frustration, even before Thomas. I scared myself a few times, Allie."

"It's going to be all right." Allie tried to convince herself. "You want to go back to college, you go back. Put both kids in preschool, and hand Randy a honey-do list. But, please, get over this mall masher guy. He's going to do nothing but rip your heart out and make you nuts."

"Spoken like the Dear Abby of romance you aren't. Since when did you get enough experience to pass out advice? And while we're on the subject, how's Jack?"

"I don't know. He hasn't called since I told him about the baby. Nothing. It's probably over." Allie's eyes started to leak. "What am I going to do? I'm in love with him, Sooz. He's gone."

"He's a fool if he lets you get away. You're a single mother who just doesn't need a babysitter yet when you go on a date." Soozi tried a feeble joke. "I'm sorry I didn't tell you about Thomas sooner. I wanted something special for me. Your life was heading toward happily ever after."

216

"I can't blame Jack for running. It's a pretty big shock. I knew this would happen. I mean I didn't know I was going to meet Jack or anything." Allie wiped her face and picked up her hamburger for something to do. "Who would have thought."

"Take a bite, give the baby some nourishment." Soozi nibbled at one of the chips from her basket. "I'm not too hungry myself anymore."

"Men. You'd think God would have planted a warning label on their foreheads or something. Warning: early edition model, socialize at your own risk; management cannot be held responsible." Allie bit into the sandwich, the famous grilled flavor made her mouth water.

"Hey, any chance of you playing hooky? Let's go shopping. I can call the babysitter and see if she'll watch Zoe a little longer. You get something for the baby, and I'll get a new outfit for school."

"Gillian will gladly take over the office solo; he's been pestering me about not carrying my weight. Hey, even *he* was worried about you."

"No! The Ken Doll has a soft side to him?"

"Just don't tell him I told you, or I'll fill him in about Thomas and you'll never hear the end of it."

Soozi threw up her hands in surrender. "I'll leave him alone."

Each of them grabbed their cell phones.

Gillian punched a button on the phone. "Novel Software, may I help you?"

"Gillian, it's Allie. I'm taking the rest of the afternoon off. Soozi and I are off to do some major shopping."

"I take it you two have kissed and made up?"

"Yeah. And thank you for your concern. You're getting a little pompous for your thong. So, can I go, Mother?"

"You might as well. You're useless to me here. At least one of us should get some work done." Gillian leaned back in his chair and propped his feet on the desk. The delicious wine at his own lunch with a certain male someone had relaxed his demeanor. "Tell the wicked witch of bad make-up hi for me." Gillian could afford to show a little extra generosity to Soozi. Let her try to top this one. Gillian marveled at his own brilliance.

"You're being awfully charitable. Should I be concerned about leaving you alone with my company?" asked Allie.

"Go, play. Frolic and be merry. All this kingdom will be here tomorrow for you," Gillian assured her with a laugh.

"Okay. Thanks, Gillian, see you in the morning."

Chapter 17

"Enough wet stuff, this rain is getting on my nerves." Soozi shouted at the dark sky as she flipped her umbrella up over her head. "Who said it never rains in Southern California? That's why we have sprinklers everywhere, stupid weather."

"It's just rain, girl, granted a drenching rain. You won't melt, trust me on this one." Allie reached over with her free hand and awkwardly gave her friend a hug good-bye, clashing the two umbrellas together above them.

"Nope, I was a very wet birth for my mother."

Allie felt lighter in spirit than she had for days as the two of them walked toward their cars. Soozi's confessions released a ten-ton brick from her shoulders. Sooz promised it was just a Fabio phase of fantasy.

"Hey, model for Randy tonight after the kids go to bed—one of those cute school outfits you bought." Allie teased her friend.

"You want me to come out in knee socks and pigtails for him? I don't think so. But I do love the wardrobe. I never thought buying school clothes could be fun." Soozi had splurged and bought a mix and match quartet of casual wear for the upcoming winter quarter at school.

"A New Year, a new you."

"Are you wearing your new dress tomorrow?"

"I don't want to frighten Gillian." Allie had bought her first official maternity dress, a darling jumper in red plaid and black accents with a black T-shirt to wear underneath.

"He'll probably pout because I got to pick out the first outfit, and I love you for that. But you know with his incredible tastes, you'll be the best-dressed expectant woman in Southern California."

"I hope the sitter doesn't mind we're late." Allie opened her car door and threw her purse and sacks onto the passenger's seat.

"Nah, Randy should be home already. I'll call you in the morning," Soozi threw back as she put her keys into the car door lock.

Allie and Soozi followed each other out of the mall's parking lot and into the sluggish evening traffic. Two soggy stoplights up the crowded boulevard and they entered the freeway heading east behind one another. Their windshield wipers swiped across wet glass. Allie had hers on high, a fast Jimmy Buffett staccato, as she drove. The last of the rush hour traffic glowed around them.

Soozi waited until they merged onto the highway then passed her up, blinking her headlights. They followed each other playing cat and mouse in traffic for a few miles through the downpour on the familiar route.

Allie punched at her dashboard CD player with her finger, switching Buffett tracks. Love songs didn't do a thing without Jack around. "Don't go there," she mumbled to herself. Don't start a pity party for yourself after the good news of getting Soozi back. One crisis at a time is all you can handle. Allie's heart squeezed with a twinge of sadness. She found a favorite song and cranked up the volume, drowning out the rush of water under her car and the vision of Jack from her heart. Slapping to the beat on her steering wheel with one hand, she came around Soozi's car once more.

Allie glanced in her rear view mirror as Soozi started her right blinker to move into the transition ramp for the I-10 freeway. This is where they parted directions.

"'Bye, sweetie," Allie whispered out loud in the car. "Good luck tonight with Randy." Allie blew a kiss to the mirror before she looked back at the night's traffic in her own wet lane.

A huge explosion behind her rocked the car. She gripped her steering wheel with both hands, trying to stay in her lane, as the body of the car moved hard with gusts of wind from the deadly force. The inside of the car lit up like broad daylight as Allie heard the shrieking of brakes on wet pavement and the unforgettable screams of metal on metal. Truck horns blared like Godzilla through the night.

Allie, her foot already slammed on her brakes at the onset of the explosion, twisted the steering wheel to the right, sending her car into a nosedive off the freeway toward an emergency call box. The car smashed into a dirt embankment, and mud splattered the windshield from the force, slamming Allie's head against the side window and shattering the glass. Allie saw stars, and a blinding pain shot through her skull.

After a long minute, a blurred vision of the yellow call box appeared through the rain-soaked windshield in front of her. Her wipers still were slapping in double-time. The blinding light from the fire made her shrink inside her car, and she put her hand up to her throbbing head. The continued sound of screeching brakes seemed further back, as traffic around the inferno pileup of lives and vehicles began to stop in the oncoming traffic lanes.

Allie didn't notice the blood on her shaking hands as she forced herself out of her seat belt. I've got to get out of the car; I have to get help. Allie held onto the open car door, trying to steady her rubbery legs, then let go and stumbled her way through mud and ankle-deep puddles. Her hand trembled violently as she wrenched open the metal box and pressed the red call button inside. Holding the receiver tightly with both hands, she waited for a dispatcher of the California Highway Patrol to answer.

"There's been an accident, a multiple car accident. Listen to me, it's on the interchange of the #15 north to the westbound lanes of the #10. Get the fire department out here. Looks like a holocaust of trucks and cars and…and injuries." Allie didn't give the dispatcher a chance to respond or herself a chance to breathe.

"I said, there's been an explosion, we need the fire department and ambulances; I'm on the northbound #15. The wreckage is right behind me," Allie shouted into the receiver. "Do you hear me? We need help out here, damn it! Do something."

The roar of the fire and sporadic passing cars made it difficult to hear any response. "I need you to stay calm. Is your car out of a traffic lane? Are you on the shoulder, ma'am? I have a traffic accident located at the…" The composed voice of the female dispatcher infuriated the rain-drenched Allie.

"We need lots of ambulances. People are hurt on the transition road off the #15. Can't you hear them screaming? Are you deaf? My best friend is in there. My friend…" Allie stopped her frantic yelling into the phone and stared back at the blazing wreckage and thick, acrid smoke in front of her. Soozi's in there.

The downpour of rain blinded her eyes like a veiled curtain; parts of her hair mixed with blood plastered over one eye, making the sight more frightening and surreal. Somewhere, lost in the middle of the vicious flames of fire streaking the black sky in colors of yellow and red, was her best friend. Her hand slowly dropped to her side, the weight of the phone too much to endure. The dispatcher's voice disappeared as the cold receiver rubbed against Allie's leg. Soozi. Oh God, no. Sooz.

Allie felt the first crunching pain of a contraction come from somewhere far away. It couldn't be her body. Not now, she had to help Soozi get out of the fire. Gotta help Soozi. The twisted wreckage and carnage spread across two lanes of freeway. People were out of their cars, standing on the edges of the devastation. It was too late for anyone inside.

The next pain doubled her in half as Allie grabbed her waist. Soozi, the baby. "Somebody help me," her voice strangled in despair. "I'm losing the baby." Allie leaned against the metal pole too weak to stand alone. Her teeth chattered from the cold and fear, and she bit her lip.

Another explosion rocked the area as a gas tank from one of the involved cars blew. People shouted and scrambled, the frantic activity in front of the flames looked like toys scattering in the rain. She barely acknowledged the blast, as another wave of pain inside her started to recede.

She closed her stinging eyes against the blood and the rain flowing down her face, yet the glow from the fire came through her eyelids. A few cars flew by in the lane next to Allie, rushing away from the disaster, thanking any higher power above they weren't involved. Air from the passing cars smacked against the bedraggled woman, over and over. Allie slid heavily to the wet ground below. The paved shoulder and gravel bit into her body. A chorus of sirens blended with the faint dispatcher's words as Allie sank into darkness.

Allie tried opening her swollen eyes. She blinked once with difficulty against the florescent light overhead, and then rested from the strained effort. The rain stopped, she thought. A grogginess weighed heavily on her body and mind. I'm not wet anymore, came through as a conscious thought. She felt warm and dry, but how? Her eyelashes fluttered again and she tried to focus on her surroundings through a haze of throbbing pain in her head. Her hands lay outside a thin blanket, one arm stiff with an IV needle and bandages.

She stretched her legs with some difficulty and soreness against crisply starched sheets. "Where are my shoes?" she struggled to say out loud, in confusion. Who took my shoes? She blinked again and winced with pain. The stark painted walls with a single framed print of a boat on a lake came into view. An electric IV stand next to the bed flashed red numbers. A striped curtain hung from the ceiling surrounding one side of the bed.

I'm in a hospital? What's happened; how long have I been here? Allie sucked in her breath and grabbed at her stomach. The baby. The rubbery IV cord snagged on the sheet as she tried to feel if her stomach was any different, and she winced at the pull of the adhesive tape. She remembered contractions and cramping, bending over in the rain outside. The incessant rain, and standing on the side of a freeway in the night when the frightening pain had started. She could taste blood in her mouth as the pain had crippled her in the dark.

Allie shivered as she recounted the electric pain shooting through her while she leaned against a call box on the freeway, just as it had in her bathtub months before. She must have fainted, she had no memory of getting here. Tears started trickling down her face before the racking sobs began.

The wooden door to Allie's room opened slowly. A bouquet of brightly colored flowers came around the edge first. The bearer of the flowers stepped around the door into the semi-private room and carefully placed the vase on Allie's table.

"Jack," she said, staring at him. Sobs caught in her throat as she tried to speak. "What are you doing here? How…how did you know I was here?" she whispered. Her mouth felt dry, yet her eyes kept filling with tears, spilling over and soaking the top of her hospital gown. "The baby's gone. I was on the freeway, and contractions started…" Allie's voice trailed into a heart-wrenching scream.

"Shh. It's okay. You're going to be okay." He carefully sat on the edge of her bed and leaned over to brush a strand of hair off her forehead, away from blood-stained bandages. The blue of his eyes deepened as he stared hard into hers. He stared at every inch of her bruised face, ensuring himself she was all right. "You gave us all quite a scare last night." His fingers traced along the edge of her wounds, ignoring the plea in her eyes. He blinked back his own tears with effort.

Tears gushed unchecked down her cheeks, blinding her view to his concerned face. "I don't know, I guess I passed out." She tightened her arm across her waist. Everything inside her was gone. She'd miscarried. A groan from the darkest corners of her soul escaped through her lips as she tried to breathe between the sobs.

"Allie," his soft breath saying her name caressed her mouth as his rough hand wiped against the tears on her cheek. "Listen to me, listen."

Her head pounded as if sledgehammers were beating the sides of her face. She tried sinking deeper into her pillows, to escape the torture. She couldn't hear Jack through the pit of her grief.

"Allie, you didn't lose the baby," Jack's voice became sharper, trying to penetrate the veil of anguish in front of him. "You smashed the door window with the side of your head. You've been out for quite a while." Jack pushed his words to get her attention. "But you're okay, and the baby's going to be okay. The doctor says you'll be fine, he wants you to stay here for observation and rest." His eyes took on a somber cast.

Allie tried to take a deep breath, her body shivering. What was Jack saying? She grabbed his hand still touching her face, clutching it with a force surprising them both.

Jack laughed softly at her reaction as he tried to ease her crippling grip on his fingers. "Yes. I spoke with the doctor myself a couple times since they brought you in. And if it wasn't, we'd make more babies." His eyes searched for a response, drinking in all of her.

"What?" The throbbing of her head came faster as her heart reacted to his words. Her mind had yet to catch up to the conversation.

"I've been a fool, Allie. I let my male ego block everything," Jack continued. "Walking out on you that night was the stupidest thing I've ever done.

I got scared and just plain bolted." He tucked his head down. His brown hair fell forward, shielding his face from her view. "So many times I wanted to pick up the phone, but I didn't know what to say. I thought the worst when I heard about the accident. That it would be too late, and I might have lost you forever."

Allie wiped her runny nose with the back of her hand, without moving more than she had to.

"I love you, Alissa. Would I have introduced myself if your cart was filled with baby formula? I don't know, my hindsight is pretty nearsighted. But I know I love you, and I want to be a part of your life." The man changed positions carefully, trying to avoid the IV tube as he moved closer to her.

"Look, I know this isn't the best time or place to talk about this, but I've been without you too long. Not being able to touch you, I can't be responsible for my actions." He bowed his head. "I'm not good at speech making, Allie. I'm probably botching this whole male apology routine."

He shifted his weight on the bed, bracing himself on one arm across her body. "You didn't lose the baby, and I'm glad." He took a short breath, wishing he could erase the baffled look on her face. "And we can practice for the next baby, Allie. If you want to, I mean." Jack reached over and caressed her cheek with his fingertips.

"The next baby?" she whispered disorientated, trying to take in his ramblings. The look in Jack's eyes sent a shiver of excitement through her numb body. "I'm still pregnant? I didn't lose the baby?"

"Poor Allie. This is too much for you right now. Yes, you're still pregnant, sweetheart." Jack leaned in and pecked her dry lips with his own before he spilled the rest of his thoughts. "Maybe the little blanket hugger you're carrying wouldn't mind a dad, and he's going to want a brother or sister someday. If you'll have me, I want you both to be happy. Please let me try." Jack tried to smile through his own nervousness. Breathing became difficult; the room seemed stuffy and closed in.

"You're not upset with me? It could be our baby?"

"What kind of drugs are they giving you? I'm trying to tell you in my own demented way that I've fallen in love with you, and it's a package deal." He closed his eyes briefly. "Allie, I love you—if you want to be a mom with all your heart, who would deny that rug crawler a practically perfect parent?" Jack's voice cracked with emotion.

He leaned in closer, and Allie noticed he hadn't shaved in a while. His ruddy complexion now held the shadows of waiting around the hospital for hours. Allie tried to stay focused on Jack through the blurred vision of drugs and confusion. Her heart felt as if it would break through her chest from pounding so hard.

"Why don't we get married when they let you out of this place?" He tenderly kissed her parched lips. When he pulled away, fresh tears were running down her cheeks. "Hey, I thought you'd be happy."

"I feel like I'm on some kind of roller-coaster, and I don't know when I'm supposed to get off." Allie's hands covered her face, and muffled the sobs. "I'm so confused. I can't believe you want to marry me," came out in a pitiful whine.

"Whoa, the dam's breaking. I'm sorry. Here, here's a box of tissue. Geesh, I've had a lot more time to think about this, I guess. It's all kind of sudden for you. I'm such a dunce." Jack scrambled to give her a box of Kleenex off her side table, slapping his forehead with his hand. "You cry for a while, and I'll come back with a Big Mac or something."

Jack ran his hand down her tangled hair, then nervously through his own. "Let the waterworks go, kid, you've been through a hell of a lot and a good cry will do you good. I shouldn't have said so much yet."

Allie tried to stop the flood; she wanted to tell him she loved him, too. Yet, it was all too much. Finding out she was still pregnant was one thing, but Jack's sweet proposal sent her sobbing over the hysterical edge.

Jack started to move away from the hospital bed, tripping over his big feet in the attempt. "I'm sorry for just dumping my feelings out like this." Jack leaned back toward her, he couldn't make up his mind to leave or to stay. "Allie, I love you."

The sudden moment of silence between them didn't last but a split second. Sheer terror painted across her bandaged face as she dropped her hands. "Oh, Jack, the explosion. Soozi. I remember, I remember everything. Oh, my God, Soozi's dead."

Chapter 18

Allie's voice crescendoed to a scream, and she started hyperventilating in the hospital bed. "Jack, Soozi…horrible car accident on the freeway…fire," her voice echoed loudly in the room. She choked as her body started to vomit from the nightmare of the memory. Her face drained of what little color was left. "She's dead, Jack. I saw. Soozi's dead!"

"Allie…" Frightened, Jack rushed quickly back to the bed and took her stiff shoulders roughly in his hands. "Allie, don't."

"Allie, don't what? What did I miss?" Soozi barged through the door in a hospital-issued wheelchair with Randy pushing from behind. Her hair stuck out in odd angles, spots of dried blood in it, giving her a freakish, adolescent look. Her left arm, molded in white plaster, bent across her chest, and various bandages spotted the rest of her.

Allie screamed in terror and dug her fingernails deep into Jack's arms. She looked at him, quickly over at Soozi, then back to Jack's face. He nodded slowly, unsure if he should breathe or not to keep her from ripping the flesh off his upper arms. "She's okay, she made it through the crash. I thought you knew, babe. I'm so sorry," Jack forced his voice out in a soothing whisper, like trying to calm a frightened pit bull.

"Thanks for the warm welcome, girlfriend." Soozi waved her hand at

Randy to push her closer to the bed. "I threatened my nurse with bodily harm if she didn't let me come see you just now, and this is how you react? Ask Randy how I fought to come here, didn't I, love? I knew you'd be worried about me, but really, girl. Get a grip, this is a hospital. You're scaring the other patients."

"Uh, she didn't know you survived the crash," Jack explained to both Allie and Soozi at the same time, afraid he was going to lose whole patches of skin in the vice grip.

"Oh. Surprise! Thank goodness for heavy-duty suspension in that green tank of mine. I got knocked out of the way of the worst of it. Can you believe it?" Soozi tried to scratch her nose around a thick bandage with little success.

"One minute I'm changing lanes and like the next this person in a red pickup truck just rams the side of my car with a huge heave-ho, throwing me far enough over so I was out of the way of the explosion. Yet, when I talked to a highway patrolman, this cute guy waiting with me for my turn with the paramedics, there was no red truck involved in the accident. No one remembers seeing a red vehicle of any kind around there. Seems my guardian angel drives a pickup. Can you believe it?"

Allie released her hold on Jack and he rubbed the sore spots, hoping he was out of harm's reach. "Sooz, you look like hell, and I can't think right now of when you've looked lovelier." Allie broke eye contact with her best friend only to blow her nose. She tried to take a deep breath, and didn't know whether to laugh or cry. Soozi was alive. She looked back at her bedraggled friend, and put her hand over her mouth. Soozi. The waterworks started all over again, she couldn't help it.

Jack realized it was safe to move again, and took advantage. "And Jack wants to marry this pregnant angel as soon as they release her from here, and live happily ever after." Jack tilted his head. "I think she said yes, but I'm not sure, come to think of it."

Soozi squealed in delight. "That's terrific—I am so happy for you! Ow, ow, I think this excitement is giving me more of a headache than I already had." Soozi reached with her hand toward her bandaged skull. "If you two love birds will excuse me, I'm going back to my room and hang out for a while with a pain shot. I don't know that I was ready for quite all this. I just wanted to come and see how you were doing."

Soozi took some shallow breaths. "It's going to be okay, Allie. We're going to make it even under these crazy circumstances. I'll see you tomorrow sometime." She carefully turned in the seat of the wheelchair to look behind her. "Back, Randy. Jack, take care of that girl, would you?"

"My pleasure," Jack said. He reached down to the wheelchair and planted a kiss on Soozi's bandaged cheek. He looked straight into her clear eyes. "I will take care of her for you forever," he promised. "You get yourself all better, too, Aunt Soozi. We'll need you for babysitting, you know."

Randy reached over and patted Jack's shoulder before he started to maneuver the wheelchair back through the room door. A nurse held open the door and bustled in after them. She stared at Allie's swollen eyes.

"I think visiting hours are over," Jack whispered.

Allie nodded, and wiggled her fingers at him.

"I'll be back later," he said, then noticed the glaring eyes of the nurse. "Uh, tomorrow." Jack rushed out the door.

The next morning, the door to Allie's room swung open and in walked Aunt Kitty. How long had it been since she'd seen her? A wave of guilt washed over her. They hadn't managed to coordinate their calendars together after the Oak Glen trip, and she blamed herself. Allie tried to conceal her surprise at how old and shrunken her aunt seemed, slowly coming into her room. The tip of a black cane tapped on the hospital's tile floor with purpose as she walked directly toward the bed.

"Aunt Kitty, how did you know I was here? How did you get here?" Allie reached her hands out to her favorite relative, grasping the warm, thin-skinned hands of her aunt.

"They showed this terrible, terrible accident on the freeway over there in your area on the eleven o'clock news, and there was a shot of paramedics working on someone on the shoulder near an emergency telephone deal, you know, off to the side. It looked just like your car in the distance. I called your house after that, sweetie, and there was no answer. I got worried.

"I started calling hospitals when you didn't pick up the phone." She moved a chair from the side wall of the room closer to the bed. Her arms strained at the effort of dragging the single chair.

"I almost lost the baby, Auntie." Allie's eyes reddened at the memory. "I couldn't hang on, and I thought Soozi was dead." Allie broke into fresh sobs despite her best efforts. She reached over to the side table and grabbed a handful of tissue.

"Hush now." Aunt Kitty patted Allie on the closest leg. "Nature takes care of what it wants to, sweetie. You can't argue with forces stronger than us about what's to be. I'm glad they decided to spare the baby."

Aunt Kitty continued, still patting her niece's leg in an absent-minded way, "I never got to have any children of my own. Lord didn't see fit to grace me with any. You were the closest thing to heaven I got."

"You were always there for me," Allie whispered.

"So was your mama, child. My sister was so proud of you with all them plays you wrote and put on with all them neighbor kids. What a pistol you were in them days. You gave me more trouble with that artistic temper of yours." The aunt chuckled at the memories. She bent her head, coughing, drawing a lace-edged handkerchief to her face. The harsh racking motion shook her fragile body.

Her mom proud of her? Allie blew her nose, and hiccupped back a sob. "They locked themselves away with their work, and I thought I was a bother to them, a thorn in the side of their careers. A freak oops of nature interfering in their life together."

"What's the matter with you? You were their child." Aunt Kitty stared hard at her niece. "Maybe they didn't plan you like so many people do nowadays, especially you with this idea of do-it-yourself pregnancy. But they loved you, thought you were the cutest thing to hit this valley."

"You were the one who took care of me, Aunt Kitty."

"While your folks worked and all. That's what people did, child. Their work and sacrifices were how they loved their children. I could see the look on your mama's face when she'd be sitting on a chair in the backyard watching one of your plays. It shined, Allie, it shined watching her baby."

A new wave of sadness broke loose. Allie brought the fistful of tissues to her face and cried for the emptiness. All these years she thought she wasn't wanted by the two people most important in her life. An accident of birth only tolerated, and now her aunt was handing her the knowledge to soothe her wounded heart.

"Your mama always carried a picture of you somewhere close by wherever she went, Alissa. She had a couple snapshots in her briefcase, in her purse, just about all over. She never left without you keen to her heart. Don't you remember me always about with that Kodak camera? Most of your life is photographed; I made sure."

"Obsessed is more like it. You followed me everywhere with that dang thing." Allie blew her nose.

"I never had much, growing up. Our mama raised us to work hard and live later, though she never told us when later was. Times were hard for everyone and you didn't give fate a chance to send you to the poorhouse. Your mama did what she knew how in raising you. We never had any of this touchy-feely stuff in our house. By the time you finished your chores, you were too tired to wonder about anything."

Aunt Kitty opened her handkerchief. "I still miss my own mama. It's been nigh-on forty years, I guess. She died shortly after you were born, though she got to hold her grandbaby in her arms. She's the one that named you. Your parents couldn't agree on a name for you, and here comes your grandmother just as strong and proud as always. She held you tight and looked down in those dark eyes of yours and said you were Alissa Marie."

"I've never heard that story, Auntie. I didn't even know Grammy saw me before she passed away." Allie sighed deeper into the hospital pillows. She rocked her head from side to side, overwhelmed with the family sagas.

"You never asked. You caught the work bug from your mama. Always had your nose in some book or working on a class report yourself after a while. You took to school like a duck to water. I guess there's a lot you don't know, seeing as how your parents were taken away sudden like. I'm sure your mama would have shared stories, you getting pregnant and all."

"It's strange thinking she would be a grandmother. You'll be the baby's grand aunt," Allie said with a smile.

"Kids ain't the be-all and the end-all of life, sugar. They do make the world a little sweeter to live in, and yet they can break your heart six ways to Sunday, too. But don't you go crawling under some rock if it don't happen the way you think it oughta." Aunt Kitty sat up straighter in her chair, dabbing her nose with the tissue.

"Guess what, Auntie?" Allie wiped her face with clean tissues. "The baby's going to have a daddy." Allie squeaked out the good news.

"It had better be that Jack fellow you're always mooning over, or I'll be sorely disappointed in my old age."

"Oh, Auntie, of course it's Jack." She smiled at the thought of him. "He wants to get married as soon as I get out of here." Her bottom lip trembled and the tears threatened to overflow again. She couldn't believe his love for both herself and the baby.

"Gracious goodness. A wedding and a baby." Aunt Kitty noticed the tears welling up in Allie's eyes again and felt it was time to leave. "Your parents would be proud, you count on it. You best get lots of rest now, like the doctors say.

"Mrs. Johnson's waiting to take me home, so I'd best get back down to the lobby. You mind them nurses, you got a baby to take care of, and that Jack fella." She struggled to her feet and, in a slow, shuffling gait, pushed the chair slowly back across the floor to where she'd found it.

"Don't go laying there feeling sorry for yourself. You do what the doctor tells you, and call me when he lets you come home. I can stay with you for a while, if you want." She leaned on her cane near the bed.

"Thank you, Aunt Kitty. I'll call you as soon as the doctor lets me know anything." Allie opened her arms for a hug. Her aunt's body felt like brittle toothpicks under the polyester pantsuit. "Thank you for letting me know about Mom."

"Don't start up the leaky faucets again. You just rest up." Aunt Kitty bent over for one last kiss on Allie's cheek and was gone.

Allie's head throbbed from the onslaught of tears. She felt drained and at peace. A dry well somewhere inside her heart had filled with fresh rain. She thought about turning on the overhead television to check out some of the soap operas the rest of the group always nagged her about. She sighed loudly and blew her nose again. *I don't even know if the soaps are on.*

Before she could reach over and press the button on her panel for the television, the room door opened a few inches, followed by a clunk. Another few inches wider, and another clunk. Allie sat up in the bed, curious.

Soozi finally pushed the wheelchair through the door by herself. "Ta da. Hey, girlfriend. How do you like my new wheels? I couldn't find a floor nurse, so I did it by myself. I'm not too good driving this stupid thing one-handed, though. They'll never notice the dents I put in the door."

Allie hiccupped a grateful laugh and clapped her hands together for her friend's efforts. "I wondered what was bouncing off the door; you're dangerous with that thing, woman. You sure you should be driving so soon?"

"Hey, get in a car accident, get right back behind the wheel, or in this case, pushing the wheels. Whatever." Soozi took several difficult tries maneuvering the wheelchair closer to Allie's hospital bed.

"Look, I got my hair washed this morning. God, how one simple act can make you feel good." Soozi fluffed her short hair with her good hand. "Not as good as Total Look, but it'll do. Still look pretty beat-up around the edges though, don't I?" Soozi fussed with the variety of bandages and gauze on her body. A tug here, a pat there.

Allie pressed a few buttons on the control panel and moved the hospital bed lower, closer to her banged and bruised best friend. "Well, yeah, you do. But I'm not complaining." Touching her own bandaged head carefully, she raised the head of the bed up further and got herself more comfortable.

"Hey, I got a basket of flowers from Gillian this morning. Can you beat that?" Soozi looked around the room and snickered. "Oh, I guess you can. The Easter Bunny's been here, too. Geez, it looks like the Rose Parade in here."

Allie ignored her. "Did you see Aunt Kitty in the hallway? She just left."

"No, I would have loved to see the old sweetheart. How's she doing?" Soozi winced with pain. "Excitement isn't allowed quite yet under all these bandages."

Allie winced with her. "Pretty good, compared to you. She looks so frail I was almost afraid to hug her. She's going to stay with me for a while after I get out of here, though I don't know who'll be taking care of whom. You should bring the kids over and visit. She'd love to see them." Her voice trailed off as she played with the tightly-stitched edge of the hospital blanket. This was the first time they had been alone since the accident.

Allie's vision blurred in an all-too-familiar wave, and her nose began to run as the tears overflowed quietly down her face. Soozi tried to avoid looking at her friend, but she too started to crumble. "I thought I'd lost you forever—the explosion was deafening. My whole car shook, and I thought you were in the middle of it," Allie tried to hold back the sobs, but they refused to retreat once the dam cracked again.

"I know. I couldn't believe it was happening, and all I could think of was Randy and the kids waiting for me." She put her head in her free hand. "My kids are my life, Allie. I love them so much. Maybe I shouldn't be thinking about going back to school. Maybe I'm being selfish. Maybe this accident is trying to tell me something." She wiped the back of her hand across her face, smearing the tears.

Allie reached over and handed her the box of Kleenex, after taking a handful for herself. "Don't start thinking like that. The accident has nothing to do with you wanting your master's. That's ridiculous. Someday the kids will be older and off doing their own things, and where will you be? Lenny won't make you feel guilty because you're going back to school, in fact the two of you can do homework together in the evenings."

"Allie, he's in preschool. I don't think he'll have any major homework for a while." Soozi chuckled and blew her nose.

"Let him pretend he's doing homework with you; give him some notebook paper and a pencil while you're studying. Let him be like Mama. Zoe, too. Look how fast she'll probably pick up the alphabet and numbers. Lenny can teach and work with his baby sister. See?" Allie got into the role of storyteller. "Randy gets to bed down a hot and bothered coed and the kids get new educational entertainment that's not on television or a computer. Sounds like a win-win situation." Allie stretched her leg under the hospital covers. She laid a protective arm over her barely rounded stomach. "Someday, Lenny and Zoe can play school with mine, too." The last part came out in a hoarse whisper.

"I'm so glad you didn't lose the baby, Allie. I don't think I could have forgiven myself if you had." Soozi blew her nose again as the tears kept leaking down her face.

"It wasn't your fault. Pouring rain, trucks and cars on a slick freeway—who knows what triggered the whole thing."

"But if I hadn't insisted we go shopping after lunch, you would have been safe in your office and I would have been chasing Zoe somewhere in the house. None of this would have..."

"There you are," a large nurse barreled into Allie's room, interrupting the two of them. "We've been looking for you, you have a date in x-ray." The nurse grabbed the handles of the wheelchair with briskness and turned Soozi around, ignoring the sniffling women.

"Guess this is good-bye. Talk to you later." Soozi waved her handful of tissues toward the bed as the nurse held the door open and expertly pushed the chair through the opening.

Only Soozi gets herself into trouble wherever she goes, even in a hospital. Allie played with the bed controls, trying for a comfortable spot. The doctor had said she would probably go home tomorrow, but her blood pressure had remained fairly high through the night, which caused him some concern. Allie knew between the accident and a proposal from a certain gentleman, she was surprised she wasn't bouncing off the walls.

The cabinets under the window along the side wall of her room created a shelf that looked like a florist shop. Two very large arrangements had been delivered late this morning from Gillian, after a near-hysterical phone call early in the morning to convince himself she was all right.

He had entered the dark office this morning, thinking maybe she had actually overslept. Then after getting her answering machine at home twice within an hour, panic set in. Gillian immediately called Soozi's house, and Randy had filled him in on the night's gruesome details.

"Gillian, I'm fine, really, just bruised here and there. The baby's going to be fine. The doctor wants me to take it easy for a while. I have a few stitches on my head, but nothing serious."

"You and Soozi are walking magnets for disaster. I can't believe she survived the accident. I see it made all the morning headlines, now that I've taken time to open the paper. Thank God I didn't do that first thing this morning. I'd have fainted away, alone in here."

"Calm down, breathe. It's over."

"For you, maybe. You've had all night; this is a brand new nightmare for me." Gillian took a sip of coffee to soothe his nerves. "You both could have been killed."

"I'm sorry. You're right. Look, I don't think there's anything on my calendar for today. Do what you have to, and then close up shop and take the rest of the day off."

"Excuse me? I was talking to Allie Thompson a minute ago, operator, who's this?" Gillian mocked concern.

"Gillian."

"That must have been a nasty bump on the head, the boss saying take the rest of the day off? With pay, I'm sure you meant to say. I'll take care of the office, you take care of you. And try to do a better job of it than you have lately. You're getting frightful bags under your eyes."

"Thanks a bunch, flattery will get you nowhere. Stay out of my high heels while I'm gone. You stretch them out of shape."

"Party pooper."

"Before you hang up, I have a delicious piece of news that will brighten your day." Allie dangled the hint like a carrot.

"You're pregnant." Gillian laughed at his own warped sense of humor.

"That's pitiful. When I came to last night, Jack came to see me."

"The cat man turned up at the hospital? I knew the man had quality in those tight pants. What did he have to say for himself?"

"He proposed!"

"Get outta here." Gillian smiled a wicked Cheshire cat grin, but kept his voice sincere. Someday she'd thank him for his little part in the cosmos of true love.

"I'm still in shock myself. He said he's in love with a package deal, me and the baby." She looked over to the floral display, dropping her voice to just more than a whisper. "Gillian, he wants to get married as soon as I get out of here."

"*Au contraire*. That's impossible, it will take months setting up a decent ceremonial affair. Is the man insane? There's the caterer and the winery to contract. We'll need a string quartet reserved..."

"Gillian—," she tried interrupting, but he was in matrimonial nirvana.

"…and the invitations need to go out at least a month before the date, if you can wrench them from the printer in a decent time period." He paused for a breath. "I'm simply glowing. A wedding, my gawd. Little Jack and you."

"Gillian. I am not having a huge, fancy ceremony like Carrie and Adam. We'll talk about this more when I get out. Don't get carried away while I'm gone. If you're going to stay at the office today, I expect work. That's what I'm paying you for, not as a wedding coordinator. I'll talk to you tomorrow."

"Ta-ta, O betrothed one. I have a million calls to make, details to arrange. I'm flushing," he said, and he hung up.

Allie hung the phone in its cradle and shook her head. Maybe she should have waited until after marrying Jack to tell him the news. No, heavens, he'd have pouted forever.

Allie leaned back into the pillows and stared at the pageantry by the window. Gillian's extravagance had impressed most of the nursing staff. This kind of floral decadence reeked of Gillian's signature style.

"See what Uncle Gillian did for us?" she whispered. "Can you imagine what he's going to do with a wedding?"

Her room door creaked open again, and Allie tiredly turned her head, expecting a nurse. Her head throbbed from all the excitement of the day, and Allie shifted her body under the white sheets trying to get comfortable. Instead of the floor nurse, Jack poked his head around the wooden door.

"Are you decent in there?" Jack hesitated, then walked into the room with a gift-wrapped box in his hands.

"What do you mean by decent? I didn't expect to see you until tonight," Allie whispered as he came to the side of her bed for a quick kiss.

"What would you like me to mean by decent?" Jack teased. "Here, I got you something you can share with the baby."

Allie blushed a light crimson. "Jack, you shouldn't have. The doctor said I might be allowed home tomorrow and maybe back to work soon, too. I have to get back before Gillian thinks he owns the place."

Jack leaned over the bed and kissed her before sitting on the edge of the bed.

She carefully slipped the bright ribbon and bow from the box. Jack watched her with fascination as she lifted the Scotch tape from the papered sides, trying not to tear the pattern.

"Are you always this meticulous about opening packages?" Jack hooked his foot on the metal bed frame and clasped his hands around his knee.

"Yes, get used to it. Christmas morning can take forever with me. I was an only child, remember, and I made the moments last." She lifted her bandaged face from the pillow with some effort for another quick kiss.

Allie folded the gift wrap into fourths and stored it on the table with the ribbon. Jack rolled his eyes to the heavens. "I also keep everything, too. It's a girl thing, trust me." She shook the box on her lap, lifting the lid. Nestled in white tissue paper she found a portable CD player with headphones.

Allie squealed. "How perfect, music for me and the baby. Thank you, Jack. This is so sweet of you." Underneath the portable equipment peeked the corners of two CDs. She lifted the player out of the box and saw the bright printed covers of Jimmy Buffett's collection *Songs You Know by Heart* and his Christmas CD, *Christmas Island*.

Jack cleared his throat. "I hope you don't mind my selections. I, uh, got you some of my favorites. He's kind of an upbeat sort of guy. Maybe it'll brighten up this place for you while you're here." Jack ducked his head, embarrassed by her prolonged silence. "Allie, you okay? I can exchange them if you want; I kept the receipt and all."

Allie stared at the plastic CD cases sitting at the bottom of the box. Her eyes filled with tears, blurring Jimmy's face on the cover. "I love his music," she whispered hoarsely through the tears. "Don't you dare exchange these."

"I didn't mean to make you cry, Allie. Okay, the Christmas one is a little early. Come on, don't make me feel bad. I've gotta run back to work before the boss misses me. I don't want to leave with your waterworks running. You gonna be okay?" Jack stood up, shifting his weight uncomfortably from one foot to the other, checking his watch.

"I'll be fine." She ran her fingers over the player, never taking her eyes off the bottom of the box, which was spotted with teardrops. Jimmy Buffett. Jack's a Parrot Head? "Honest," she said as she sniffed against her runny nose, "I'm fine."

"Okay, uh, I'll come back tonight." Jack watched Allie's damp face in concern. She didn't move other than nodding absently in his direction, still staring at the CDs. He gave her a quick kiss on the forehead. "Well, uh, I gotta run." Jack made a dash out the door.

Heading toward the elevator, Jack pulled a black cellular phone out of his back pants' pocket. He pressed the down arrow on the wall, and then punched in a phone number. He ran his fingers through his hair as the number rang.

"Gillian? Yeah, it's me, Jack." The elevator doors quietly opened and Jack stepped inside the carpeted empty car. "You were right about the gift. I owe you one, buddy, big time. She started crying when she saw the CDs in the box. Who is this Buffett character anyway?"

Acknowledgments

Listing all who have been with me on this magical journey, or helped out along the way, would take us to Key West and back.

From a disbanded group in Rancho Cucamonga headlined by Kay to a fun, intimate critique group in Olympia—Lee, Nicki, Becky and Pat—fellow writers have encouraged, read and helped edit this book over time.

My deepest thanks for the quality polishing of my manuscript goes to Barbara Fandrich. She not only wreaked professional havoc on my grammar, but laughed in all the right places.

Again I bow to the talented staff at Gorham Printing for another great production process. A great bunch of people to work with.

To my mother who had the sweet chance to be at the beginning of this journey and who has continued to cheerlead from her heavenly post.

And finally I owe a debt of gratitude to Jean, who has cracked the whip of friendship and support, never letting me forget the joy and passion of writing. Jean may be gone from this world, but is raising cane and laughter in the next, I'm sure.